Joel Lane lives in Birmingham. He is the author of a book of short stories, *The Earth Wire*, and a book of poems, *The Edge of the Screen*. His first novel, *From Blue To Black*, published by Serpent's Tail, was set in the world of post-punk rock music. He and Steve Bishop have edited an anthology of urban crime and suspense fiction, *Birmingham Noir*.

Also by Joel Lane and published by Serpent's Tail

From Blue To Black

'Lane's writing is faultlessly immediate . . . (with) a simple, unforced vividness and clarity of perception' *Guardian*

'Music is notoriously difficult to write about, but this novel pulls it off triumphantly' *Daily Telegraph*

'Psychological depth, human compassion, sly wit and the observational power of an entire network of security cameras characterise Joel Lane's fiction . . . To this powerful and moving narrative of life lived on the knife edge between creativity and madness, he also brings an infectious enthusiasm for indie rock' Nicholas Royle

'A doomy and deeply felt debut which combines bleak despatches from the early '90s sub culture with a relentless emotional pulse. The best novel about rock 'n' roll since Jonathan Coe's *The Dwarves of Death*' DJ Taylor

'Joel Lane is a master at creating a mood of disturbing and disorientating strangeness set against backgrounds of urban decay' Karl Edward Wagner

the blue mask

....

Joel Lane

Library of Congress Catalog Card Number: 2002110981

A complete catalogue record for this book can be
obtained from the British Library on request

The right of Joel Lane to be identified as the author of
this work has been asserted by him in accordance with the
Copyright, Designs and Patents Act 1988

First published in 2003 by Serpent's Tail,
4 Blackstock Mews, London N4 2BT
website: *www.serpentstail.com*

Printed by Mackays of Chatham, plc

10 9 8 7 6 5 4 3 2 1

For Nick Royle –
greetings from the heartland

contents

What did you say to solitude
Did you fall down on your knees
That's all right, you got blood in your eyes
It just won't let you be

— Dan McAlister

chapter 1

our little group

1

The queue on the staircase was like a line of silhouetted trees bent by the wind. Hairspray and lacquer held the twigs in place. The distant rumble of bass guitar vibrated the bare steps. Neil felt a draught as the door behind them opened, letting in more shadows. Beside him, Matt was shivering; Neil restrained the impulse to warm him up. In front of them, Stefan and Theresa stood impassively: Stefan already drunk, Theresa still locked in her own silent world. Neil wondered if seeing despair mimicked as a style would help to lift her mood. Slowly, they climbed towards the admission desk. Beyond it, a red light shone through an open doorway.

Because of the stairs, you reached the upper dance floor first. Neil remembered it as a gig venue. He'd seen Electrafixion here. Ash. Marion. A tiny stage, framed by speakers that poured out jagged noise. Now it was covered with swaying black-clad figures. The crowd at the bar was three or four deep. Something by the Sisters of Mercy was playing, a hollow vortex of brittle drums and synth-effect guitars. The lyrics were about drowning. Matt said something none of them could hear. He pointed to a doorway beyond the bar. The other three followed him.

The next room was quieter. It had low black tables, and a small bar selling bottled beer and spirits. There was a half-price offer on double vodka that Neil and Matt took advantage of. Theresa and Stefan selected beers. They sat around one of the tables, feeling the pulse of bass in their drinks. Goth Night at Edward's No. 8 was on alternate Fridays. Matt had been trying to drag them along here since the end of last year. 'You don't have to be into the music,' he'd said. 'Just soak up the atmosphere.' Grudgingly, Neil had to admit that he was right.

'What's it like downstairs?' Stefan asked. 'Don't say *more Gothy*, 'cause I won't believe you.'

Matt shook his head. 'Nah. It's more a metal, grunge, hardcore type thing. And kids snogging in the corners. Not much light. If we keep together we'll be OK.'

'What if we don't?' Theresa said quietly. 'Might be interesting.' Stefan looked at her, miming astonishment.

'Down there you won't know who or what you're running into,' Matt said. 'One minute you're in a slow dance, the next you're carrying an alien-human hybrid embryo.'

'I suppose so,' Theresa said. 'One baby Goth's enough for any household.' Matt looked away. Neil listened to the wordless roar of guitars coming through the wall.

As they went down the staircase at the back of the club, Neil was aware of drawing a few covetous glances from white-faced, hollow-eyed girls. Perhaps from boys too. The hair and clothing made it hard to tell the difference. He liked that. In terms of physical attraction, faces were more important to him than bodies. He couldn't understand men who were fixated on breasts or cocks. What expression could a boneless organ have? And those size-queens he'd met were only too aware of the practical drawbacks of their fetish.

The light changed from red to blue, and a raw blast of Soundgarden derailed his train of thought. The lower dance floor was wilder: lads in T-shirts, sweat glittering in their spiky hair, jerked and twisted as if the music were literally an electric charge. Plastic glasses scrunched under his feet. Beyond the bar was a darker, less crowded area where couples formed distorted sculptures against the walls. He thought of the Cure song 'Siamese Twins', which Matt made a point of playing whenever they'd had a row. Cohabitation had its drawbacks. But this place reminded him why it was worth it. The blue-lit faces on the dance floor made him feel a kind of panic. If a fight started, would anyone notice the difference?

After a while, the combined effect of alcohol and noise made him feel stunned. Midnight passed and the club was still filling up. Where had all these people come from? Where did they hide during the day? He and Matt went back to the upper floor, drank more vodka, danced to 'Walk Away' and 'The Unforgiven'. They never danced at the Nightingale, because the music was shit. Stefan and Theresa had drifted off somewhere. Neil wondered if Theresa was serious about finding someone new. People often used one-night stands to try and get over someone. It never seemed to work.

In the quiet bar, Matt got into a long discussion about hair with two of his Goth friends from the University. Neil went for a piss. The Gents was a murky lake of beer, piss and thin vomit. He didn't like using urinals, but the state of the cubicles left him no choice. The harsh smell of the soap reminded him of primary school. His image in the mirror was more a shadow than a reflection.

Feeling a little disorientated, he made his way back to the tables. A hand touched his arm. 'Hi.' A thin girl, sharp-featured, about nineteen. 'Are you and your mate on the pull?' she said.

'No, actually we're together.'

The girl shrugged. 'Oh well. Can he spare you for a dance?'
When he hesitated, she grabbed his hand and led him out
through the doorway. It was weird how many people seemed
to find him attractive these days. Hardly anyone had bothered
with him as a teenager. But then, he'd had longer hair and
no social skills. If anyone had tried, he'd have been too
wrapped up in himself to notice. Going out with Matt had
given him more confidence.

They danced to a mid-tempo Siouxsie and the Banshees
track. The voice sounded lost, terrified, its message impossible to decode. The girl was hammered; she wove her arms
in the air between them, staring at Neil's face. They moved
closer together until they were almost touching. In the brief
quiet between tracks, she grasped Neil's shoulders and kissed
him fiercely. Then she pressed her mouth to his ear, said 'See
you,' and was gone.

Neil could feel the reality of this place slipping away. The
girl's loneliness had infected him; the crowd suddenly felt
like a vast, hostile creature that could trap you, nudge you
into a corner and drain the life from you. The floor was
vibrating with a slow distant beat, like a bridge over a
motorway. He needed to get home. The house in Moseley
village. The four of them in the kitchen, sharing a late-night
snack that was more of an early breakfast.

Matt was still talking with his friends around a black table
that reflected the overhead light. 'We'd better make a move,'
Neil said. 'Night bus in twenty minutes.' It was too cold
outside for walking home, and they were too drunk.

They found Stefan drinking on the staircase, looking tired
out. He'd worked some late shifts at the hospital recently,
and never seemed to sleep. Theresa was harder to find. She
was on the dark side of the lower floor, sitting alone.
She didn't notice the others until Matt touched her shoulder.

'Are you OK?' Neil asked her as they queued for their coats. She smiled vaguely. Stefan gripped her hand.

In John Bright Street, they saw a thin boy being held back by two friends. The lower half of his face was glossy with blood. The man he was trying to reach stood calmly in a doorway, weighing his fist in the palm of his left hand, ready to strike again. Drops of blood shone like coins on the pavement. The boy's eyes were pale blue and wide open, as if he were staring at something too bright and terrible to look away from.

2

It was only warm when the sun was shining on you. Matt was glad of his fluffy black sweater, though he'd still have worn it in an August heatwave. He'd been outside all morning, leafleting in Sparkhill and buying vegetables from the cheap greengrocer's along the Stratford Road where the window displays were on the outside: boxes piled high with chillies and root ginger. Three hours later, here he was in the Physiology lab, staring at a decerebrate rabbit.

The creature was, for all ethical purposes, dead. Its cerebral cortex had been removed through the front of its skull, leaving the sluglike cerebrum intact behind a red curtain of tissue. The heart and lungs would keep going for a few hours, which was the point of the exercise. Maybe the exposed back brain harboured some dim, atavistic longing for the chance to do what rabbits normally did in the springtime. But Matt doubted it. Even dreaming was a function of consciousness. Still, he could have done with some warning before today's practical.

Fighting back nausea, he picked up the scalpel and inserted it into the warm sternum. You were supposed to peel back the ribs like an eggshell to get at the heart and lungs. The steady heartbeat shuddered through the stiff points of the creature's bloodstained fur. At least there wasn't a face looking back at him. Carlos, Matt's partner in these practicals, stopped filling syringes and glanced anxiously at Matt. 'Y'all right there?'

'Suppose so.' Matt swallowed a burning thread of bile. 'I don't know. It's ironic. The only time I touch meat is in the lab. Except when I'm in bed with Neil.'

Carlos nodded philosophically. 'Yeah. I worry sometimes, what this does to us. Did you hear about that med. student last year who stuck a dead rabbit up his arse?' Matt stared at him. 'It's true. Exam fever, I guess. Just flipped. He couldn't get it out again. Spent the night at the QE, having this rabbit removed with forceps. He quit after that, never took his Finals. You might have met him. His name's Warren.'

'*Whaaat?*' Matt cracked up. 'You *bastard*. Fuck!' The laughter brought more bile into his mouth. Lucky it was cold in here. But time and the rabbit's heart were ticking away. They'd better get on with it.

Afterwards, they had a fifteen-minute break. Matt went for a walk. A prickly light rain shadowed the campus, blurring its shades of grey. He knew Neil would be in the library, but there wasn't time to look for him. Poplar trees shivered in the vast courtyard as if stepping out of the shower. He brushed droplets of water from his cardy, which was more resistant to penetration than its owner. A smear of light glistened from the wet sky.

The second practical was another heart-lung experiment; but this time, they were the subjects. You had to put on a plastic mask with a breathing-tube, then ride an exercise bike. It seemed pretty kinky to Matt. As usual, Carlos took care of the measuring and recording while he did the messy stuff. The mouthpiece tasted vile, rubber overlaid with chlorine. He shut his eyes and cycled down the long, tree-lined road from West Bromwich to Handsworth. Every two minutes, Carlos measured his heart rate and changed the airbag. Quite what this was meant to prove, Matt wasn't sure. No doubt he'd make sense of it when revising for the exam.

To finish with, you had to keep cycling with the same airbag; then, when you started to feel dizzy, you stopped. The abnormal readings at that point would bring home the physiology of asphyxia. Matt grinned at Carlos. 'Just like old times.' But with the mask in place and the pedals going round as if driven by themselves, it seemed about as sexy as an operation. After a few minutes, the air in his mouth tasted stale; but he wasn't tired. The rain must have stopped: sunlight was pouring through the long window, drifting past his face. He was swimming in it, his legs kicking behind him as he rose to the surface. But something was pulling him down.

'Matt! Matt, are you OK? Jesus Christ!' Matt felt the floor against his back. Carlos was crouching beside him, his hand on Matt's chest. For a moment, Matt thought he was taking the heart rate. 'You blacked out there, man. Got off the bike and just collapsed.' His eyes searched Matt's face with a mixture of concern and secret curiosity. 'Are you OK?'

'Fine.' The dense sunlight had been replaced by the lab's pale electric light. Matt's face was wet. He took a deep breath, drinking the air.

Dr Finn was striding towards them, looking panicky. 'Matthew, isn't it? Are you all right, son?'

'Mmm.' Matt stood up, brushing the dust from his jeans. 'Never got the warning signals.'

'Don't take up diving.' The lecturer glanced at Carlos. 'Is he always this pale?' Carlos nodded. 'OK. Do you want to take him outside and get a cup of tea? I'll clear up your stuff.'

'Cheers.' They walked together down the half-lit corridor to the exit. Matt felt hungover. Not only the last few minutes but the whole day seemed blurred, less than real. Outside, the rain had stopped but the sky was still dark with bruises. Worried-looking students, weighed down with shoulderbags full of books, scurried between the redbrick faculty buildings. At Derek's Café in the Guild, Carlos bought Matt a black coffee with lots of sugar. *I should get a tan,* he thought. *As long as I look like a Goth, everyone thinks I'm ill. I've only got to frown and they assume I'm suicidally depressed.*

The café was rapidly filling up with students: bright-coloured sweaters, ethnic jewellery and unimaginative haircuts. A group of SWP members were agreeing with each other about the election. 'If New Labour wins,' one of them was saying, 'all the anger will be forgotten. The only reason the ruling class will let things get any better is to stop the revolution evolving from a dream into a programme. It's the good cop–bad cop strategy: first Labour, then the Tories, then Labour again. Same shit, different arse.' Matt drank his coffee and tried not to listen. The hard left depressed him. Did they really think Thatcherism had brought the revolution closer? Neil had said once that any popular revolution in England would be fascist, not socialist.

'Are you off home now?' Carlos said.

'No. I'm meeting Neil in a bit. Then I'm doing Nightline. Neil's got a rehearsal. This play he's written.'

'What's it about?'

Matt shrugged. He wasn't really sure what *Nights of Insult* was about, though he knew what happened in it. 'It's about some tenants in a house. They're in all kinds of trouble. It's almost like the house is under siege. Then they work together and begin to sort things out.'

Carlos grinned at him. 'You're like a married couple, you two. I'm a bit jealous. Heterosexuality is so fucked up, men and women can't even be friends. Still, I can't change the way I am.'

'I wouldn't want you to. I mean, I *really* wouldn't.'

Carlos raised a finger, laughing. 'Sit and swivel.'

After he'd gone, Matt settled down with a horror anthology he'd found in the second-hand bookshop in Selly Oak. It was one of the *Not at Night* series, with blood-red covers and thick, dusty paper, dated 1932. He shared Neil's love of old books, though their reading tastes diverged somewhat. 'You don't understand,' he'd said to Neil that morning over breakfast. 'This is the first time these stories had been published in Britain. Before that, they'd all appeared in the now-legendary *Weird Tales* magazine.'

Neil had perused the red jacketless cover, the heavy black print on the cheap paper. 'Yes, but they're shit.'

Arguments of this kind were more playful than the earnest mindfucks Matt was used to getting from older lovers. Indeed, one of the things he loved about Neil was his total lack of any compulsion to pass on wisdom. Most of his exes were mature men who'd lectured him on the meaning of love before sinking their world-weary cocks into his slightly plump arse. Neil didn't try to mould him or use him to prove a theory. There were only six years between them, though in the student world that was like two generations. They took it in turns to do the housework: Matt was more domesticated, but Neil was at home more.

And despite his advanced years, Neil was stunning. His face combined the best features of Morrissey and Johnny Marr: dramatic eyebrows, gentle eyes, fine cheekbones, a soft mouth, a firm chin. His hair was red with black growing through, like a flame above charcoal. Theresa was so taken with Neil that Matt had threatened to break her arms if she fucked him. He didn't quite trust her not to. Whether he trusted Neil, he didn't like to think about. Matt himself looked like an adolescent Robert Smith: spiky black hair, a semi-skimmed milk complexion and a tendency towards flab.

Just after six o'clock, Neil's crimson head passed through

the doorway. Matt closed his book (part-way through 'The Creeping Horror') and waved across the crowded room. They kissed briefly – not so quickly as to be furtive, but not so slowly as to provoke a reaction. You had to be aware of these things. Matt told him about the decerebrate rabbit and the blackout. 'Not one of my better days, so far. You?'

'Been in the library, mostly. Reading *Mein Kampf.* They should print *Now wash your hands* on the back cover. It's so obvious, from the book, what he'll do if he gets into power. But the book was translated into English years before the war, and all those fucking American and English intellectuals were praising Hitler's *scientific insights.* It's like there were Nazis everywhere, but after the war they'd all magically disappeared.'

Neil had been writing this Ph.D on fascist ideology for more than three years now. At times, he seemed to talk about fascism as a universal human tendency, like murder; at other times, he saw it as an exceptionally warped and deceitful kind of political organisation. He couldn't make up his mind whether the causes of fascism were in people or in the capitalist system. Anyone else would have chosen an explanation and then tried to justify it. That was what politics was all about. But being Neil, he couldn't.

They walked together down the steep footpath that curved around the playing field, more for the view than for speed. In front of them, the sunset rusted the tall University gate; the field was a lake of shadow. Poplar trees swayed uneasily, waiting for the band to come on. It was cold out here. As they stood among the blacked-out shapes of trees, Neil put his arm around Matt. 'Are you feeling OK now?'

'Sure. Nothing a good curry won't put right.' Outside the gates, the Bristol Road was the curry equivalent of Sunset Boulevard. But this time, it let them down: the restaurant they chose served up two dilute, warmed-over kormas with pilao rice that was garishly multicoloured, like confetti. At least it was cheap, though not as cheap as better food in Sparkhill.

They walked back up to the Guild by the side road. Neil's rehearsal was in the Muirhead Tower; Matt's Nightline shift was in St Francis' Hall, the chapel building. They kissed goodbye in the dark. There was something weirdly exposed about the University campus: the huge brick buildings, the blank sky in between, the bare ground. And the silence. It was like being upside down. As he rang the bell and waited to be let in through the locked entrance to the Nightline offices at the back, Matt couldn't help feeling comforted by the stone crucifix and narrow stained-glass windows. Even though he'd not attended a church service since leaving school, he still thought of them as places of safety.

Comfort was important, because answering Nightline calls was a pretty weird experience. Like being stoned and listening to a Spacemen 3 album: you didn't know what was coming next, but you knew it would sound lonely and fucked up. And it would be in your head for some time. Most of the female callers preferred to speak to a woman, so Matt ended up with lads who were drunk or drugged and losing their grip. Some were sexually confused, and he tried to reassure them that it was not only all right to be queer, it was all right to be confused.

But the one overwhelming problem was money. Debts, loans, jobs, evictions. When you got through the course, you'd spend the next ten years paying for it. Which meant a bad result really *was* the end of hope. One plaintive caller the other night had said: 'Of course, it'll be different when Labour get in. Won't it?' Yeah, right. It was a good job the Nightline volunteers weren't expected to solve anyone's problems. You just had to sit and listen, give out relevant information, be helpful without getting involved. Then walk or cycle out into the unexpectedly peaceful night, with the city's lights spread around you like a distant galaxy viewed from a satellite.

3

The Studio Theatre was in the base of the Muirhead Tower, a shaky concrete and glass building that, like the Eiffel Tower, had long outlasted its planned demolition date. Unlike the Eiffel Tower, it housed three academic departments. Including Cultural Studies, where Neil spent quite a lot of time. Being up there on a windy day was like being inside the head of a schoolboy on his first encounter with Special Brew. The tower was fenced around with wooden platforms held together by scaffolding, preventing anyone from getting close enough to be hit by falling windows. To get inside, you had to go through a concrete-roofed tunnel with scaffolding walls. The tower was rumoured to have been the point of departure for a number of suicides, though in reality it was hard to see how anyone could get far enough out to hit the ground. Working in the Studio Theatre, you had a constant sense of social and economic structures being about to col-lapse around you.

Gary and Tim were already in the rehearsal room when Neil arrived. Tim unrolled a sheath of pencil sketches for sets and lighting plans. He wanted the basic scenery to be three walls, a bed and a chair. No windows. Rachel's room had a small dressing-table with a mirror and a cot in one corner; Corin's room had an exercise machine; Dave's room had a collection of videos and framed pictures. Mr Y would be in a blue spotlight; the other characters would be lit by a floor lamp or a fixed overhead light.

'That looks good,' Neil said. 'I'd actually meant the set to stay the same, with all the different props there at once. After all, the broken glass and other rubbish stays around from scene to scene.'

'That reminds me,' Tim said, 'we'll have problems using real glass. Let alone razor blades. Too many risks. Anyone gets hurt, there'll be hell to pay.'

'Isn't Theresa doing most of her scenes barefoot?' Gary asked. 'And then Sean and Michael rolling around in every other scene. Could take the Theatre of Cruelty to a new level.'

'Smart one,' Neil remarked wearily. The coolly ironic tone that Gary brought to his nameless role was fairly tiresome in real life. 'Look, we'll put down rugs or something, mark off no-go areas on the stage.'

Gary lit a cigarette with an air of frosty detachment. At that point, the opening and closing of several doors announced the arrival of Sean and Michael. That was the whole cast apart from Theresa, who wasn't coming tonight. Sean played Corin, a bruiser hiding from his former criminal associates. Michael played his boyfriend, Dave: a petty thief and full-time fantasist. They'd met in prison. Theresa played a stripper, Rachel, who was still mourning the loss of a child a year before. Gary played the narrator, a phantom figure who stalked the other characters and spied on them. He was never entirely offstage. Neil had started calling him Mr X in rehearsal, but Gary had changed it to Mr Y. 'After the chromosome. And the lack of motivation.'

Tonight they were rehearsing two of Dave's scenes, with Sean playing both Corin and another thug. Tim dimmed the lights in the rehearsal room, creating a sense of imprison-ment. The distant chime of the University clock was an appropriate touch. Gary started reading from his crumpled copy of the script. *On an early morning in January, someone knocked on the house door. It was the agent Dave had been waiting for. But the part he was offering wasn't one that Dave wanted to play.* Michael backed into the room. Sean walked in slowly after him and closed the door, his face completely expressionless.

The visitor was an associate of Corin's who was anxious to contact him. At that time, Dave really didn't know where he was. *Robbed of the opportunity to betray his friend, he improvised a grief too perfect to be convincing.* Sprawled on the floor, face tilted downward, Michael told the story of how Corin had been found hanging in an allotment shed. *There was no funeral service. The body was cremated. I kept the ashes. Scattered them in the Sandwell Valley on Christmas Day. He used to cruise there. The ashes were a black frost on the grass. They didn't blow away. They probably still haven't.*

Without saying anything, the visitor began to smash up Dave's room. The idea was that Sean would break some framed pictures and lamps, scattering broken glass over the stage. The only light remaining would be a faint red glow from behind the audience, representing the dawn. Then the visitor pinned Dave to the wall and beat the shit out of him. *I don't know where he is! I don't know if he's still alive. If he comes back, I'll tell you – I'll set him up for you – I'll give the cunt to you, I swear.* The visitor tossed a card on to the floor and walked out. Dave huddled in the corner, shaking. The narrator moved to centre stage. In the dim light, Gary was hardly more than a silhouette.

This was a speech Neil was quite proud of, though Gary was still pushing too hard, hiding behind bits of arch mime. *Keep still,* Neil jotted on his copy of the script. It had been Gary's idea to play these scenes cold, with no visible emotion; but then he'd got bored. *I thought he was going to kill the boy. Another picture for my winter archive, my extended family of the dead. But that would have been too easy. It would have made no difference. The daylight flickered on bloodstained fragments of glass, like rose petals. Stooping over the boy's frozen body, I saw a pale cloud of breath leave his mouth like cigarette smoke. Every breath he took was a final breath.* Gary stood for a few seconds with his eyes shut. Then he looked straight at Neil. There was something hostile and questioning in his face.

They broke off for a beer from their little store in the backstage fridge. Sean, who'd been even more wooden than usual, emptied his bottle in a few aggressive gulps. 'I know you don't think so,' he said to Neil, 'but this play is a party political broadcast for New Labour. Crime is bad, families are good, the working class are mindless thugs.'

Neil bit his lip. They'd been over this ground before. 'It's not about the family you're born into, it's about the family you make. A family that has whatever meaning you bring to it. The criminals represent the ethos of capitalist society.'

'You can't rise above class by ignoring it, you know.'

'I'm not trying to rise above it,' Neil said. 'I'm trying to say something about domination.' Gary cocked an ear, feigning interest. Neil ignored him. 'What happens between Dave and Corin . . . I'm trying to suggest that relations of power can be subverted, played with. Exposed as social constructs. And ultimately, changed.'

Sean crouched in his chair, looking unimpressed. Being in this play was difficult for him, of course, now that he and Theresa had split up. Even if she wasn't here tonight. And he was obviously finding the Blair circus a bit hard to stomach. Even Neil was getting rather sickened by it all.

'I don't know which of you has less of a clue,' Gary said in a tone of mock boredom. 'What do you know about domination? S&M isn't some kind of clever political thesis. It's not about fucking semiotics. It's about giving up control, or taking control. In a world where pain is the only currency. But *you*' – he glanced at Sean – 'wouldn't have the first idea about that, and *you*' – that look again, directed at Neil – 'just try to sentimentalise it. You think *relationships* are the great answer. Going home every night to play mummies and daddies with that little boyfriend of yours. You think you live on the edge, but you know fuck all. Vanilla's too dangerous for you.'

Sean flushed with a mixture of anger and embarrassment. 'Tell me something,' he said quietly to Gary. 'Since you're explaining the mysteries of the universe, maybe you could explain to *me* something I've been wondering ever since we started working on this play. Why are you such a cunt? I mean, what is your problem with everyone?'

Neil stood up and walked to the door. 'Here's an idea,' he said. 'Why don't we save the amateur dramatics for the fucking rehearsal?' Rather awkwardly, the others followed him back into the half-lit room. But as they took up their positions, Neil wondered if Gary had been winding them up in order to inject some tension into the acting. He was one devious queen.

The next scene they were working on involved sex between Dave and Corin. They were both staying in to avoid the gang who'd threatened Dave. It was meant to be a fairly brutal scene, with the narrator doing most of the talking. Tim lit a cigarette and blew dry smoke across the room. Michael lay on the bed, while Sean paced tensely up and down. Gary began to read: *Night and day were becoming hard to tell apart. While the boy took refuge in his celluloid dreams, Corin tried to think of a way to escape. The gaps on Dave's shelves, where pictures had been broken, showed Corin the shadowy, patient faces of his past.* A strange tone had crept into his voice, somewhere between disgust and compassion.

I'm going to leave, Michael said. *I don't belong here.* He made for the door. Sean took hold of him, gently at first, then cruelly. They fell on to the narrow bed. In performance, Sean would tear off Michael's shirt. Gary's voice became deeper, breathy, a monotone breaking the silence of the struggling bodies. *As Corin's fear and rage spent itself in Dave's body, it gave way to a strange tenderness. They lay in the dark for a long time, holding on.* He clearly didn't need the script for this scene. The words seemed to be drawn out of him in a long, painful string. Then he snapped out of it, waving a hand to dismiss the still figures. Sean backed off, doing up his belt. Michael stayed on the bed, curled up on his side, like a child.

Neil felt at once part of the scene and cut off from it – more like a *voyeur* than an audience member. Somewhere at the back of his mind, he knew that this was pants. It had no dramatic tension, no real life to it. But somehow, the contrast between Gary's obsessive narration and the awkwardly non-erotic movements of Sean and Michael was exciting. It was like the contrast between the profane dialogue in a Fassbinder film and the demure subtitles – *Ich habe ihn im Arsch gefickt, und ich habe sein Scheiss noch auf meinem Schwanz* being represented as 'I've had him.' Maybe you had to be English to find that not only funny but profound.

'Time for a swift pint down the Gun Barrels?' Tim suggested as they locked up, closing the door on a darkness that looked infinite. Sean and Michael agreed; Gary shrugged. It was quarter to eleven; they'd have to run.

Neil put his script down on the reception desk. 'I've got some points from this evening to think about. See you Monday, lads.' Michael took off down the walkway between two dark buildings; Sean and Tim raced after. Neil looked at the script for Scene 9, the beating. It needed more reaction, less commentary. He didn't immediately notice that Gary was still there. A thin hand brushed across the paper, making him look up.

'You can't write what you don't feel.' Close up, Gary's narrow face was a mask of tension. 'Try it some day. A walk on the secret side. The wrong side. Or you'll go on thinking you know, but knowing nothing.' Neil stared at him. 'What

have you got to lose?' Gary almost whispered. 'I mean *really*
got to lose? Apart from your cosy game of happy families?'

If that was meant as a pass, it fell flat. Neil smiled, then
looked back at his script. 'Save it for the rehearsals,' he said
wearily. Gary slammed the front door of the Studio Theatre
behind him. Neil settled to a few minutes of quiet work:
jotting points in the margin of the script, crossing out lines
of text, inserting pauses and silent movements on the narrator's part. He no longer had a sense of the character as
someone distinct from Gary.

In a way, this had all started with Gary's seminar on Jean
Genet the previous autumn. Gary had focused on the themes
of death and faith in Genet's novels. *You have to take the titles
literally. They really are about miracles, roses, funerals. Genet's
writing breaks down the walls between the sacred and the profane.*
Sean had argued that Genet's work was secretly fascist, an
endorsement of power and oppression. Neil had wondered
then what it would be like to get the two of them on stage
together.

Nights of Insult owed a lot to Genet: the role playing and
transformations, the idea of a lonely narrator obsessed with
the characters. There were bits of Neil Bartlett and Philip
Ridley in there too. Maybe it should have been a novel. But
he'd needed the actors to make it real. The faces and voices
brought it to life. At the end of the play, the characters
banished the narrator from their world. The chains of fantasy
were broken.

Too late to join the others, he unchained his bicycle from
an alcove under the road bridge and pedalled through the
silent campus. The sky overhead was completely blank.
Towards the city, the Bristol Road was a dead-straight dual
carriageway; even this late, it was packed with roaring traffic.
Trees shattered the yellow light. The bank of undergrowth
behind the fence to his left smelt of rot and shadows. Sud-

denly he remembered cycling up the long straight road from Macclesfield to Alderley Edge. It was the same road that Ian and Deborah Curtis had been walking along when they had the row that led to them splitting up. Neil turned off at the crossroads, passing the dark emptiness of Cannon Hill Park and climbing the long, steep hill into Moseley Village.

He'd moved here in October from a flatlet in Acocks Green that had begun to feel like a cell. Acocks Green was an industrial district, filled with the dull rumble of cars and the barking of dogs. Phoneboxes never lasted through the weekend. Matt and some of his friends had moved into this converted three-storey house on Trafalgar Road, and there'd been one empty room. It wasn't quite a communal household, just as he and Matt weren't quite living together. Gary's jibes had unsettled him. He knew there was more between him and Matt than domestic fantasy. They'd still be lovers in a tower block. But he couldn't help wondering how Matt would react to a crisis that couldn't be sorted out by a long talk, a plate of Jaffa cakes and a hug.

When he reached the house, all its front windows were dark. Neil let himself in quietly and climbed the narrow staircase to the first floor. He and Matt had separate rooms, but they rarely slept apart. From behind Matt's door, he could hear the low, ominous rhythm of Simon Gallup's bass and Lol Tolhurst's drums. He knocked. 'Come in.' Matt was lying in bed, reading the red-covered *At Dead of Night*. Neil bent over the side of the bed and kissed him.

The medic's face looked brittle in the red light of the bedside lamp. His eyes were stamped with darkness. A smile flickered in his open mouth. 'How did it go?'

'Not so bad. Sean's in a weird mood, probably over Theresa. And Gary's still bitching about you and me. I can't believe him sometimes. But his acting's come on a lot. He's beginning to sound like he means it. Only on stage, mind.'

'He's just jealous. The closest he ever gets to a relationship is meeting in the same cubicle twice.'

Neil raised his eyebrows. He knew Gary and Matt had had a disastrous fling back in 1995, but Matt had been vague about specifics. 'How was Nightline?' he asked.

'Same as ever. Bit sad, but nothing too heavy.' That was as much as he was likely to say, unless something had really got to him. 'I bet medieval sin-eaters were bored to death half the time.' He put the red book down by the lamp. 'Come here. Give me something to confess.'

The hollow beat of the Cure's 'All Cats Are Grey' filled the darkness as they pressed together, kissing slowly. The air was slightly chilly; it smelt faintly of cigarettes, like a jacket brought home from the pub. They rubbed each other with practised urgency, legs entwined to capture the tension and share it. The constant possibility of going further gave this childlike act an edge of passion. As Matt came, Neil pressed him down against the bed and covered his mouth with a kiss. He felt the cry rising from Matt's throat and shaking through his own. The last three piano notes of the Cure song faded like stubbed cigarettes. The tape player clicked off.

For some time after Matt had gone to sleep, Neil lay on his back and listened to the house. Floorboards creaked; water-pipes groaned softly. The sounds of people were at once sharper and more obviously distant. In the back garden, a pigeon called from its smoker's throat. He couldn't help wondering about the families who'd lived here in the past. Before the house was converted to bedsits. What children had crawled up the winding staircase, played in the narrow garden? Maybe they were in his dreams, the past owners or tenants of the house: the faceless, shadowy people he glimpsed or touched at night, but never spoke to. Yet the place of his dreams wasn't here. He didn't know where it was.

The next thing he knew, a blade of daylight had slashed the curtains. It was nine o'clock. Saturday morning. Matt was still hiding in sleep, his back curved away. Neil listened as the house came to life, one room at a time: the sounds of music, sex or arguments. None of it was quite real. Like the memories of his childhood. Maybe that was why Thatcher had always seemed like a ghost to him: he'd been seven years old when she'd come to power. For years he'd half-expected her to vanish with the dawn, like the distorted shadows thrown by the bedside lamp. There were only five days to go, not counting Election Day itself; and then they'd all be gone. The end of an era. The lifting of the shadow. Perhaps.

4

'Trafalgar Road? Why bother? There's a Labour Party poster in every window.'

Mary nodded patiently. 'It's just as important to reassure supporters that they're not being taken for granted. After all, a lot of the national campaign's been aimed at previous Tory voters.'

'I know,' Neil said. 'And it's been persuading them to change their vote, not their politics.'

'Surely that broadcast last night was intended as a message to the faithful?' It had featured Pete Postlethwaite as a taxi driver who gave a young couple a free ride to the polling station just before it closed, for which good deed he was rewarded with a pair of wings.

'Do you think it was patronising enough for that?'

'Now you're just being bitter and cynical,' Matt said. 'I thought it was lovely.'

'Matthew, sweetheart, you're either very good at irony or a complete zombie.' Matt turned away and stared grimly at the map Sellotaped to his pile of leaflets.

They were in Mary's house, allocating batches of leaflets for delivery. Which was as exciting a prospect as counselling paint on its solidification issues. Nobody read the leaflets. Supporters let them pile up in the kitchen; non-supporters used them to line the cat litter tray. Mary, a grey-haired activist with steel-framed glasses, radiated a kind of quiet optimism that always made Neil feel brittle and inadequate.

Matt was sulking as they left the house and walked up to the Moseley end of Trafalgar Road. They took opposite sides, judging the number of leaflets for each house by the number of doorbells. Neil watched his lover's short figure scurrying from door to door; not for the first time, he admired Matt's ability to let the practicalities of a situation distract him from doubts about its meaning. When they'd got together, Matt's efficient hospitality had helped to cement the relationship while Neil was still walking in circles around the concept of it. The first night they'd spent together, Neil had praised Matt's cooking. 'I was brought up on proper food,' Matt had said. 'I've had more hot dinners than you've had blow jobs.'

Beyond the pub and the initial line of shops, Trafalgar Road had a strangely Edwardian feel. The big houses had bits of neo-classical frontage, leaded windows, dwarf conifers or monkey-puzzle trees. Black fire escapes clung to the side walls like burnt skeletons. Most of the houses had been converted into flats or bedsits. There was an atmosphere of faded grandeur, lost scale. But Neil suspected that, given the choice, he'd rather live here now than seventy years ago.

The election result was almost a foregone conclusion. But party activists, at least in Moseley, didn't seem euphoric. There was a cold determination to get the job done, linked to an unease about the price of victory. Both feelings were in some way coloured by the death of John Smith. Neil had attended a branch meeting that evening, two years ago. All of the agenda was cancelled. They sat in silence for a while.

Some people cried. Everyone seemed older; there wasn't enough light. The meeting had ended after half an hour, but its aftermath hadn't gone away.

Student politics was different. There were no compromises, since it was all about words and abstract principles. No wonder Barthes was so popular among student radicals: how could they resist a philosophy that made language out to be the most powerful thing in the world? The academic left regarded itself with such absolute seriousness that it was a kind of escapism, the mirror-image of stealing a traffic cone or wrapping a Villa scarf around a statue. Or those public schoolboys last year who'd put up a candidate for the Moseley ward in the council election to represent the Avatars of Yog-Sothoth. Matt had explained it to him: something to do with a 1920s pulp horror writer. 'If we vote for them, we might be allowed to live when the Ancient Ones return to the Earth.' Not even Paxman could have summoned enough disbelief for that.

Near the Balsall Heath end of Trafalgar Road, trees framed a children's playground. On the far side, there was a ratty scrapyard with a wrecked pram and bin-liners full of rubble, overlooking the backs of terraced houses. A condom-littered alley led through to Brighton Road, where they finished the round of leafleting. The Malt Shovel pub wasn't open yet. Matt smiled at Neil. 'Could murder some lunch after this.' They stood close together, almost touching. You didn't touch in the street.

'Are you OK?' Neil said.

'Yeah. I was just seeing how tall you are.' That was an old joke between them, referring to Neil's one-time job in a garage. 'Let's go home.'

They walked back up the Alcester Road. Most of the Asian shops were open, selling videos, music, clothes. Neil loved the way fragments of the inner city and the suburbs were joined together around here, like a hybrid jigsaw from several different pictures. When he'd first come to Birmingham, Balsall Heath had been its red-light district. Every night, the streets were scattered with motionless figures wearing tank-tops and miniskirts. In 1995, a team of Moslem vigilantes had driven out all the prostitutes and kerb-crawlers. They'd also driven out practically every unmarried woman under fifty who'd lived there. Including his ex-girlfriend Anne, who'd been working for West Midlands Arts. Something about Anne seemed to antagonise fucked-up men, because she wasn't afraid of them.

Neil and Anne had got involved in their first year at the University. She'd been his last girlfriend; but that wasn't her fault, and their relationship hadn't been a pretence. Some-times he still missed her. And he missed being able to hold hands or kiss in the open air. He felt vaguely disloyal, thinking about her while walking along the road with Matt. But it was better to be vaguely disloyal than to build up walls you'd tear down in your sleep.

Neil spent most of Election Day in the University Library, reading Adorno's contribution to *The Authoritarian Person-ality*. Bookcases towered around him like office blocks in a city of wood. Someone had carefully engraved the first verse of Joy Division's 'Passover' in the wooden support of the desk, at eye level. It must have taken hours. He followed the intricate spirals of Adorno's text, trying to keep the image of Tony Blair out of his mind.

By ten o'clock, the whole household were gathered around the TV set in the living-room. There was Andy, the middle-aged Scot they rarely saw. He wore clothes from charity shops and hung around the park with other alcoholics, looking rough. But once, Neil had seen him leaving for work at seven a.m. in an old suit. There was Clare, a music student at the Birmingham Conservatoire; and her boyfriend Mark, who was there most weekends. Clare's room was the attic. Every night, around nine o'clock, she opened her door and played REM's 'You Are the Everything' very loud: the sound drifted down three flights of stairs. For four minutes, everything else stopped.

Then there was Stefan, a nurse who worked in the Trauma Ward at the General Hospital. Theresa, a psychology student. She was playing Rachel in *Nights of Insult*. There was David, an architecture student with bleached hair who did some modelling on the side. And Matt and Neil.

There was some communal food: crisps and chocolate provided by Clare and Mark, Jaffa cakes provided by Matt. They took turns to make a round of coffees every hour or so. Alcohol, on the other hand, was subject to private ownership: Andy had a bottle of vodka, which he polished off as if it were wine; Neil and Matt shared their Johnnie Walker with Theresa; the rest had cans. The tenants were sorted. It was time to stop arguing about what New Labour stood for and just watch the Tories get shafted. Five years earlier, similar hopes had met with bitter disappointment.

One of the first blue-rinsed heads to roll was Dame Jill Knight, Edgbaston MP and architect of Section 28. A lot of West Midlands results came in early; the Tories were practically wiped out of Birmingham. Two spectacular ogres, Sir Rhodes Boyson and Lady Olga Maitland, became unemployed. There was particular joy when Neil Hamilton lost his seat in Tatton, next door to Macclesfield: a symbolic defeat for the smug prick who'd personified Tory corruption. By midnight, Neil and Matt were cuddled up on the floor in front of the sofa, kissing tenderly. Neil tasted whisky in his lover's mouth, the warm flavour of malt and decay.

It got better still. The appalling Dr Adrian Rogers, renta-quote spokesman for homophobic bigotry, lost his seat to an openly gay Labour candidate. David Mellor bit the dust. And Edwina Currie, who'd been kind of fun. The high point came after the overall result was beyond any doubt. From early on, they'd been suggesting that Portillo's seat was vulnerable. Around three o'clock, Neil watched in a haze of drunken ecstasy as that most hideous of proto-fascist militia men bent over, grabbed his own ankles and was shafted by a small hamster; another openly gay Labour candidate. David, Matt and Neil argued briefly over who was more desirable, Ben Bradshaw or Stephen Twigg. Afterwards, Neil was unable to remember who'd got his vote.

The whisky bottle was empty. Outside, trees were creaking in the wind. Neil and Matt staggered up to Matt's room, took off most of their clothes and collapsed into bed. They agreed to celebrate the new dawn by fucking each other senseless – but not just now. The immediate priority was to lie side by side and watch the ceiling become the cosmos.

chapter 2

....

underneath the bridge

1

On Saturday morning, the Jesus Army were out in force in the city centre. A group of them by the fountain were chanting over a tape of synthesiser music. Others were standing around their green bus, handing out pamphlets. As Matt climbed the library steps, a young man in a white shirt stepped in front of him. 'Excuse me. I wondered if you'd mind telling me something.' Matt nodded. 'What do you think happiness is?'

I don't know, Matt thought. *But I look in your eyes and . . . it isn't there.* The boy had grey eyes and a pale, nervous face. He looked like he didn't sleep well. 'It means being loved,' Matt said. 'And being at peace. Living in a just and peaceful world.'

The evangelist shook his head tensely, like a glove puppet. 'No, that's not happiness. It's running away. Letting yourself rot. I'll tell you what real happiness is. I want you to know.' Matt shifted uneasily. Why did he always walk into these things? Sunlight flashed from the plate-glass window of the library, dazzling him.

'I used to live for love,' the boy continued. 'Or I called it love. It was pure selfishness. I can't believe the harm I did.

And the sick things I was into.' He lowered his voice. 'Like *masturbation*. I was dying inside. Then I found someone whose love could heal me. Someone who truly cared. And his name is Jesus Christ.'

'They all say that.' The boy looked bewildered. 'Sorry, I just think the solutions to ... those kind of problems are actually in human relationships.'

The same mechanical headshake. 'You mean, putting it into practice? That's a loser. I've tried it.'

Matt was getting bored. This was like the Nightline calls he sometimes got from Christian Union types: they'd pour out their woes, then twist the discussion into an attempt to convert him. The things people did to feel better about themselves. 'Can I ask *you* something?' he said. 'I saw a TV programme about the Jesus Army. This guy was saying that you don't eat toasted cheese. Because it turns the bread to carbon and the cheese to fat. But does that also mean you don't eat pizza? Because if so, I can't join you.'

The boy didn't smile. 'Oh, you can mock.' From the fountain, the hymn-singing swelled to a mighty chorus. There must have been vocals on the backing tape.

Matt browsed through the horror section of the lending library. He felt vaguely spooked by the encounter. It reminded him of the time he and Neil had paused to listen to a particularly manic evangelist in New Street. *Why do you think you know better than God? You'll have to accept the truth soon.* His finger hovered, then jabbed towards Matt. *When you're dying and you know it. You're dying already, but you don't know it yet.*

He took out a couple of novels: Harris' *Red Dragon*, Campbell's *The Face That Must Die*. The main reason he was here was to visit that shop in Paradise Place, next to the library, that sold silk shirts at half price. One of those would be perfect for the post-election party tonight. A black one, obviously. Not that he was a fascist. And not really because black was how he felt inside. It was a tradition, something that he could belong to.

2

The post-election party was at a house in Prospect Road, on the Kings Heath side of Moseley. The huge trees flanking the roadway cast distorted shadows in the lamplight. Matt and Neil had walked here from home. They were both a little subdued, a reaction to Friday's euphoria; but the party would take care of that. Besides, Neil reasoned, you didn't need to be a New Labour android to feel relieved that those twisted gargoyles were no longer in control. The air felt cleaner somehow, the distant bassline of traffic less threatening.

Sean answered the door. His hair was cut aggressively short, and he looked pale. 'Come in.' Behind him, a dozen or so brightly dressed undergraduates were talking over a drowsy REM track. The air smelt of wine and cheap after-shave. Matt deposited their two bottles of cheap red in the kitchen, where an impressive array was already glittering with condensation, and poured glasses for himself and Neil. Over the fireplace in the living-room, someone had put together a huge picture of Tory faces going up the chimney in a river of flames and smoke. Each face overlapped its own double.

There were four people living in the house, including Sean and Perry, a Goth friend of Matt's. Every room was given over to the party. Neil recognised people he hadn't seen in years, graduates he'd thought had left Birmingham. And there was Anne, smiling through a glass, already looking woozy and unfocused. After a quick tour of the house, Neil went back to the kitchen and refilled his glass. Matt was upstairs somewhere. The doorbell rang every couple of minutes, admitting more wire-framed glasses and nervous smiles.

So many students, he thought. But whatever got learned

was also an unlearning. Reification. Forgetting. After a generation of ignorance, was it possible to start again? He was standing in the living-room, his hand on the election frieze as if it were a real fire. The surface behind it was brick. He felt a hand on his shoulder, and turned round.

Sean. His eyes were bloodshot, fires above mounds of ash. 'Hey, Neil. How many Marxists does it take to change a lightbulb?'

'No idea.' They were standing close to the wall. Neil could smell whisky on Sean's breath.

'Three. One to change the bulb. One not to change the bulb. And the third to both change and not change the bulb.'

Neil raised a plastic cup full of wine and gulped slowly. It tasted faintly metallic, like fermented blood. 'Did you ever read Adorno's *Negative Dialectics*?'

'Too difficult for me. I read *Minima Moralia*. The subtitle would have been a better title: *Notes from damaged life*. It was pretty bleak, but good. Like the whole of Europe was in pain, and he was trying to give it an X-ray. You know, I was talking to James from *Redbrick* the other day. He kept saying Marxism's a perfect theory, doesn't work in practice. Like saying an X-ray can't do as much for pain as morphine.'

'He's a wanker. You know, Foucault said it wasn't possible to be a historian and not be a Marxist.'

'Tell that to the fucking history department here.' Sean gripped Neil's arm. He was strangely physical when he was drunk, but there was nothing sexual about it. He made emotion out of politics. The opposite of Gary, who made politics out of emotion. 'Do you think we should be celebrating?'

'For the moment, yes. It's a victory for democracy. Besides, now the wankers are actually in power, we can stop supporting them.' They emptied their glasses and went back to the crowded kitchen for a refill. As they wandered through to the front room, Neil asked: 'Are you and Theresa still not talking?'

'Well, she thinks the sun shines out of Tony Blair's arse, so there's not really a basis for meaningful dialogue.' Sean grinned, but there was a twist of pain behind his eyes. He was drinking too much these days. 'Politics as a displacement activity, volume nine. Trying to stay friends isn't always the right thing. Don't worry about the play, we'll be fine for that. I find it quite therapeutic, playing love scenes with Michael. Have you ever been with a girl?'

'Yeah. Wasn't much else happening in Macclesfield. Even when I came here, took me a while to get sorted out. It's not like I threw up whenever I kissed a woman.'

Sean nodded thoughtfully. 'I never tried it with a man, you know. Had offers, but couldn't see the point. It would just be shagging. And I'm not into that.'

'I think that Julie likes you. From the Drama Soc.'

Sean winced. 'Do you think I could go out with a woman who wears a teddy bear in place of a rucksack?' The stereo in the front room was playing the Dead Kennedys' 'Moon Over Marin', a song that lurched from absurdity to naked horror. Already, some of the partygoers on the couch and the floor looked like they'd passed out.

Upstairs, Perry's room was misted over with smoke. A couple of joints flickered in the haze. The red eye of the stereo was the only fixed point. The Cure's *Entreat* was playing at a low volume: jagged guitars over sleepy rhythm, an atrocity in slow motion. Matt was sitting by the bed with three of his Goth friends. His eyes were already bloodshot. As Neil crouched beside him, his mouth gradually stretched into a smile. A boy in a faded Sisters of Mercy top was saying: 'This song reminds me of when I took acid for the first time. Stripped myself to the bone. I looked in the mirror and there was no face.' It didn't remind Neil of anything, except a kind of comfortable depression that would never need to change. He finished his glass and signalled to Matt that he was going to refill it.

At the top of the stairs, he passed a lad he'd never seen before. He was exactly Neil's type: short, stocky, with pale skin and heavy black eyebrows. He was rolling a thick joint on a copy of *The Face*. As he looked up, Neil noticed that his T-shirt bore the message DEAD GIRLS DON'T SAY NO. For a moment, Neil gazed into his dark eyes. Then he blinked, glanced away and hurried down the stairs. *Hope Anne doesn't see him. There'll be a bloodbath.*

Anne wasn't known for her tolerance of sexist males, whether or not they came with quotation marks. When they'd been undergraduates, she'd poured beer over a Trotskyite for insisting that the class struggle was ontologically prior to the struggle for women's rights. When Neil and Anne were going out together, he'd played her a Springsteen album and her only reaction had been: 'Why's he singing about making love to a *little girl*? Sounds like child abuse to me.' Not that she was entirely humourless. At that seminar where a visiting feminist historian had said 'You need post-structuralism to talk about differences between women,' she'd been the only one in the audience to laugh out loud.

It took him half an hour to find Anne. She was in one of the bedrooms, curled up on the floor, her eyes wide open. He knelt beside her, feeling suddenly like a visitor to a hospital. 'Anne. Are you OK? What's the matter?'

Her eyes searched for his image. 'Neil. Oh, you have already. Sweetheart.' She looked exhausted; her face was like paper, the lips flaking. 'I'm fine. It's just these pills I'm on. Tranquillisers. You're not supposed to drink.'

'Do you need to get home?'

'No, it's OK. Really.' She pushed her shoulders against the wall and twisted upright. 'How's the play?'

'I don't know. Last rehearsal was a bit stormy. Ideological differences. Sean thinks the play is secretly reactionary.'

'Yeah. He thinks everyone is secretly reactionary. At least Gary can't insist it's a disguised treatment of gay themes. Not when he gets to watch two guys fucking like pitbulls on amyl nitrite.'

Neil stared at her. How much had she drunk? Anne touched his hand. 'Sorry, Neil. I'm not getting at you. How's Matt?'

'Currently off his face. He's with Perry's mates. Smoking dope and reliving the eighties. Can't think why. I mean, he was a child.'

'There you go.' Anne picked up Neil's half-empty cup from the carpet and drained it. 'Everyone wants to go back to a time of innocence. But they don't know how to.'

She brushed her short auburn hair nervously with one hand. Although her face was blank from alcohol, Neil could see things moving behind it: tensions, shadows. 'You didn't use to talk like that,' he said. 'You said every sane person was driven to learn.'

'Yeah, well that was *my* innocence. Before I encountered the real world. Except it's not real. There's more lying and delusion and fucking ignorance in the world of work than I ever thought there was at university. Everything is so false. There's no theory could deal with it. And no practice either.'

'I thought you liked your job.' Anne worked as a sub-editor for a local newspaper.

'I do. It's just the management. There's this guy, Malcolm. Head of department. Hates women. In six months, he's corrupted the whole system. He plays people off against each other. Lets things get fucked up, then starts handing out blame. He's got no idea about work, but he's good at meetings. You know, when people talk about *office politics*, they mean office corruption. There's no real politics. If I had

something to make a case over, victimisation, sexual harassment, at least I'd feel I knew what to do. But it's not that.
It's insidious, undermining, twisted.' She raised her arms
tensely, then crossed her wrists at the base of her neck.

'Sounds like you ought to leave,' Neil said.

'It's not easy. You get into something, you start to rely on
it. Hard to get out. Even when what you think you've got
turns out to be something else.'

She was looking hard at him now. 'Anne, I'm sorry.'

'It's OK. I'm pissed. Run along and play. I'm going back
to sleep.' Anne settled in the corner and closed her eyes.
Neil watched her for a couple of minutes, then went back
downstairs to the kitchen.

The red wine was gone, but there was lots of cheap white
left. Neil filled a glass, gulped it down. It tasted acidic. He
couldn't feel the alcohol. All around him, students were
laughing, arguing, flirting, snogging, dancing. The wall of
voices was as impenetrable as a foreign language. A few words
broke loose from it: *Did you see the results come in? – No, I
missed it all. Went to bed early with a headache. – What's his
name?* He refilled the glass and went back upstairs to look
for Matt. Then a hand grabbed his arm and pulled him into
the spare room.

It was Gary. He was wearing a white frilly shirt with a red
cravat, and drinking vodka from one of those small frosted
bottles. 'Neil darling, there's someone I'd like you to meet.
This is Raymond.' He gestured towards a younger lad who,
like Gary, was tall, thin and very pale; unlike Gary, he was
beautiful. Raymond shook Neil's hand, gripping the fingers.
He was wearing a blue–black shirt of some iridescent
material, and tight jeans. 'Raymond's an actor. A real one.'

Neil became aware of how drunk he was. He couldn't look
away from the boy's face. 'I've been in a few films recently.
You might have seen me. Things on Channel 4.'

'Sorry. I don't see a lot of TV.'

'Just made this film with Anna Friel. And Johnny Lee Miller. And Ewan MacGregor. Me and Johnny Lee Miller, we're rivals for Anna Friel. I get to do this slow dance with her. And Johnny's watching, but is he jealous of me or her? And then she goes off with Ewan, and I'm left with Johnny, just walking off together. It's all very . . . ambiguous.'

'Yeah? That's cool.' Neil swallowed another mouthful of wine. His stomach felt tight. 'Have you met Sean and Michael? They're in the play that Gary's in, at the Uni.'

'We're in no hurry to go out there,' Gary said quietly. 'It's full of straights in rugby shirts, drinking Grolsch. This is our little queer bunker. Our cubicle.' He laughed, stumbled, and steadied himself against the wall.

'Gary, we don't need a bunker,' Neil said. 'There's all kinds of people here. It's not them and us.'

'It's always them and us.' He glanced at Raymond and made a small hand signal. Neil felt sure he'd been meant to see it. 'But maybe I *will* go and talk to someone. Leave you two to get to know each other.' He slipped out, like rain passing between houses in the dark. A shift of the light, and he was gone.

Raymond touched the fabric of Neil's shirt. 'Gary talks a lot about you.' *That's news to me,* Neil thought. He felt Gary's will numbing him like kevlar, like wine. 'You know, I used to be in other films. Hardcore. I was the one who took it. But I always gave it in the end.' His gentle fingers traced the line of buttons down Neil's chest to the navel. 'There's a garden round the back. I could give you a screen test.'

'Ray, I'm here with my boyfriend. It's not . . .'

'If he comes along for the ride, that's cool. I don't mind sleeping in the middle of the bed.'

Neil shook his head. 'Sorry.' He didn't want to share Matt. Or even Raymond. He reached up and touched the boy's cheek, tracing the bone with one fingertip. They kissed slowly, deeply. It was lucky he was too drunk to get a hard-on. Then Neil closed his eyes and turned away. 'I've got to go.'

'Gary was right about you. He said you were a coward.' Neil tried to drown his voice in the thudding of bass guitar that filled the stairwell. His mouth felt dry, alien. He stumbled into the kitchen, which resembled a concrete bottle bank, and eventually located a half-full bottle. Some first-year queens were attempting group therapy on the staircase. *People can only like you if you like yourself. Do you like yourself? – Does self include hair?* Neil realised he had to stop walking. He sat down in the living-room and watched blurred figures dance with deliberate awkwardness to 'Common People'.

'All right, darling?' It was Gary again. 'Don't tell me you walked off and left him. And after I'd worked so hard to set you up.'

'I'll bet you did.' Neil felt confused and angry. The kiss was still numbing his lips. 'Next time, don't bother.'

'Look, I know that Johnny Lee Miller stuff was just bullshit. But he *is* a real actor.'

'You're telling me.' Neil stood up, then almost blacked out. Gary put out a hand, supporting him. He took a deep breath. The dark patches faded from his eyes. Gary's hand was still on his arm. 'Cheers.'

He was vaguely aware that most of the people had gone. It was very late. He passed the spare room, noticing that its light was off. Perry's room was still a twilight haze of smoke and hair. A Goth was crouched over one of the speakers, using a straw to inhale the fumes from a crumpled piece of tinfoil. Robert Smith was wailing, trapped in a fugue that could never end. *You know I believe you, but faith isn't everything.*

Matt hadn't moved in however long it had been. For a moment his face was a skull, caught in a twisted wrap of smoke. Neil touched his arm, gripping black silk. 'I want to go home.' His boyfriend stared at him. Eyes streaked with red, black coals in rings of fire.

'Chill out,' Matt said eventually. 'There's no rush. We're having a good time.'

'You could have fooled me. It's the land of the dead in here. Why do you go on hiding in this . . . miserable crap? This is a new era. Everything's going to change.'

'Neil, you're hammered.' Matt sucked the remnant of a dead joint. 'I'm just too tired to move.'

The room was half full of drowsy, insomniac students. Their dreams streaked the dense air. Neil felt a kind of senseless, vacant rage. 'Fuck this. I'm going. See you tomorrow.' Matt stared at him, a flicker of panic crossing his still face. Then he closed his eyes, no longer there. Though he knew it wouldn't take much to persuade Matt to come back with him, Neil felt his own anger steer him away like a hand between his shoulder-blades.

In the spare room, Neil switched on the light to find his coat. Raymond and another boy were lying together on the floor, asleep. A duvet covered them below the waist. Their shoes and trousers formed a small heap at the foot of the bed. Neil felt a pang of lust, as pure and bright as a melting ice crystal. He pulled his coat from the heap on the bed and walked out into the night.

Cars scraped the darkness. A shadow melted from a garden wall and landed on four legs. A young couple got out of a taxi and helped each other along the street, their laughter shattering against the cold air. Distant streetlamps flickered like dying torch batteries. Neil didn't know how he was getting home, but somehow he was. Instinct. Every moment brought new images and sensations, but they weren't connected. It was like the night he'd walked home through

Alderley Edge, only seeing in the flashes of lightning. At last his key was gripping the lock, turning.

He woke up several times in the night, convinced there was someone in the room with him. Yellow light filtered thinly through the curtains. Someone leaning over the washbasin, combing his hair or cleaning his teeth. When daylight washed the pale walls, he got out of bed and drank three mugfuls of water. His mouth tasted as if it were coated with a thin film of shit. But the hangover hadn't really kicked in yet. After a while he undressed, washed, made some coffee.

Matt probably wouldn't emerge until lunchtime. Neil missed waking up next to him. He opened the curtain; sunlight dripped like pure water through the dusty glass. His eyes drifted over a shelf of books, a lower shelf of records and tapes. Matt was one of the few lovers who'd had the curiosity to look right through his record collection. Who'd surveyed the 45s all the way down the stack, from the limited-edition indie coloured vinyl of Marion and Tindersticks down to the hidden singles of shame: the tear-stained, scratchy copies of 'Only You', 'To Be Reborn' and 'Every Loser Wins'.

Neil drank black coffee and listened to *Nebraska* as his brain slowly re-engaged. Through the gaps in the sparse instrumentation he could hear voices in the house, cars in the street outside. It was past midday. He went to Matt's room and knocked on the black-and-white zombie poster. The door swung open. Inside, the curtain was still drawn. The bed hadn't been slept in, since the clothes Matt had been wearing before the party were scattered across it.

Irritably, he went downstairs and made himself a sandwich. There was no-one about. Somebody had left a slice of blackened toast and some almost homogenised beans on a plate by the cooker. Neil suspected he'd done that himself; but his memories felt like rumours. An afternoon of serious work beckoned. Adorno, Marcuse, maybe early Foucault. A shot of righteous anger.

3

The pillow was smeared with ash. Matt slipped out of the bed. His eyes were sore. Something glinted on the carpet by his feet: a torn piece of foil. Perry was still asleep, a tangled mass of black hair on the other pillow. The curtains let in light, but not colour. Matt dressed as quietly as possible. He didn't feel hungover or guilty. He felt numb. There was a knotted condom near his shoes. He considered flushing it down the toilet, but in the end left it. As he opened the bedroom door Perry whispered, *Matt?* He turned and said, 'I've got to go. Take care.'

'And you.' The house was still marked by the party: cigarette stubs, plastic cups, the stink of wine. It had been almost dawn when he and Perry had slipped into bed. They'd been discreet; nobody had seen them. Neil didn't have to know. But hadn't he said that honesty was the first principle of a meaningful life? It hadn't been planned. He'd just felt a bit down, with Neil storming off like that. He wished he'd never gone to the party.

It was warmer outside, with sunlight trapped in the damp air. The trees were glistening. As he walked, Matt felt a twinge of pain in his gut. Perry had been his first student lover, back in their first year. He wasn't beautiful, but he was tall and sensitive, and had a nice sense of humour. He wore a black cloak and a smoking-jacket, like a Victorian gentleman. Last night seemed to close a chapter in Matt's life. It had been somehow a way of confirming that he wanted to be with Neil. You had to go away sometimes to come back. It was something Matt had done all his life, finding emotion in the negative.

By the time he got back to Trafalgar Road, it was two o'clock. He'd not eaten since around four, when Perry had defrosted a pizza for them and two other stoned children of the night. Lunch could wait until he'd talked to Neil, but not long beyond that. Red placards were still attached to most of the lamp-posts, which cheered him up.

Neil was in his room, taking notes from a library book. His handwriting was tiny and neat. 'Are you OK?'

'Fine. Sorry I didn't make it back. How are you?'

'All right. Sorry I left like that. I was pissed. And pissed off.' They embraced. 'Where have you been?'

'Nowhere. I mean, I stayed at the house.'

'With Perry?' Neil knew Perry was Matt's ex. His stare was questioning, but not hostile. Matt kept up eye contact for slightly too long, knew he'd have to say it.

'Yeah. Neil, I . . . You know you said telling the truth was the only way to live?'

'I didn't mean it.' Neil's tone was flat. His eyes were beyond reach. 'Go on. You and . . . Perry. Well?'

'I'm sorry. It wasn't planned. Old habits, you know? Look, we talked about . . . you know. If something happened.'

'Yeah, I know. That was when you were scared of losing me.' Neil's voice had no inflection. He was hiding somewhere inside himself, only just in touch. 'Did he fuck you?'

'We were careful.' Perry was always good like that. He'd taught Matt a lot in the old days. A year and a half ago, a long time.

'I'm sure you were. I wasn't assuming you'd gone mad. The point is, you let him *fuck* you.'

'Why's that so important?'

'Trust, intimacy . . . I don't know. You're right. We agreed this could happen.' Neil's face was blank.

'I'm sorry. But I don't want you to see more in this than

there is. It's not the start of something. It's more like the end
of something else.'

'The end of what, exactly?' He came towards Matt, as if
about to hit him; then he put his arms around him. 'It doesn't
matter what we say, you know. It's what we do that counts.
Words are no protection.' He kissed Matt slowly, his tongue
reaching deep, his fingers digging into Matt's shoulder-
blades. Then he stepped away. 'Your mouth tastes of come.'
Matt flinched. It was a lie.

They stared at each other for a few seconds. Then Matt
said, 'I'd better get some lunch. Do you want anything?' Neil
shook his head.

Matt went downstairs. He was trying to light the grill when
he heard the front door slam. The sound seemed to echo, as
if the house were both larger and emptier than it was in
reality. He still felt numb, in a way that had nothing to do
with dope. The grill lit up. He watched the toast brown, char
and burn.

4

The bar was below street level, at the bottom of a twisted
flight of stairs. It was arranged like a studio theatre: an oval
bar in the middle, small tables all around. Wherever you
were, you could see everybody else. Not that there were many
people to see at this time. It was more of a night place. But
then, it was always night here. A few middle-aged men in
suits were sipping at pints of Guinness. A skinny boy was
staring into the juke-box as if someone might be hiding inside
it. Another boy, wearing a blue denim shirt, was examining
his face in a pocket mirror. A thin trail of smoke rose from
an abandoned ashtray.

Someone coughed at his shoulder. Neil looked up. 'Can I
get you a drink?' It was one of the suits. He had a plump,

almost jowly face with worried, childlike eyes. He looked like
he might have been good-looking once and had never quite
got over losing it.

'No thanks. I'm OK.' The man gazed at him as if to
question his statement, or just to fix Neil's image in his head
for future reference. Neil knew he wasn't looking his best:
crumpled shirt, pale skin, streaks under his eyes that could
be mistaken for badly applied eyeliner. He wouldn't mind
being propositioned by someone dodgy. But this guy just
wasn't dodgy enough.

The juke-box shifted from nameless disco fodder to something breathy and tearful – Patsy Cline, maybe. Neil sipped
the last of his whisky. It tasted of smoke. Did Matt understand that being told the truth was no comfort when you
couldn't stand what you were hearing? It would be easier to
live with silence. He didn't want to talk to anyone. He just
wanted something to happen that would make this morning
the past.

Eventually he got up and went to the bar. The barman
was chatting with two homely-looking leathermen on the far
side of the optics from Neil. As he was waiting, the boy who'd
been holding a pocket mirror came and stood beside him.
His hair was spiked, the pale tint of fool's gold. Slowly, he
raised his mouth to Neil's ear and whispered: 'How long is
it?'

Just as slowly, Neil shifted along the bar until their arms
were touching. He breathed gently into the boy's pale ear:
'Since when?'

'Since you were last here.' The boy was smiling. 'You look
like you're waiting for someone who hasn't turned up.' Neil
shook his head. 'Maybe not. Let me tell you something about
this place, anyway. Nobody ever makes a date here. If
someone says he'll meet you here, then he won't turn up.
Even if he was your boyfriend before that. Anywhere else on

the scene, if someone makes a date, he might keep it. If he doesn't, you might find him in here.'

'Cheers.' The barman was still gossiping with the twins. 'Do you want a drink?'

'Since you're asking.' They sat down together at the back, near the juke-box. The boy who was standing there gave them a contemptuous glance, then crossed to a pile of *Boyz* magazines and started reading. They talked for a few minutes. Then the bleached boy touched Neil's hand. 'No offence,' he said, 'but I'm not trying to pick you up. I'm into older men. My ideal man is like Haagen-Dazs ice-cream: soft, rich and thick. Don't get me wrong, I don't do it for money. But I like being given things I couldn't buy. Nice clothes, holidays.' He smiled again. 'What do you look for in a man?'

'Don't know. Youth, energy, charm. Sense of humour.'

'So what are you doing here? This is the pit, babes. Anyone with a sense of irony would set off the smoke alarms.'

'I wondered what would do that. The smoke doesn't.'

'Are you just here because you're pissed off about someone?'

'Well, yes. But also . . . I can't decide what's right for me until I know what's wrong.'

'Well, be careful.' He kissed Neil gently on the mouth. 'See you around.'

The kiss left Neil's face stiff with energy. There was so much he didn't know about this city, though he'd lived here nearly six years. He might as well have been living in Macclesfield. He'd only been here once before, with a group of friends. At the time, they'd discussed how the dark stairs to the basement bar were symbolic of oppression. Now it seemed exciting. But maybe that was lack of sleep, and drinking on an empty stomach. He needed some fresh air. Then he'd find another bar, and decide what to do about Matt. Or not.

Outside, the late-afternoon chill made him feel like a scrap of paper. He wished he'd thought to bring a jacket. As he turned away from the pub, a figure emerged from the carpark. It was the juke-box boy: cropped hair, a grey jacket, artfully ripped jeans. He wasn't tall, but he stooped as if he were. Neil watched him disappear into the underpass that led through to the two glittering tower blocks. The sky behind them was flecked with blood.

He was about to go into the Fountain in Wrentham Street when the boy reappeared from the shadows, smoking a roll-up. From the way the boy avoided his eyes, Neil knew he was being stalked. He stopped, took a step forward. Brown hair, high cheekbones, papery skin, a thin mouth you couldn't imagine kissing. The boy was thin; his jeans were loose on him, the belt holding them up. He looked at Neil and breathed a knot of smoke. Then he gestured *this way*, and started walking towards the Chinese quarter.

They walked on together in silence. The boy's gait was nervous, jerky; he kept stooping and then straightening up again. 'What's your name, man?'

'Neil. What's yours?'

'Neil. That's good. Do you?' Neil didn't bother replying. 'Where you from?'

'Macclesfield. Where are you from?'

'I been everywhere, man.' The boy dropped the roll-up and twisted it under his foot. 'You gonna come with me, then? I want to show you something.' His fingers touched Neil's arm; the tension in them was like a static charge. He was eighteen, maybe younger. 'I been everywhere, but I started here. Everything goes back. True?'

'Maybe.' Neil had no intention of going home. They walked past a series of boarded or shuttered factories. A torn bin-liner flapped in an empty window. 'Were you following me from the Jester?'

'I wanted to talk to you. But it's no good in there, man. Fuckin' queens talking about their salaries and their houses, man. Make me sick.'

Neil smiled. 'Property is theft, yeah?'

'You calling me a fucking thief?' The boy's eyes were like flints, ready to spark off anything they touched.

'No. Sorry . . . I was trying to say I agree with you.'

The tension in the boy's face eased only very slightly. 'Are you a student or something? Bet you are. You're cheap, but you've got no idea how to handle yourself.'

'Does it matter what I am?'

'It matters to you. I don't give a shit.' The boy paused under a railway bridge. Its sides were lined with steel panels, bolted into the brick, and it stank of piss. Neil didn't know exactly where he was. He watched the boy unwrap a tiny string of tobacco, divide it lengthways with a fingernail and roll an impossibly thin cigarette. In the shadows, it was like a concentrated point of energy that could feed them both. The boy reached up and touched the side of Neil's face. His fingers traced the jawline to the neck, then slipped away.

'I saw you in that pub,' he said. A puff of smoke made his face invisible. 'You looked like you wanted to be shown the rules. But like you also thought you knew, and you'd forgotten. I couldn't stop looking at your face, man. I want to show you . . . something.' And he was off again, walking faster than before.

They were heading further into some bit of Digbeth, or maybe Highgate, that Neil didn't recognise. He saw a boarded-up pub with the word WELCOME sprayed across the blackened frontage; a salvage yard where rusting car bodies were slowly crushing the ones below. Chicken wire broke up the reddish glow of the setting sun into random flashes. It was getting colder.

Then the boy stopped. He touched Neil's sleeve and

pointed below their feet. 'Are we gonna make a go of it, then?' Neil looked down: a muddy slope led to the pale towpath beside a tight, glistening skin of dark water. He felt a blind impulse to go through with this stirring in his groin. This desire had nothing to do with fun. It had to do with anger, and hurt. He nodded.

'Do you like playing rough?' the boy said.

Neil blinked at him. Was this some kind of test, a question at the gate? He didn't know what to say. 'Maybe.'

The boy laughed. 'Maybe? Take it or leave it?' He shook his head; dropped his cigarette on to the slope, where its grey smoke blew away in a moment. Then he slipped through the gap in the metal fence and began stepping carefully down, as if looking for footholds that he already knew. Neil let him reach the towpath before following.

It was darker by the canal: the sun had already set. To their left was a corrugated-iron wall riveted to concrete posts, with coils of razor-wire above it. To their right, across the still water, were the backs of living and dead factories. Pipes stuck out through gaps in the brickwork; extractor fans turned slowly; shattered windows had been bricked up from inside. A rusty fire escape reminded Neil of Moseley. He had the sensation of having fallen. They passed under a bridge; the canal reflected scraps of graffiti. Just beyond that, a hazel shrub poked its thin silver-tipped buds through a wire fence.

'There's nobody down here this time of day,' the boy said. In the stillness, his voice seemed louder. 'It's too late for the guys walking their dogs, and too early for the others. It's a city down here at night, man. Beggars, queers, smackheads, prostitutes. Bet you'd love it. You'd write a poem about it.'

'What's your name?'

'I'll write it down for you,' the boy said. 'Wouldn't want you to forget.' He paused and rolled a final, matchstick-thin cigarette, then threw the paper into the canal. It floated. 'You ever been inside?'

Neil wasn't sure if he was talking about prison or anal sex. 'Inside what?'

'I'll show you what it's like.' He glanced at Neil. It was getting darker now. 'Has anyone ever told you you're beautiful?' His tone was flat, neither hungry nor tender. Neil didn't know how to answer. 'A man told me I was beautiful once,' the boy said. 'I didn't feel beautiful when he'd finished with me.'

'I'm sorry.'

'Fuck it. Let's do the business. We're here now.' Another bridge. The wall had alcoves on the far side. On the near side, they were bricked up. The boy stopped just beyond it. Neil could see the wall was hollow. An arched entrance led into the sealed-off alcoves. The other side was solid wall. A low arch framed each alcove. The boy stopped to go in. Neil followed him. Just a few feet from the entrance, they were in darkness.

A trace of light filtered through gaps in the brickwork at the top of each alcove. In the one nearest the entrance, Neil could see a heap of old clothes and burnt paper. It smelt of soot, wet ashes, dead fire. The boy clicked on his lighter; a thin oval of light framed his bony face. 'Just like a cell. True?' He stepped forward. 'Look.' The flame illuminated a message scraped into the brickwork: KAZ SHAGED MARTIN HERE. 'Must have taken ages to write that.' The lighter clicked off.

Neil reached out. His hands found the boy's shoulders. They kissed. The boy shivered. 'It's as cold as fuck.'

'How cold is fuck?' Neil said.

The boy laughed flatly. 'You're about to find out.'

'Look, I don't want to . . . you know. Go all the way.'

The same empty laugh, like bad acting. 'You haven't got

any fucking idea what *all the way* means.' A taut hand stroked him through his shirt, his jeans. 'Told you I was gonna show you something, Neil. I didn't just mean this place. Or what's in my pants. I want to make you see.'

'See what?'

'Come in here.' The hands guided Neil into an alcove, almost out of sight of the entrance. The boy smelt of old sweat and smoke. They kissed again. 'Neil.' He did. Fingers gripped his hair. He reached up to touch the boy's crotch, and heard glass breaking against the wall behind them. His fingers brushed denim. Then pain tore across his face.

He couldn't move. The hand in his hair stopped him even falling. He tried to scream, but there was something wrong with his mouth. 'Can you see now?' The darkness had become a red blur, like a fingerprint in blood. 'What the rules are. Can you see?' The hand pulled his face back, and the glass stabbed again. It twisted, striking bone. He still couldn't scream. He knew there was no face left. The boy stooped and muttered something in his ear, then stepped past him. He forced himself upright. The entrance was a dark flame. He tried to walk towards it.

His shoulder smashed into the wall. He turned to face a paler strip in the curtain of blood. It opened to let him out. Now he could see, like a faint cartoon or a double exposure: wall, towpath, canal. He was on his feet, moving. His shirt was soaked with blood. His left eye wouldn't open. He didn't dare touch his face. The pain was a riff in his head, a scream of feedback, the worst guitar he could imagine. If he stopped moving, or lay down in the canal, he knew the pain would go on forever. He had to find the boy and beg him to finish the job.

Up ahead, a yellow light was glowing on the canal bank. It shimmered in the water. An angler was hunched by a wooden box. He looked up as Neil came towards him. And

it was the look on the angler's face that finally made Neil
lose consciousness, falling on to a path that felt no more solid
than the blank water of the canal.

chapter 3

....

place of recovery

1

The hospital was a group of red-brick buildings close to the Bristol Road. Outside, there was a modernist statue of an injured man sprawling on the ground and another man reaching out, helping him to stand up. The late-afternoon sun blinked from the windows of the main building, a dazed red light. Matt rubbed his eyes, then stood there and tried to make his hands stop shaking. If he was going to be a doctor, he'd have to do better than this. The call had come early this morning. Neil had spent the night in A & E. They'd had to wait for him to regain consciousness before they could find out where he lived.

Quite badly cut up, the nurse had said. Matt didn't want to imagine what that could mean. His mental image of Neil's face was blurred. Theresa had wanted to come with him, but he'd said it would be easier for him and Neil to talk if they were alone together. He wasn't sure that Neil would even want to talk to him. He didn't know if the things he'd brought – books, chocolate, orange juice, a copy of *Mojo* – would be appropriate, medically or emotionally. He didn't have a clue.

The receptionist directed him to the Maxillofacial Unit,

where a nurse led him through a ward of curtained-off beds.
Neil was in a tiny side room with a door. He was sitting up
in bed, a drip attached to his wrist. He had a patch over one
eye. The lower half of his face was covered in bandages. The
room was so dark that Matt could only make out that much.
'Neil.' He sat on a chair by the side of the bed. 'How are
you?'

'Matt.' A black mouth opened. Neil reached out; their
hands linked. Neil's fingers traced his palm, his knuckles, his
wrist. 'It's good to hear your voice.' His voice was slurred,
maybe from drugs. It sounded like an echo.

'What happened to you?'

'I don't remember.' He paused. 'There was a boy. He
followed me from the Jester. Picked me up. We went down
by the canal. Then he went mad.'

'Oh, Christ. Do you know his name?'

'He wouldn't tell me.' Silence drew out between them like
a thread. 'I'm sorry.'

'I'm sorry too. It was my fault.' He couldn't look at the
single, dark eye watching him above the bandages. 'If I hadn't
been so fucking stupid – '

'We were both stupid. We are. Both stupid.'

'It doesn't matter now. Are you going to be all right?'

'How do I know?' Matt looked at him. The eye was bloodshot, scared. 'My left eye ... they think it's just some
blood. The sight will come back. But the doctor's not sure.
There's damage on both sides. It's not as bad as I thought.
There's still a face, not a skull.' His hand shivered. 'Or maybe
it's just the bandages holding it together.'

Matt felt himself starting to cry. 'You'll be OK, Neil. I
know you will.' He took Neil's other hand, as if they were
about to dance. 'I love you. You know that, don't you?'

'Yes.' Neil looked at him as if preparing to say something

else, then looked away. In the half-light, his torso seemed impossibly thin.

'You'd be amazed what they can do with facial injuries. There's hardly anything they can't repair. It just takes time.'

Neil drew his hands away, let them fall in his lap. When he didn't speak, it was easy to believe that he wasn't Neil at all. His mask of bandages tipped towards his pale chest. Then he shook his head, wincing from the pain. 'I can't keep awake,' he said. 'It's the drugs. You'd better go.'

'Brought some things. I don't know if you . . .' Matt placed them on the bedside cabinet.

'Cheers. I can't read just now, but it's good to have them. You know? Reminds me what there is to come back to.' He lifted an unstable hand to brush Matt's cheek, his lips. 'Thanks for coming.'

'You're welcome, babe. I'll see you tomorrow.' Matt hesitated, wondering if he should kiss Neil's forehead. It seemed too formal a gesture. Instead, he lifted Neil's hand and kissed the narrow fingers. 'Take care.'

Before leaving the hospital, Matt had a word with the staff nurse. Neil was on a very low dose of morphine. Enough to disconnect him from the pain, but not from reality. His injuries weren't serious, the nurse said, but they would leave a lot of scarring. The main worry was Neil's left eye. 'We'll have to wait until the blood drains away before we can assess how much damage there is. There's no point frightening him by testing his vision now.'

Outside, Matt felt the noise of traffic hit him like a wave. Yet the hospital hadn't been quiet either; it wasn't a physical silence that he felt ebbing inside him, fading away. It was the silence of illness, a pattern of missed notes that you never got used to hearing. Cars and lorries were roaring down the Bristol Road. He waited at the intersection until the green

man stuttered into life, then crossed. The sky was beginning
to fill with darkness.

2

After Matt, there was another visitor. Detective Constable
Willetts, a young man with curly hair and an expression of
deep-seated bitterness. His accent reminded Neil of lads
looking for trouble in Macc pubs. They'd spoken briefly in
the morning, when Neil had muttered a description of the
attack and sketched his attacker with a shaky hand. If Willetts
had been offended by the story, or by the illegality that had
almost happened, he'd given no sign of it. Now he looked
like he might have some news to impart. 'How you feeling?'

Neil shrugged. 'Don't feel much. I'm on morphine.'

'Since you came here, or is that normal for you?' Neil
lifted a weary finger. 'Got something for you to look at,' the
policeman said. 'Is this the guy who attacked you?' He lifted
a small photo to Neil's good eye. On cue, the nurse turned
up the light.

A teenager, cropped dark hair. Similar cheekbones, but
otherwise nothing like. Neil shook his head. 'How about this
one?'

Neil flinched. The room blurred; he could see a deep red
glow through the wall, a furnace. Involuntarily he put up a
hand to shield his face. Too late. *Can you see now? What the
rules are. Can you see?* Under the bandages, something
touched him.

'Are you OK?' Willetts was still holding the photo. Neil
forced himself to look at it again. It was obviously a police
mugshot. The boy looked younger, maybe sixteen.

'Looks like him. I'm pretty sure.' He winced at the word
pretty. 'I'm sure. Who is he?'

'His name's Ian Moore. He's not long out of prison. Went

in for six months, stayed three years. Went down for shop-lifting. Then he got a name for beating up queers. No offence, like. He cut up one with an empty tin can. The guy fought him off, broke his hand. It happens all the time. Moore was in solitary for a while. He said the man he attacked had raped him. There was no evidence. And the incident was mixed up in his head with something about a juvenile detention centre two years before. Two stories tangled up. The prison governor decided it was a cover story.'

'What do you mean?'

'Something he'd made up to justify himself. Why he hated queers. Why he was so violent. Just about everyone in prison's got an abuse story. A lot of them are true. But even so . . . You remember when there was all that crap about Satanic abuse in the Orkneys? Winson Green Prison had seven guys in one year remembering how they'd been raped by devil-worshippers. The prison psychiatrist told me. Seven versions of the same story that was going round the prison. All involving a child called Mike who was buried under the M6.' Willetts smiled bleakly. 'Anyway, nobody believed Moore. He was released in February. Six weeks ago, he broke his pro-bation and disappeared. We didn't know where he was.'

'Do you think he's still here?'

'Doubt it. But he's a local boy, so he might not go far. Or he might come back.'

Neil closed his eyes. The morphine was starting to wear off. He could see the furnace, feel its breath melting the hard mask his face had become. The blank wall cracked, revealing layers of images and words packed tight as asbestos. From somewhere, he heard the policeman saying 'I'd better go . . . I'll come back another time.' He hugged his bruised arms to his chest and tried not to shake.

Through the roar of the furnace, he could hear the nurse saying 'Take it easy.' There was a hand on his arm, then a needle going in. His mouth was dry. He must have been screaming. Gradually, the heat and the terrible glow faded. But the crack in the wall remained.

When he opened his eyes, both Willetts and the nurse had gone. The light had been turned back down. In the far corner by the door, he could just make out a figure, standing. It moved into the doorway, and its shadow reached the edge of his bed. He couldn't see its face.

As clear as a photograph: the blackened church tower in the centre of Macclesfield. Four spires and four little crosses. Behind it, a distant hillside with trees and fields. As if the tower belonged to another landscape. A childish thought he'd never quite shaken off. You needed something to lift your gaze. Otherwise, the town enclosed you.

The streets were narrow and crooked, built on a steep hillside. Some of them were just staircases. A lot of the buildings were unstable, and they were always being torn down and rebuilt. Throughout his childhood, there'd been scaffolding everywhere. It was like a town someone had started and not finished.

He'd loved it then. The strange angles, the unpainted stone buildings. The museum with its Egyptian treasures looted from a vault: the painted empty sarcophagus, surrounded by carved tablets and lapis lazuli figures. And miles away, but always in sight, the bony ridges and green skin of the Pennines. The rocky footpaths that led in all directions, but there was nowhere to get to except back to the town. The villages were ghosts: if you caught the bus to Prestbury or Alderley Edge, there was hardly anything to show you'd got there.

After he'd reached puberty, he'd begun to see the other town. The people who'd lost work or never found it, or settled for jobs they hated. The weekend violence. The girls wearing heavy make-up to disguise the bitterness in their faces. Macclesfield was a tiny island of working-class life: three housing estates in a sea of wealthy commuters and Tory landowners. It was built on the silk industry – but a town less like silk was hard to imagine.

Neil's father was a scientist at ICI's Mereside site off the road to Prestbury. He'd started working there when Deborah Curtis was in the accounts department, but he'd never spoken to her. Martin was a good company man. He had no time for politics, voted Tory, always said the anger and violence in the town came purely from drink. At least he didn't beat up Neil's mother. They'd found much subtler ways of hurting each other, over the years.

At sixteen, Neil and some of his friends had started drinking in the local pubs. Des usually bought the drinks, because he was tall and had a bit of a moustache. It was easier at the weekends: the bar staff were too busy to ask questions. One night, they'd been huddled in a corner of the Queen's Hotel opposite the station, watching a crowd of sweating drunks. They were trying to copy the mannerisms: shouting, swaggering, drinking in frantic gulps. Neil couldn't hear their voices above the beat of New Order's 'True Faith'. They could have been miming.

Near the bar, a young couple had got into an argument. He was trying to pull her towards the door, she was refusing to budge. Another man squared up to the first. They began a slow, deliberate choreography of threat. Other men backed away, hands spread out. Silence fell over that side of the bar.

Then, suddenly, there was a crash of breaking glass from the far corner. A man staggered out of the shadows, screaming. His face was a mask of blood. A glittering triangle of glass was embedded in his cheek. Weaving between invisible trees, he reached the door and crashed out into the street. Nobody followed him straight away: people finished their drinks and then began to leave. Within five minutes, the bar was nearly empty. When Neil and his friends left, the man who'd been glassed was gone. A trail of burning coins led across the road and down an alley.

Did it really happen like that? Or was the shadow walking through his memories, pausing to stab, moving on? He'd spent less time with the gang after that, made new friends at the sixth-form college in Stockport while they'd stayed in Macclesfield to work or not work, using male bravado as a mask for creeping alcoholism. He still had Des' phone number somewhere.

Just after the GCSEs, a boy called Alan at Neil's school had thrown a party. It was really Alan's older brother, who was hoping to get his hands on some schoolgirls and was looking after the house while their parents were away. The house was at Alderley Edge, not far from the hotel where Neil and his friends sometimes drank.

That night was warm and cloudy, as if you were standing at the bottom of an unchilled glass of beer. Neil felt uneasy, not part of any group, aware of too many things going on that didn't include him. He drank at least a bottle of white wine, danced with a girl and snogged her against a wall in which red shadows lived. He didn't have the nerve to take it further; the sight of a couple in the bathroom, his bare arse between her skinny knees, left him disorientated and faintly nauseous. Maybe it was the booze. Around midnight, he decided to walk home. The air prickled around him; stars flickered in and out of sight.

He took a wrong turning on the country road, following a side road that became a footpath. He could see the distant cluster of yellow lights that was Macclesfield, ahead and below. It started to rain – unevenly at first, large drops hitting him like flob, and then steadily. The sky was a thick, starless grey.

The first flash of lightning lit up the trees around him like stained-glass windows, curtained by a fringe of rain. He started to run, looking for an open space, and almost stumbled over the Edge into thin air.

A steep footpath led him down, back into the trees. His jeans were heavy with splashed mud. When he reached the foot of the slope, he knelt and vomited. The rain washed his face clean. He thought of buried knights, blind ghostly dogs, the percussion of Alan Garner's words. Lightning struck close by, several times; it was like watching a flock of birds fly across a steady white light. His clothes were soaked through.

The dawn reached him on the edge of Macclesfield, fatigue making him drunk all over again. The angular buildings cast long shadows across the roads. He was thinking of the girl at the party, his first real kiss. The rain had stopped; his shirt was steaming in the pale light. His feet were aching. He was trying to remember her name.

The shadow was still there, at the foot of his bed, half turned away. Beyond it, he could see through the layers, see the cut edges of memory. Everything was here at once, frozen in time. There was nowhere to hide.

3

In the morning, his face was drier. The swelling around his left eye was going down. The nurse took off his bandages so that the doctor, a thin man with a beard, could look into the ruins of his face. 'Starting to heal up.' He spoke with a high-pitched, nasal Brummie accent. 'We'll leave the patch on your eye for a bit, but you should be OK there. Have you tried talking?'

'Yeah. Had visitors.' Neil's mouth felt dry, the lips stiff. Like a puppet. 'It's OK, I can speak.'

'You're just not feeling too chatty right now?' The doctor

eyed his face with the calm intelligence of someone reading a computer screen. 'Does it hurt?' Neil nodded. 'Of course, there's some bruising as well as the actual wounds. And your brain tends to interpret pain in any part of your face as injury to the whole face. Subjectively, there are no regions in the face. Too many nerves.

'There's some damage near the mouth and the left eye, but I think they'll recover. It's probably best not to operate. We'll give you a few days to heal up, then send you home. You'll need a few weeks, probably, before you go back to work. Oh no, you're a student, aren't you?' He smiled. 'Even so.'

The nurse wrapped Neil's head in a fresh set of bandages. He felt relieved, as if his missing trousers had reappeared in one of those train journey dreams. When he opened his good eye, the doctor was sitting beside him. He could just make out the shadow standing by the cracked wall. It reminded him of somebody.

' . . . too early to decide,' the doctor was saying. 'You'll notice the avulsion – that is, the wound area – looks quite rough. We need to let the scar tissue form, then use it as a source of material. Like Polyfilla. If we tidied the wounds up too much, you'd be losing tissue that could still be saved. It's how you're going to look a few years from now that really matters.'

After he'd gone, Neil sat up in bed and watched the reddish light seep through the walls. He had nothing to fill the cracks with. After a while, he switched on the weak overhead lamp and read slowly through the magazine that Matt had brought. The text seemed to hang above the pages: something important, permanent, whose true meaning he couldn't quite get.

*

When the door opened, Neil was expecting Matt to come through. But his first visitor was tall, thin and fair-haired. Gary. He brushed the chair with his hand before folding himself into it, then said: 'I heard you were having a bad hair day.'

'Got caught in the rain. You know how it is.'

'Not really, no.' Gary touched Neil's arm. His eyes were dark with fury. 'So what the fuck happened?'

'Boy. Jester. Canal. Mad.' He was getting tired of telling this story.

Gary shivered. He suddenly looked much younger. 'What did he look like? This boy.'

Neil shrugged. 'Skinny. White. Dark hair.'

'That narrows it down.' Neil didn't say anything. 'Sorry. There are some fucked-up people out there. You have to protect yourself. If you leave with someone, make sure someone else sees you together. If he seems crazy, you walk. Use your instincts.'

'I don't believe in instincts.'

'I don't give a fuck whether you believe in them. Just get some.' Gary blinked. Tears stuck to his eyelids, glittering. 'Why did you do it? I thought – ' He broke off. Into the silence, he said in a low voice: 'Neil, if what I said had anything . . .'

Neil shook his head, feeling a loose flap of bandage brush his lips. 'It had nothing to do with you.'

The door opened again. It was Matt. Gary stood up; he and Matt exchanged awkward greetings. Behind them, the shadow created a triangle of unease: it turned to face the shivering wall. Gary said goodbye, kissing the back of Neil's hand. Matt sat down. 'How are you?'

'Not great. How are you?'

'All right.' Matt's eyes were bruised. He'd brought his own Walkman and a shoebox. It was full of tapes, including some that he'd recorded off Neil's LPs. 'Can you wear this?' Neil nodded. The glass had missed his ears: the only sense he could still trust.

'Your Dad rang,' Matt said. 'They're coming down to see you tomorrow.'

'That'll be fun. Not.'

'Try to think positively.'

'Bullshit. It's only negative thinking that can keep me sane.'

They talked for a while, reliving some of the highlights of Election Night. 'Things are looking really good,' Matt said. 'Prescott's talking about taking measures against the car lobby, putting public transport back on the road. Cook's promising no more arms deals with regimes that violate human rights.'

'Sounds promising.' Neil closed his eyes. He was feeling visited out. 'Thanks for the tapes, Matt. I hope you weren't up all night recording them.'

'I had an essay to do.' Matt stepped towards him. They hugged gently for a couple of minutes. Neil wanted to kiss him, but couldn't. How long would it be like this? Matt stared over Neil's shoulder. His face was pale and miserable. But then, it usually was.

After Matt had gone, Neil turned off the overhead light. Carefully, he fitted the Walkman headphones behind his bandages. Then he slipped in one of Matt's D90 cassettes. The sound of chiming guitars and soft, echoed keyboards filled his head. The magnificent seven: Brittan, Clemens, Federici, Springsteen, Tallent, Van Zandt, Weinberg. In the end, there was no comparison. Neil let the imagery of open roads and deserted towns dissolve the rotting wall, the distant fires, the thin shadow of his companion.

*

The next morning, as he washed, Neil looked carefully at his face in the rust-streaked mirror. It was held together by stitches and black scabs, a patchwork in various shades of blue. He wondered if anyone could recognise it. He only could because there wasn't much choice. *The blue mask.* He wanted to take it off and see his real face underneath. It sickened him.

By the time his parents came, he'd made himself a second face under the damaged one. His whole body felt like a chrysalis, stiff and awkward. Inside, he felt the tender shape of his true self. He realised he'd not had an erection since being admitted to hospital. Morphine had wiped out his sex drive. The thought depressed him; but what point could desire have? The life of his skin seemed to be over.

His parents arrived promptly at the start of visiting time. The half-light in Neil's room made them look sketchy, unformed. Neil's mother hugged him cautiously; his father gripped Neil's hand. Their expressions reminded Neil of how he'd felt in the morning, seeing his own face. He wished the bandages were still there. His father brought a second chair next to the first one and sat down. 'How did it happen?' he asked. 'Your . . . Matthew said you'd been attacked. Were there any witnesses?'

'No. We were alone. On the canal. Me and this guy.' The air thickened with embarrassment, his parents' faces blank. Asbestos glittered in the exposed wall cavities as the cracks widened. Why did he have to say that? He'd rather have had them visit him in prison on a charge of molesting cats.

'This is a violent place,' his mother said. 'I could tell, driving here. You have to be careful in a city like this. It's not like home.'

Neil stared at her. They lived in the street violence capital of the North, and she was still implying that he'd put himself at risk by moving here. 'I think you'll find it's a lot safer here.'

'Well, I'm not the one sitting in a hospital bed. Do you see me holding my face together with stitches?'

'No, only with comforting delusions.'

His mother raised a shaking hand. 'If you weren't in such a state . . .' His father coughed, and she slumped against him.

'It's not where you live that matters,' his father muttered softly. 'It's what company you keep.' Neil couldn't see his eyes. This was not going well.

'Did you watch the election?' Neil said. His mother looked disgusted. His father smiled.

'Nice to see Hamilton go down,' he said. 'Fat pig's been playing lord of the manor for long enough. As for the rest of it . . . If Blair knows where he's at, he'll run things just the way Major did. If not, it'll be a disaster. I can't see anything changing.'

Neil shook his head furiously; before he could speak, pain washed his mouth. He glanced at the clock. There were cracks all around it, shadows jerking in the first stiff movements of a dance. A thread of bile stung the back of his throat.

They sat for a while, exchanging platitudes. Neil found their blank sympathy harder to take than their criticism. He withdrew behind the mask. His mother said he could come and stay with them for a while, if he wanted to. 'It's OK,' Neil said. 'I'm going back to Moseley in a couple of days. Want to get back to my thesis.'

'No time to waste,' his father said. Neil didn't rise to the bait. He appreciated their coming to see him. He just didn't appreciate their actually being here.

As it grew dark outside, he listened to *Unknown Pleasures* on Matt's Walkman. The crash of breaking glass made him feel sick. The pale buildings and steep streets of Macclesfield trembled in the grey air. He saw the primary school where he'd made a papier-mâché head on a wire skull around a balloon. The secondary school where he'd been shit at games and passed around socialist pamphlets in history lessons. His best friend at thirteen, Victor, had been an army obsessive. He remembered arguments about China and Cuba – Victor saying smugly, 'You haven't studied Cold War tactics.' They'd lost touch by the time the Berlin Wall came down, which was probably just as well.

Victor was thin, with blue–grey eyes and an air of sardonic detachment. Neil had been conscious of desiring him, but had never said anything. The closest he'd ever got to sex in those days was the time he'd been sitting in a toilet cubicle at the bus station and two men had got into the next cubicle. He'd sat there for half an hour, listening, the messages scrawled on the metal door suddenly given an aching reality.

Then there was the time he'd answered an ad in the local paper for someone to do casual work in a garage. The mechanic had got him sandpapering metal pipes for half a day, then said to him: 'Stand up. I just want to see how tall you are.' They'd stood back to back. Then he'd said: 'Your jeans are fucking tight. Aren't they?' Nothing had happened. Sometimes the feelings you didn't act on stayed with you far longer than the ones you did something about.

Near the end of visiting hours, the door opened slowly and Anne came in. They hugged briefly. Close up, she looked pale and tired. 'I've come from work,' she said. 'Matt called me. How are you feeling?'

'I don't feel very much. Drugs. A bit woozy, most of the time.'

'You'll be OK.' Anne squeezed his arm. 'Once the bruises fade. Scars aren't so bad. How do you feel inside?'

'My ribs are sore. I think I fell. Otherwise no damage.'

'I meant . . . how you feel about things.' Fatigue had taken the edges off Anne. Looking at her now, he remembered her as an undergraduate, before anger had become the only emotion she trusted. He wanted to stroke her hair, but knew she'd feel it was taking a liberty.

'I don't know. I'm trying not to be in touch with my feelings. It's not safe.'

'Bit late to think that, Neil.' He looked away, chasing the shadow in his left eye. 'I'm sorry. Didn't mean to . . . I'm just tired. Don't know how to behave.'

'Are things any easier at work?'

'Not exactly.' A flash of rage crossed her face, then disappeared. 'Have the police got the guy who did this?'

'Not yet. He's on the run. Broken parole. But they know his name. Bit of a lunatic, apparently.'

'And you thought he'd just cut up your face because he'd mistaken you for a fish supper.'

Neil smiled. 'You were going to tell me about work.'

'It's not important. Well . . . That manager I told you about, Malcolm. He lost some work I gave him. Maybe on purpose, maybe not. But he pretended he'd never had it. I had to do it all again, late. So I was a bit quiet, you know. Not laughing at his jokes. The bastard had me formally reprimanded for my attitude.'

'What a cunt.'

'My sentiments exactly. If he pinched my arse I'd laugh. I'd laugh out loud, then make a formal complaint. But what he's doing . . . it's not harassment, it's like he's trying to drive me out. Just because he can.'

'He's really got to you, hasn't he?'

'You know me. I take pride in my work. I'm good at it. This is the worst thing that could have happened. And it's something I can't give a name to. It's not discrimination. It's just poison. I don't understand it.' She ran a hand tensely through her hair.

'The important thing is to protect yourself. You need a plan. Honesty's no use against a liar. Look at how Thatcher – '

'Neil, is there any situation you can talk about without referring to Thatcherism or the Third Reich or the assassination of Trotsky? I mean, just for once?' Her sudden anger relieved him. At least she seemed more in focus.

'Sorry. All I meant was, you need to think about tactics rather than justice. Are there people in the office who'd support you?'

'I don't know who I can trust. Feel so isolated. This *attitude* thing is such crap. I'm sure if I jumped out the window, they'd record *Suicide while of unsound attitude. Suicide while the balance of the attitude was temporarily disturbed.* No-one would question it.'

'Don't let it get like that. Remember, "attitude" is a pretence.' He held up his hands, one in front of the other. 'Here's your face. And here's what you really feel. Keep them separate and you'll be OK.'

'Maybe.' Anne shrugged and smiled wearily. 'Why do liars always contaminate the people around them?'

'They don't always. Neil Hamilton didn't get away with it.'

Anne looked unconvinced, but then cracked up. 'That was so brilliant. It was like Sylvia Plath's "Daddy". There's a stake in your fat black heart, and the villagers never liked you . . .' Their shared laughter faded to silence. 'What are you going to do now?'

'Go back to Matt, try and sort things out.' He gestured towards the lower part of his face. 'Don't know what this is going to be like. He can always put a paper bag over my head. Doctor said I might need plastic surgery.'

'Sooner or later, we all come to a time when we stop

looking pretty.' Anne put her arm across Neil's chest. 'Well, I'd better go home and commune with Tori Amos. Take care of yourself.' She leaned forward and suddenly kissed him on the mouth. 'Love you.'

'Love you too.' As the door closed, Neil lay back and shut his eyes. Shapes floated in the dark like boats in a harbour. Then the quiet tide of sleep surged past them to fill the room.

The next morning, the doctor took off the patch from Neil's left eye. The shadow that had crouched on the far side of the room dissolved into frail sunlight. The walls still looked about to crack, but he found it easier not to stare at them. He read the *Guardian*, which had a front-page story about Jack Straw's intended crackdown on beggars, drug users and young offenders.

Later, they gave him a sight test and some speech exercises. His left eye was still a bit slow to focus and his voice was still thick, but the doctor seemed happy enough. 'There's nothing that requires immediate treatment,' he said. 'We'll take out the stitches next week and keep an eye on how your face is healing up. But for now you should go home. Is there someone who can pick you up from here and then stay with you for a few hours, just to check you're OK?' Neil said there was.

He phoned the house and spoke to Theresa, who said she and Matt would come for him straight away. He dressed and began to pack his bags, trying not to panic at the thought of leaving the hospital. His left wrist hurt where the drip had been inserted. How many mirrors were there in the house? How many windows? What kind of summer was it going to be? Still, at least he could work on his thesis. And his antithesis.

chapter 4

and one who cried

1

It was a warm night. Matt had left the window open, and the sound of passing cars fell like handfuls of gravel into the room. Neil had spent half the evening in the garden, where years of unregulated growth had nearly concealed the evidence of the family who'd once lived here: the swing, the little climbing-frame, the bird table. They'd eaten late; Matt had cooked a vegetable korma that wouldn't hurt Neil's mouth. They'd shared a bottle of wine. The plates and glasses were still on the bedside table. Neil was sitting on the bed, untying his shoes. 'Turn off the light,' he said.

The red eye of the stereo watched them embrace. Lamplight glowed through the curtains. Neil's body was a thin shadow against the pale wallpaper. Matt stroked Neil through his shirt, feeling his nipples harden. He kissed the sweat from the hollow of Neil's throat, then licked down his chest, fingers unbuttoning the shirt to his crotch. Neil gripped him with hands that were as tense as wire. 'Stop. Put the light on.' Matt hesitated. 'Now.'

Light snapped the room into cold focus. Neil turned away. He was shaking. Matt sat beside him and stroked the back

of his neck. Neil leant back against him, breathing deeply.
Matt gently pulled his shirt away from his tight-skinned ribs.
He'd lost weight. The pale torso made the cloudy bruises
and blue stitched-up cuts on his face look much worse. Matt
hated himself for being put off, but couldn't help it. 'Are you
OK?' he said.

'Sorry. I just panicked.' The injury was thick in his voice.
'The first time since . . .'

'I know.' He thought of Perry and felt numb with guilt.
'I'm sorry.' He sounded like a child apologising for breaking
a window. But that was how he felt. The whole *betrayal* thing
didn't make sense to him.

The only sound in the room was the passing traffic. Matt
pushed Neil on to his back and undressed him, then kissed
his chest and belly. He could count Neil's ribs in the dark.
Neil stroked Matt's hair, but made no sound. Matt took
Neil's thin penis in his mouth and worked it slowly, moving
back and forth. It took a long time, as if something inside
Neil had to fight its way to the surface. Just when his mouth
was becoming uncomfortably numb, he felt Neil's back arch
and heard him cry out in apparent pain. Semen flooded his
mouth. He managed not to gag.

Neil lay there as if stunned. His eyes were closed. Matt
watched him for a few minutes. He couldn't read any
expression into the torn face. It made his body seem so
vulnerable that Matt wanted to cover him up, protect him
from contact. He went to switch off the light, but Neil said
'Come here.' They lay together and Neil caressed him,
exploring with his fingertips, then slowly and carefully jerked
him off. In the stillness that followed, he could hear the clock
ticking.

Neil got up to go to the toilet. Matt heard it flush; then
there was nothing. Then he heard the door to Neil's bedroom
close. Eventually he realised Neil had gone to bed. Their

clothes were still scattered over Matt's floor, like dried-out replicas of their bodies. He turned out the light and lay on the duvet, trying to sleep. A cat screamed from the back garden.

Neil stood in the bathroom, naked, trying to piss. He needed to take some painkillers. A streetlight made a pale angel shape in the frosted glass window. He could hear music from the floor below, something acoustic with a lot of minor chords. Finally, his bladder unlocked itself. He pulled the chain flush, then turned to wash his hands. There was someone standing by the washbasin, in the dark.

He was tall and very thin, and seemed to be cleaning his teeth. Neil had no idea who it could be. Was there a new tenant in the house? Then the man stood up, gesturing at the wall. In the light trapped by the frosted glass, his mouth appeared to spread. There was something wrong with it, like a growth. He bent over again and spat repeatedly into the basin. The sound was like rain on a tin roof. It was too loud for the room.

Neil glanced at something on the wall where the thin man had pointed. Dark words on the pale wallpaper. Dark blood on the pale washbasin. He couldn't see the man any more. Perhaps his left eye was playing up again. Biting his lip, he switched on the light.

There was no-one else in the room. Neil glanced at his reflection in the grimy mirror, then looked away. The washbasin contained nothing but some traces of stubble. The words on the wall by the cistern were an advert cut out of *Viz* magazine: YOU CAN'T MISS WITH ARMITAGE SHANKS.

Neil stumbled back to his own room and closed the door. He swallowed two of the red plastic capsules the doctor had given him, then chased them down with a few painful mouthfuls of cheap vodka. His face ached as if all the bones had become rotten teeth. He felt the cold of the vodka melt through his chest, then soak upwards into his mind. Clouds drained the blue from the night sky. He shut the curtain, got into bed and lay in a half-crouched position, as if tension could protect him from bad dreams. He wasn't sure exactly what he was afraid of. The only way to be safe was to stay on his own.

2

We're living at a time when the only acceptable face is a mask. The lies of politicians are no longer meant to be believed. They're acts of duplicity that the public appreciate as such, finding their own hypocrisy and cynicism validated. A generation of liberals and radicals tried to 'unmask' Thatcher with facts and reason, to prove that she was insane and dishonest. They won the debate, but lost the vote. Because Thatcher was mask all the way through. That was the key to her appeal.

In Blair, who balances the image of ruthlessness with the image of compassion, we see a similar process. There is nothing to be exposed. Yet Blair's masks will rub against each other and force him to improvise, to generate new possibilities, even if there is no head in between them. It's rather like the way that Madonna's magpie sensibility led her, almost by accident, to make better records than those singers wedded to a static notion of authenticity. Like music, politics has become a tissue of samples and overdubs. The best we can hope for is a decent remix.

What a load of toss, Neil thought wearily. James at *Redbrick* would never run this unless he was well desperate for copy. Then again, he wanted a range of different viewpoints for the feature on the new government. Sean and Neil were supposed to be representing the socialist perspective. Was this the best he could do? He'd been trying for hours, alternating between postmodern cleverness and Frankfurt School gloom. He had nothing to say.

That was the problem with his thesis: it was too clever. He'd spun out a web of theory so fine it hardly had any substance. If fascism could be diagnosed in every abuse of power and every form of propaganda, then there was nothing that wasn't fascism. And that was bullshit. Fascism was pain and terror, rifle-butts smashing cheekbones. It wasn't a language to be decoded in every word of the middle class. Maybe Adorno had gone down that road, but then he was trying to deal with losses and traumas that had almost driven him mad.

How you related fascism to other political systems was a factual question, not an abstract one. You had to talk about fascism as a reality in the world. What lay behind it wasn't some dark secret of fascist ideology, but lots of ordinary stuff. Trotsky called fascism 'a chemically pure distillation of the culture of imperialism'. More pithily, Engels called anti-Semitism 'the socialism of idiots'. Either way, you didn't identify fascism from its ideological essence. You identified it when it was breaking your face.

Outside, the darkness was gradually lifting. Seeing the dawn reassured him that the daylight was real, not just a slick facsimile that could tear at any moment. The street outside was quiet. He felt more human in his room, surrounded by books and records. This was his real self. Outside, you were nothing. The sky convulsed over you. Birds could shit in your hair. Polluted rain smeared your face, stung your eyes. He'd read that after being released from prison, Jean Genet spent most of the rest of his life in a room, giving his 'moral solitude' a body in physical solitude. He was beginning to see how much sense that made.

He loved Genet's early novels, especially *Funeral Rites*. He was becoming more interested in the religious side of Genet's writing, the imagery of the soul that could free itself from the body. Revolution and redemption were similar things to Genet. But he wasn't an optimist in either political or spiritual terms. The haunting bleakness of *Funeral Rites* linked it to *The Thief's Journal*, Genet's attempt to explain himself without recourse to fiction. Not that the *Journal* didn't contain stories: that anecdote about the punter whom Genet had tied up and robbed, and who'd then plaintively begged *At least let me blow you*, was priceless. But of all Genet's books, it was the least playful.

Neil picked up a copy and flicked through it, his mind filling with monochrome *film noir* images. His eyes fastened on part of a long sentence: *I no longer fear anything, I am rash enough to think that my body is free of all distinguishing signs, that it looks empty, impossible to identify, since everything about me has quite abandoned my image . . .*

He'd spent the last couple of nights struggling with Richard Coe's *The Vision of Jean Genet*, a study from the sixties that his Ph.D supervisor had lent him. The best thing in it was the photo of a middle-aged Genet, standing on a towpath close to a bridge. Coe was good on religious themes in Genet, and on the politics of evil. There was something important in his observation that all Genet's writings portrayed oppression, but mythologised it in ways that did not suggest liberation. But Coe had no idea when it came to sexuality. He described *Funeral Rites*, somewhat old-maidishly, as *pornographic*. In the middle of an otherwise fascinating discussion of Genet's sexual negativism, he remarked: *For the older homosexual, the void of despair is all but inevitable.* Tosser.

That reminded him of some of the miserable crap he'd read as a teenager, trying to understand sexuality through second-hand books. Psychologists like Anthony Storr, with their sneering descriptions of 'the homosexual'. He'd sought out books in a similarly academic style that had a less negative point of view: wasted time reading Gide's *Corydon* when he could have been reading Gore Vidal and James Baldwin. Or better still, shagging. Maybe even in garages.

As if in response to that, the bedsprings in the room above began to creak. Two voices mingled in a wordless, rhythmic song. It was Theresa and her new boyfriend, Callum. He was a psychiatric nurse and she was a psychiatry student, so no doubt they understood each other. As the tempo of their cries increased, Neil couldn't help becoming aroused. Not that he especially fancied either of them. It wasn't Callum and Theresa up there, it was a nameless couple, an abstract design of sex. And he was a nameless listener. Like true love, eavesdropping left no traces. It was the perfect crime.

Finding a version of sex that didn't upset him was getting more difficult. He still couldn't cope with being touched in the dark, and he knew Matt didn't like to look at him even though they hadn't talked about it. The bedside manner couldn't survive in bed. At least Neil was able to kiss now – but how kissable was he? Alone in the house the other night, he'd flicked through a copy of *Vulcan* and impulsively phoned a porn line. He'd listened to an Irish boy faking an orgasm, hung up, then realised the call was bound to appear on the itemised phone bill. It was shocking how the knowledge that he was listening to a tape recorder had turned him on.

As the creaking and the voices subsided, Neil lowered his face carefully into his hands. However he tried to distract himself, it always came back to the same thing. They were going to operate on him in six weeks' time. Meanwhile, they'd taken tiny scrapings from his low-relief scars to grow patches of skin in the lab. His appearance depended on a work of art – like a child making a face with torn paper and glue on a wire skull. He looked up, went to the window and drew back the curtain. The sunlight flooded his skull like an X-ray. He couldn't see anything until he turned back to face the room.

3

Theresa often wondered about the family who'd first lived in this house. Who'd slept in which bedroom? Had there been a nursery? She imagined small figures creeping down the stairs, waiting in the hallway, looking up to the lights as if watching the night sky. Light footsteps growing heavier with time. Faces in thin mirrors shadowed by adolescence, losing their raw energy. Feet weighed down with suitcases, heading for the door.

Her sadness about breaking up with Sean was making her obsess over children. She wasn't the kind who believed in ghosts. Any sign of unreason in the household made her tense. Neil was worrying her. Matt said he was becoming agoraphobic. It wasn't surprising, given what had happened. She wanted to tell him that she understood, but that he was only making it worse for himself by hiding from the outside world. He needed to get out there, be himself, stare down anyone who gave him trouble. It wasn't like he looked that bad.

But she couldn't say anything. Not after that morning when she'd got up early with a hangover, gone down to the kitchen and found Neil sitting at the table in the half-light. She'd been unable to suppress a cry. He'd got up and walked straight past her, up the stairs to his room. She'd been too embarrassed to tell him that she hadn't cried out because his face was terrible. She just hadn't known who it was.

4

It had been a painfully hot day. Neil hadn't felt able to go out into the garden. Even the stairwell made him feel exposed. The furnace he'd sensed in hospital was all around the house, slowly consuming it. He'd sat at his desk through the morning, taking notes from Adorno's contribution to *The Authoritarian Personality*. The phrase *judge, jury and executioner* had got stuck in his head. The milk in the fridge had turned to a mixture of sludge and dirty water; Neil had waited for Matt to come home, then asked him to go out for some more.

Apart from them and Theresa, all the students had gone. She'd be going home to Stoke in a week or two. There were some new tenants he hardly knew, and the landlord kept showing other people around the place. Matt was working at Freezerland to help pay the rent over the summer, coming home with horror stories about spoilt food and beetles. In the evening, he'd gone to see Polanski's film *The Tenant* at the MAC. Neil hadn't felt like going with him.

Now they were on Matt's bed. The light was off, but the curtains were open and moonlight painted the room silver. Clothes were scattered over the floor like mounds of dead leaves. Matt was lying on his front, immobile. Neil's lips moved over his shoulder-blades, down into the groove of his spine. Then he gripped Matt's ribs and blew softly on the back of his neck. Matt shivered and pressed up against Neil, who entered him easily. It helped that he wasn't built like Jeff Stryker. Music drifted from the speakers on either side of Matt's bed. It was Triangle, a local band from a few years ago. As their bodies moved together, arousal trapping them like coils of wire, the moon disappeared behind a cloud. Neil felt himself beginning to panic.

Then, suddenly, the knot of tension in his gut transformed

itself into burning pleasure. He wrapped his arms around Matt and convulsed, every muscle taut. His hand reached down to grip Matt's cock. They lay in that position for a while, their breathing drowned by the music. *Your dreams are turning into gold / The trees are mad / The streets are cold / Couples stand in the lamplight / Trying just to keep hold.* A bass riff counted down into silence; a guitar broke through with high, jagged notes. The air was thick with the smell of melted KY. His fear hadn't gone away; but it had somehow turned itself inside-out, become a need. He put his dry lips to Matt's ear and whispered: 'Do you want to fuck me?'

Matt looked at him, eyes black holes in the sketch of his face. 'Are you sure?' It wasn't something they did often; Neil found it difficult at the best of times.

'Go on.' Neil settled on his hands and knees. He could see the moon flickering behind grey clouds, like a reflection in muddy water. Was it really possible to transform fear into desire? He closed his eyes as Matt penetrated him. 'Slowly.' Nerves flared, then settled into a bright tension. Like tuning a TV set. He felt Matt's thrusts quicken, fall into a rhythm. It wouldn't take him long. Sweat dripped into Neil's eyes, into the narrow tracks of his scars. Matt cried out twice. Neil saw the moon blaze coldly through a gap in the clouds. The light revealed a figure standing just inside the window. A young woman. Her mouth was sewn shut with black thread.

The moon disappeared again. Matt pulled away and knelt on the bed, breathing deeply. Neil gazed at the cloudy sky for a moment, then turned over and looked up at Matt. 'That was really good,' the boy said. They lay side by side, legs touching. Matt's hand moved gently over Neil's body: thigh, buttock, spine, chest, throat. So lightly that Neil could hardly feel it, his fingers traced the scar tissue of Neil's face. And again, like someone learning to read Braille. Neil put out his tongue and tasted the sweat on Matt's fingertips.

As their bodies cooled, Neil began to shiver. Was he seeing people who'd died in the house? Or the nightmares of a previous tenant, drugged or going mad in a rented room? Or was it just him? It was only in horror stories that visions came trailing their own explanations like designer labels. But then, this whole night had somehow been like a vision: something more real than life. He pressed Matt's face into his chest and held him there, as if one careless move would break them both into pieces.

5

At least it was cold in the freezer room. Matt's uniform was creased with sweat after four hours in the shop, repricing stock that was on the turn. Only the desperate would buy it: the old and the broke who came in half an hour before closing time and left with a bag full of crap. How did people eat so much bread? They hardly stocked any booze, because it posed too many security issues. It was strange how alcohol made people friendly in Moseley, but made them hostile in Acocks Green. Maybe it was the heavy traffic made everyone so bad-tempered. Half the trees along the Warwick Road seemed to have some kind of leaf blight, as if they smoked.

The freezer room reminded him of the Medical Centre at the Uni, where they kept thousands of freeze-dried blood and tissue samples. The long freezers here were less reliable: they shuddered and creaked like a forest, and were caked with frost where the ice had melted and refrozen. Forcing a lid open, he loaded twenty cartons of Chicken Sava Flava into the pallet. Now he needed thirty baked bean pizzas. Why couldn't Sage Wholefoods in Moseley have had a vacancy? At least the job didn't make him feel hungry very often. This stuff didn't even smell like . . . shit, what was that?

The whole stack of pizzas was soggy, and there were

patches of fungus on the boxes. They were standing in an inch of tepid water. Matt retched, wishing he'd skipped those beers the night before. Evidently the freezer was broken. He closed the lid, trapping most of the stink inside, and manoeuvred the pallet back out through the airtight door. At once, the warmth of the shop shrink-wrapped him in his clothes. Warren's pale, bespectacled face looked up tensely as Matt approached him.

'I'm afraid Freezer 9 is broken. The pizzas are all ruined.'

Warren grimaced with fury. 'You were there this morning. Why didn't you fucking check? Too busy thinking about your fucking boyfriend, I suppose.'

'Sorry, I just didn't use that freezer this morning. You can't tell from the outside.'

'Can you go and clean it out? I'll put these Sava Flavas on the shelf.' He started doing so, calming himself with repetitive movement. 'Two hundred pizzas. That's more than five hundred quid pissed up the wall.' He blinked at Matt. 'What are you waiting for?' Nothing.

Matt threw the ruined pizzas into bin-liners and dried out the freezer with a sponge and bucket. He knew it was part of Warren's job to check that all the freezers were at the correct temperature; but the junior manager always found a way to blame someone else. Screwed-up little prick.

He should never have mentioned Neil to Warren. It wasn't so much that Warren was homophobic as that he couldn't stand to think of anyone having a partner. They'd gone for a drink at the end of Matt's first week, and Warren had poured out his heart about the castrating bitches he'd wasted his money on. Matt had felt obliged to share something of his own private life, so had told him about Neil's injury and their relationship. Warren had shrugged. 'Whatever you do. Long as it doesn't affect your work, I don't give a shit.'

Then, as if to demonstrate that he felt at home among the

gesturing cropped youths and brittle AG girls who filled the bright pub, he'd gone into a rant about students. 'Those fuckers think they're so much better than anyone else. But what do they fucking know about work? They're full of shit about *equal opportunities* – tell me, what equal opportunities have I had? The day I let some politically correct arsehole tell me how to do my job is the day you can put a gun in my fucking mouth and pull the trigger. Know what I mean?' Matt had shaken his head, dismayed and helpless.

When the broken freezer was clean, Matt went to the toilet for a cigarette. He couldn't get the reek of stagnant water off his hands. When he got home, Neil would probably be asleep. Things had deteriorated. There'd been that one night when they'd really seemed to get through to each other; but it was always brightest before the sunset. Maybe Neil's operation would change things. If only they could go out together, instead of skulking around the house and fucking in near dark like people who'd just met. It was frightening how you could slowly lose someone – more frightening than splitting up. Matt's books gave fear a meaning, a story. But the real terror was that there were no plots. He lit the cigarette and drew on it hard, trying to focus the world into one point of light.

6

Going back to the hospital was difficult. Matt and Theresa went with Neil on the bus, flanking him like under-developed minders. It was the end of July: warm, muggy weather at the edge of rain. Neil crossed his arms and tried not to shake. Bodywork, he told himself. It wasn't *him* that was being changed, it was just the chassis. He had a bag full of comfort reading (Maupin, King, Chandler), but knew he wouldn't get past the covers.

When he came round from the anaesthetic, it was night. He was in an open-plan ward that made him think of Digbeth Coach Station. The man in the bed to his left was snoring, his mouth pushed open by the sound. The man in the bed to his right was praying silently. There was a strong smell of antiseptic and cleaning fluid. Neil touched his face: it was covered with bandages, holes for the eyes and mouth. There was a prickly ache all over his face – or rather, just under it, like sunburn.

In the half-light of the ward, things were moving that he couldn't quite see. He closed his eyes, feeling exposed. Slow waves of nausea made him sweat. The drugs restored him to sleep without calming him down, so that he dreamt about faceless shadows armed with broken glass, rats nesting in heaps of rags that stank of whisky and bare stone. He fought off the daylight until he realised that it was real.

In the afternoon, they took off the bandages. Post-op scars weren't random like wound scars: they were designed to heal. His skin felt tight and itchy. To stop himself touching it, he put his hands palm upwards on the blanket and stared at them. Pale, thin hands; not the hands of a worker. Yet they were tense enough.

He was going home in the evening. Matt was coming to fetch him. They needed the bed. He didn't want Matt's reaction to be the first image of how he looked. When the consultant came round to talk to him, Neil asked her for a mirror. She fished a small make-up mirror out of her handbag and passed it to him. He snapped it open, saw one red-rimmed eye, drew the mirror back slowly.

New patches of skin covered his right cheek, the chin and the area below the left eye. They were dead-white, but their edges were red and swollen. There were streaks of dried blood across the sutures, but the sutures themselves were hardly visible. Most of the scarring was gone, except close to the mouth. It actually looked like a real face. A normal face. But not his.

chapter 5

lose the feeling

1

Birmingham wasn't the kindest of cities. When you phoned the Samaritans, you got a recorded message saying 'Tough shit.' The tranquillisers were making her feel vague and stoned in the mornings. There was always a payback. On the bus this morning, the voices of schoolkids fell around her like breaking glass, bright and meaningless. Every laugh seemed like a threat. Once she got behind the screen at work, she was OK. It was the bits in-between – travelling, meetings, breaks – that made her realise how stressed she was.

There was a bunch of girls in front of her, twisting as they carried on multiple conversations. From their clothes, they probably all went to the same school. A couple of them had tiny mobile phones. Anne heard one of them say: 'I've never had good sex on acid.' Maybe they were vying with each other to sound experienced. Maybe not. Anne supposed they were fifteen or sixteen. She doubted she'd had good sex at all by that age. If ever.

These days, she felt like a relic. The key tenet of eighties radical feminism was that all heterosexual relations under patriarchy were essentially abusive. The key tenet of nineties

Girl Power was that women didn't need men as long as they had chocolate. There weren't any oppressed women any more, just girls who hadn't made it career-wise. Just like there wasn't an oppressed class any more, just people who hadn't maximised their earning potential. It was one of the things she still shared with Neil, that feeling of being denied the right to make sense of things. There wasn't a struggle any more. There was just a world of shit.

The windows of the *View*'s office, on the second floor of a converted factory in Aston, were blazing in the autumn sunlight. But the interior was dim and vaguely museum-like, with a double row of computers circled by giant filing cabinets and artificial flowers. There was even a fish-tank outside Malcolm's office, with two thin-faced angelfish blinking at the twilight. Nobody said hello to Anne as she logged in and flicked through her copy of the paper. The printed version never seemed as real as the pages on screen. Malcolm seemed to be everywhere at once, handing out memos and timesheets, his teeth glittering with efficiency. He always expected a smile and a greeting, though he was the least friendly man on Earth.

When he reached Anne, however, his face went blank. 'Come to my office at ten,' he said. 'It's time we had a little chat.' Then he moved on, his back straight as a cardboard cut-out. Anne felt her face flushing, tension clamping her teeth like wire. The hour's delay was a typical Malcolm tactic. The bollocking might be about using too many paper clips. There might be no bollocking at all. It was the anticipation that did the damage.

Nervously, Anne checked her e-mails and scanned the printed list of things she had to get done that morning. Apart from the hum of computers, it was silent in the office. She had the feeling that something had happened before she'd arrived. But there was no sense in giving way to paranoia.

She opened the sports section for the next issue on screen and subbed energetically for a while. Like rust, misplaced commas never slept. At five to ten, she went into the Ladies to tidy her hair. Her face in the mirror looked pale and vacant. She thought she was going to throw up. The reflection of Carol, her former assistant, walked past and chirped 'Morning.'

Malcolm's office was as impeccably tidy as ever. You could see your face in the desk – or the shadow of it, at least. The Systems Manager himself was a less impressive spectacle: a short man with cropped hair and a beard shaped like a chinstrap, as if it had slipped off his face. Anne remembered him boasting at an office party that women liked him because they knew where they stood. 'Close the door behind you,' he said. As Anne sat down, he pushed a copy of that morning's *View* across the desk towards her. 'Have you seen this?'

'Er, yes. What about it?' She'd worked late all through the previous week to help get the pages ready, handling last-minute changes from the advertising department. Not to mention that police enquiry into a stalker using the 'View A Mate' personal ads page. 'Is something wrong?'

'Have a look at page 61.' Malcolm's face was expressionless. It was a standard page of adverts: cars, washing machines, massages. Anne wondered what she was supposed to see. 'Now look at page 62.' A similar page of adverts. Very similar. Extremely similar. Anne felt her kidneys turn to ice. 'I can't believe it. This isn't the page I checked.'

'Yes it is.' A familiar sneer had crept into Malcolm's voice. His accent was a pushy North Birmingham whine with a contrived hint of Essex. 'I accessed your files this morning. These are the pages you gave to production. We've lost a whole page of ads. I don't need to tell you what that means in terms of lost revenue. Not to mention ongoing contracts.'

Anne shook her head. The movement nauseated her.

Bleach was scouring the inside of her skull. 'It's not possible. Before I started, I printed them all out, marked them, I couldn't . . .'

'Maybe the car adverts put you off? All those penis exten- sions, toys for boys, you couldn't be doing with it?' There was no triumph in the manager's face: only cold rage. Anne couldn't speak. Tears swelled in the corners of her eyes. She pressed viciously with her thumbs, deleting them.

'It would be easier for me to accept this . . . balls-up if your record as a sub-editor was more sound,' Malcolm went on. 'But you've been walking on thin ice for a while. And I can tell you, I'm not the only person in this department who feels that way. I've had a lot of comments about your attitude. And now . . . well, I can assure you, even if you stay here, you're not going to be in a position to make trouble.'

Anne stared at the window behind his head. Another office where someone was talking, hands gesturing to an invisible audience. Grainy sunlight fell like rain between the windows. 'All I want,' she said calmly, 'is to do my job as well as possible.'

'Well, I'm sorry, Anne. Whoever does what used to be your job is going to do it cost-effectively.'

'You really think it improves productivity to make people feel like shit?'

Malcolm smirked. 'If the toilet seat fits, wear it.'

You really are loathsome, Anne thought. 'You know what you deserve, Malcolm? A cost-effective funeral.'

Malcolm stood up. His lack of height weakened the dra- matic effect. 'That's quite enough,' he said. 'You've added insult to injury. You're suspended. There'll be a disciplinary hearing to discuss your case. Get out of the building.'

Anne walked in silence down the length of the newspaper office. No-one looked at her. She walked into the Ladies and stared at her reflection in the mirror above the first washbasin.

Her eyes were circled with red. Spontaneously she punched
herself in the face with both hands, six or seven times, then
collapsed on to the tiled floor. But her anger wouldn't let her
be still. As she climbed to her feet, shaking, the line of mirrors
across the wall reminded her of pages set out on a desk.

The page proofs. The ones she'd printed and marked up
before working through them on screen. She never wasted
paper, always kept it in a box under her computer and took
it up to the recycling bin every couple of weeks. The pages
were still there.

The report on Port Vale's recent home defeat was still on
her screen; she switched it off and logged out in a few
seconds. Then she lifted the box of paper on to her desk.
Last week's proofs were still there. Including the highlighted
pages from the ad section. But page 62 was missing. In its
place was a typed list of the paper's staff. Someone had
crossed out Anne's name with a marker pen.

Anne sat with her head in her hands, staring at the page.
Then she searched through the box of pages, twice. No good.
A shadow fell over the pages. 'Anne, I really think you should
go.' It was Carol. 'You're not doing yourself any favours by
sitting here. Go home.'

Anne looked up, but the younger woman's face was
blurred. 'Can I talk to you?' she said. Malcolm was still in
his office, or somewhere else.

Carol hesitated. 'I'm sorry. We were told not to speak to
you at all. It's better if you just go.'

Outside, the sunlight was as thick as pollen. Anne had to
keep stopping to breathe. Cars and lorries crawled along
the main road into the city centre. Advertisement hoardings
shielded the construction sites and patches of waste ground
from view. Too angry to wait for a bus, Anne walked slowly
up the long hill to the bottom of Corporation Street. Why
couldn't Carol have said something before? Or agreed to meet

for lunch and talk it over? It was only a few months since Anne had spent an hour listening to Carol pouring her heart out about that stupid boyfriend of hers.

The truth was, Anne reflected, that behind the sensitive mask Carol had a face of reinforced concrete. She was a stuck-up little Sloane Ranger so far up her own arse, all you could see of her was the soles of her green wellies. And yet . . . at least she'd bothered to say goodbye. Nobody else in that church of truth, fairness and communication had bothered to say a fucking thing.

Traffic thundered down the steepest part of the hill; Anne felt the ground trembling. In the burning sunlight, the shadows of buildings were like crude gaps scraped off a page of film. The sunburnt flesh of the Law Courts was posed for a photograph. Anne remembered seeing them on TV seven years before, in the background as the Birmingham Six raged against a system that had allowed them to be tortured and wrongfully imprisoned. *The people in those courts don't know how to spell justice, let alone dispense it.* That had been a good day.

She wanted to go and see Neil. He wouldn't know what to do, but he'd help her to put the situation in some perspective. Although she mocked the way he used reading as a comfort blanket, that was just what she needed at the moment. The last time they'd talked about Malcolm and the *View*, he'd read her something from Theodor Adorno that described it perfectly. The insistence that everyone appear to be happy, Adorno said, was like the anger of the father when his children didn't rush downstairs to greet him the moment he arrived home from the office. *It is part of the mechanism of domination to forbid recognition of the suffering it produces.*

Maybe she'd better phone him. He wasn't keen to see anyone at the moment. Or rather, be seen by them. He was due for a second operation in a few weeks. The first one had looked too smooth, almost childlike, before the skin had crumpled. The flesh underneath was the wrong shape. Now his face looked like he'd slept in it. Anne was worried about him. Neil had always been quite narcissistic. She supposed he'd been in love with himself. Now he and Neil were breaking up. It wasn't going to be easy.

Outside Rackhams she went down into the subway, to get out of the sun for a bit. Some drunks were sitting around the raised flowerbed, arguing almost wordlessly. In the exit tunnel, she passed a middle-aged busker who was singing 'Early Morning Rain' in a flat Brummie accent. Something about the song, a kind of stillness and grief, made her fumble for her purse. It was near the bottom of her bag, buried under the photos and cards and other things she'd cleared from her desk. She pulled it out, dropped a pound in the singer's cap and turned away. Suddenly the reality of what had happened hit her. As the song ended, she pressed her face against the cold tiles and wept until she could hardly breathe. Alone in the shadows, where no-one could see.

2

When Neil got to the Studio Theatre, it was closed up. He let himself in and lit up the airless auditorium. It smelt of dust and cigarette smoke. They'd held over the production to let Neil recover. Sorting that with the University had been difficult. Picking up the threads of *Nights of Insult* was likely to be harder.

All the cast were back now. Tim was going to be in Germany until the end of the year, but Theresa and Gary had taken over most of the stage management between them. Neil and Gary had worked on the play a little before the start of term. He'd been surprised at the subtlety of Gary's insights, his sense of how the themes came across on stage. The boy was so adept at being a brittle theatre queen that you forgot he had a brain.

This was practically the first time Neil had gone out since the operation. He wouldn't have managed it at all by daylight. The skin grafts had somehow pulled down on to the damaged flesh, like canvas over scaffolding. Even Matt had had to admit he looked rough. He'd sat at the back of the bus, reading the *Independent* and feeling that not only his face, but his body and internal organs, had become old. It was hard to breathe. For years, he'd been used to touching his own face as a kind of reassurance. He couldn't do that any more.

Footsteps sounded in the hallway. Neil froze, panicking. The door opened. 'Hi.' Sean was tanned; he'd grown his hair long over the summer. He shook Neil's hand, then hugged him. 'How are you doing?'

'OK, I suppose. Still a work in progress. How was your summer?'

'Great. I joined the SWP back in Leeds. Got a job in a record shop, spent the weekends selling newspapers and protesting outside hospitals. Stirring up discontent. How many Trotskyites does it take to change a lightbulb?'

'Er, I don't know.'

'Well, it's not about one person, is it? All the lightbulbs have to be changed.' Neil laughed. Sean looked at him cautiously. 'It really is good to see you, you know. What was your summer like?'

Neil thought about it. 'Not easy. I was . . . scared. But I'm trying to move on. Thanks.'

The door swung open again. Theresa looked thin and tired. The striplight made her face seem to float above her black denim jacket. 'Hello, boys.' She embraced Neil tightly, but not Sean. There was still some awkwardness between them. But Sean seemed to have got the anger out of his system. They sat down and started to plan the rehearsal. Neil wanted to focus on all the scenes with Rachel, especially the later ones.

More footsteps. Gary. He'd bleached his hair silver. 'Hello, children.' Neil didn't think he could cope with another hug; but Gary just touched his arm and kissed him swiftly on the mouth. 'Michael's not coming,' he said. 'Poor boy's got chickenpox. We won't see him for a week at least. And then he'll need some serious make-up.'

'Never mind,' Neil said. 'Let's work through the Rachel scenes. I'll read Michael's lines. There aren't many.' The characters didn't talk much to each other, until the end. The narrator kept them apart.

Under her jacket, Theresa was wearing a loose black top and skirt. Neil set up a single white spotlight, then placed his chair in the shadows behind it. Slowly, with any number of mistakes and false starts, they worked through Rachel's story. She was the loneliest of the characters. The play began with her coming home from the club and changing out of her night clothes, taking off her make-up, touching her dolls and framed photographs. Part of her room was set up as a nursery for the child, with an empty cot. Gary's narration was less detached than for the two men, more gentle. As she slept, curled on the narrow bed, he stroked her hair.

In a later scene, two barmen from the club where she worked as a dancer tried to extort money from her. One of them held her arms from behind while the other searched her, taking the opportunity to touch her up. They always had trouble with this scene. Sean played the man who searched her, but he didn't want to act it out today. 'If I just hold on to your skirt,' he said to Theresa, 'and Gary describes it – surely that's enough.' Theresa shrugged. Neil didn't feel like arguing.

After that, Rachel slowly came apart. She paced around

the house, cleaning and tidying, carrying out unconscious scene changes. Theresa seemed depressed, even scared, though perhaps she was just getting into the role. It was the strongest performance she'd given so far. Neil noticed her looking at the cot even when she was in another room. *Good idea*, he jotted in the margin of his script.

In the last scene, she set fire to the cot with matches. Dave had to help her put it out. Corin gave her first aid. The three began talking about what was happening to them. The silent figure who stalked them, giving them comfort as long as they stayed alone. Gary's character stopped narrating then. The blue spotlight on him faded out and came up on Rachel, who was lying on the bed. Consciously or unconsciously, she'd adopted what Matt had told him was 'the recovery position'. Corin and Dave opened the curtains as Tim switched on the main light. They stood at the edge of the stage, kissing. Rachel sat up and looked into the light. She was smiling.

Gary lit a cigarette without moving from his final position. Theresa stretched, leaning back on the couch cushions they were using as a bed. In the performance, it would be the same bed that Corin and Dave had fucked on. Sean took her hand to help her get up. 'You were good,' he said quietly. Neil knew he'd chosen the right way to get them back into the play, after the long break. Rachel's loneliness was a key note, somehow. It was a play about accepting loss. He hadn't seen that when he was writing it. Theresa had found the shadow on his wall and made it real.

'That was fantastic, everyone,' he said. 'If we have a blitz on lines over the next two rehearsals, then when Michael comes back we should be ready to have a complete run-through. Thanks.'

'Are you coming to the Guild?' Sean mimed the draining of a pint. It was the best movement he'd done all evening.

Neil hesitated. Tiredness stirred behind his eyes like sand. 'Don't think so. Not while I look like this.'

Gary put an arm protectively round Neil's ribs. 'Sweetness, it's not what your face looks like that matters. Not to us. It's what you've got in your pants.' Neil punched him. 'Ouch.'

'Don't you like pain?' Neil said. 'Let me introduce you to my friend pain.'

Gary seized Neil and drew their faces close together. 'Take it easy, babe. Or else you'll damage yourself. Who are you trying to fight?' His hand stroked Neil's hair. The others had moved away, embarrassed. Neil stepped back. He was in no mood for Gary's mind games. Even the sincere ones.

In the end, Sean went back to the Guild on his own while Neil and Theresa went back to Moseley. They weren't in the same house any more; she was lodging in Tindal Street, on the edge of the student vortex. They walked up the Bristol Road together towards the number 1 bus route. 'How are you and Matt?' Theresa said.

'OK, I suppose. Things were a bit shaky for a while. But he's stuck with me through the summer. I wouldn't have blamed him for bailing out. I've not been . . . myself, you know? Matt's good at practical things.' Theresa squeezed his hand. 'How have you been?'

'Pretty good. Bit of a jolt, seeing Sean again.'

'I could tell. You were really good in the rehearsal, though.' He paused. 'Has everything been OK?'

'Why do you ask?'

'I don't know. Just thought you looked a bit stressed. And thinner.'

Theresa shrugged. 'Well, I've lost weight.' She looked out into the oncoming traffic, and Neil had to strain to catch her words. 'It hadn't really started, the weight gain. I was just eating a lot because I was hungry. By the end of June, I knew for other reasons. And there was just no way. So now . . . it's gone.' She turned to face him. 'Don't tell Sean. You promise?'

'Yes,' Neil said, confused. 'You mean . . .' They stared at each other. 'Sean. He was . . .? God, I'm so sorry.'

'I just don't want him to know. It was an accident. Like most things. Nothing's ever meant to be the way it turns out.'

They walked all the way back to Moseley together, past a series of security lights that photographed their shadows on the roadway. Poplar trees stirred like giant feathers against the blue–black sky. They walked up Park Hill Road, past the little church and its malformed tree, and hugged goodbye outside the Jug of Ale. 'Take care.'

As usual after closing time, the Alcester Road was dotted with rose-pink crusts of vomit. Were they all living on prawn cocktails? Neil thought of Michael's chickenpox. How had Gary known about it? He wondered if they were close. Did anyone ever get close to Gary? Then something moved at the edge of his vision. A shadow against the streetlight, hiding on the corner of Brighton Road. Something glittered from under the bridge: tinfoil or broken glass. He felt sure someone had been watching him. Suddenly he felt naked. He needed some protection: a knife, or even a bottle. Hands knotting painfully into fists, he stood and watched. There was no-one there.

Even so, instead of taking the next left into the long arc of Trafalgar Road, he walked up through the village and went round via Woodbridge Road. It was more central, safer. His fear of being seen was less intense than his fear of being jumped from behind. (*Oh, if only*, murmured the Gary in his head.) By the time he got to the house, he was walking step by step, looking round each time he reached a streetlamp. *Snap out of it*, he thought angrily. *This is fucking Moseley. Do you think you're going to be mugged by vegans? Drowned neck first in a barrel of organic bran?* It didn't help. The marks of violence on his face were sure to bring more violence upon him. *What the rules are. Can you see?* Even inside the house, he still felt watched.

Climbing the dark stairs, Neil could hear the Cure song 'Apart' from the second floor. His spider senses told him that Matthew might have had a few drinks this evening. It was nearly midnight. He knocked on the *Dawn of the Dead* poster. 'Hi. Come in.' A tidal wave of minor chords washed over him. Matt turned the stereo down. 'Neil. Why are you so late? I was worried.'

'I walked back with Theresa. We had things to talk about.'

'How did the rehearsal go?'

'Quite well.' Matt shifted across the bed to let him lie down. 'We left out the sexy bits, just did the miserable stuff. You have to sometimes.'

'I know.' Around them, the music was a layered web of bass, echoing drums and gently overdubbed lyrics. There was a second voice behind Robert Smith's, though you could only just hear it. The sound brought the cold breath of night into the room, into the narrow bed. 'How did you feel about going out? Was it OK?'

'It wasn't easy,' Neil said. He gripped Matt's ribs, feeling the heartbeat. 'But I can't stay here all the time. The skin grafts won't be ready for another fortnight. And even after then . . . It feels like I've been scared for so long, I've forgotten what I was afraid of. Know what I mean?' They kissed slowly. Yes, Matt had been drinking. 'How was your evening?'

'Much as usual. Alien abductions, computerised implants, beer.' Tonight was the X-Files Society, Neil remembered. 'You'll have to come along some time.'

'Why, because I look like an alien–human hybrid?'

'If you're going to be like that, there's no point bothering with anything.' Matt closed his eyes.

'I'm sorry.' The chill was between them now, gripping

their faces. Neil thought he could see his own breath. 'I'm
just nervous about meeting new people.'

'I know that. But when you don't want to be seen with
me – when you don't want us to do anything together, except
have sex – you make me feel you don't believe in me. In us.'

'But it's not like that.' Neil tried to reach with his voice.
Reaching with his hands would be too obvious. 'You know I
love you. It's just . . . I'm not myself some of the time. I feel
like something in me is changing. But it has nothing to do
with you and me. I'm still here. I'm still your lover.'

Matt opened his eyes. He looked bewildered. 'Shit. What
was . . . I'm sorry. I've had too much to drink. You just
reminded me of my dad.' He was breathing hard. 'When I
was nine or ten, my mum had a boyfriend. She went out to
see him sometimes. I never met him. My dad used to talk
about *Jane's lover*. The way he said it, like a *lover* was something disgusting. For years afterwards, the word made me
feel sick. I thought pop singers must be sick when they used
the word like it meant something nice.'

'What word do you prefer?'

'Boyfriend is OK.' They kissed for a while. 'Why don't we
get into bed ?' Neil switched off the light and they undressed,
then grappled wearily under the duvet. Matt sucked him and
he came in seconds, the relief at no longer having to argue
fuelling his pleasure like lighter fluid poured over a flame. He
felt safe in the dark, not only from watching eyes but from
the things he could only half see. Matt kissed him, the combined taste of alcohol and sperm passing between their
mouths like a message.

While he was sucking Matt's cock, Neil became aware of
a faint scratching sound behind the bed. Was it a mouse,
trapped in the wall between layers of plaster and brick? The
image of a cracked, rotting wall of secrets came back to him
from the hospital ward. But as he paused, breathless, the

regularity of the sound made him realise what it was: the needle on Matt's old stereo, trapped in the run-out groove. He'd switch it off in a minute. But first . . . The flesh in his mouth thickened suddenly. He swallowed the dense fluid, which he'd always thought tasted mineral rather than animal. Then he got out of bed, switched on the lamp and freed the needle from its orbit. Matt's face was buried in the pillow. Without any conscious intention, or indeed any thought at all, be began to put on his clothes.

He paced quietly around the house, examining each empty room. No-one else was up. There was nothing to justify his search. He felt like a house-hunter being led around an undesirable property. At last he went back to his own room, undressed again, and slept.

3

The next couple of weeks were fairly hectic. Neil worked in the University Library most days, had meetings with his supervisor, attended seminars. His thesis was falling into place. When he stepped back from close linguistic interpretation and stuck to historical record, the task became easier to focus. Psychology was doing his head in. With some relief, he realised that most of what he was trying to prove was summed up by Horkheimer's statement: *Those who would speak of fascism must first speak of capitalism.*

It was a viewpoint subtly explored by Adorno's study of American racism in *The Authoritarian Personality*. Critics of the Frankfurt School argued that, after their flight to America, a mixture of grief and disorientation made them see the shadow of the swastika in the West Coast sunlight. But there was more to it than that. They were Marxists, first and foremost. In identifying the belief system of Southern rednecks as fascist, Adorno was underlining the point that racism was historical and cultural in nature: not a product of blind ignorance or instinctive xenophobia, but an ideology crafted over the generations to justify a system of exploitation. He couldn't say that much in an American textbook; but he didn't need to.

From a distance, it was easy to read between the lines. But when the words were pouring off the TV screen, you couldn't separate text from subtext. All year, he'd been making excuses for New Labour: electoral strategy, potential coalition, the need to keep the tabloids quiet. But now the post-election honeymoon was over, Blair was talking as if the real enemy of New Labour were the party itself. Neil realised he'd been suppressing his anger at this bullshit for far too long. It was adding injury to insult.

And yet, he couldn't quite break free. It was too much. To go back into opposition, this time knowing it was forever. He felt uncomfortable talking to activists like Sean. Or Sean's friend Vincent, an ex-hippie and militant trade unionist who'd quit British Rail on the day of its privatisation and now worked in a Tyseley factory that made parts for lorries. He was also a committed stoner, which meant that he and Matt got on really well.

One Friday night, the four of them were in the back yard of the Fieldmouse and Firkin, drinking beer almost as dark as Guinness. Vincent was talking about the sixties. 'It was the last time there was any sense of community among the young,' he said. 'We were all a family. Together in the garden. After that, there was nothing but alienation or selling out. You know why the Tories hate the sixties so much? Because it was a time when everyone talked about sharing. Thirty years later, they're still consumed with rage about that.'

Matt nodded. 'Even the image of a circle of people passing around a joint challenges the bourgeois concept of property.'

'Don't bring drugs into it,' Neil said, irritated. 'That was what fucked things up for that whole generation. They could have changed everything. Grass made them sentimental, acid drove them mad, heroin killed them off. It was a massacre.'

'I know what Vincent means, though,' Sean remarked. 'There was more to it than just the Summer of Love. It was a crucial time. But you know what really killed the sixties ideal in Britain? Shit housing. All those dreams, all those hopes, and what did they build? Fucking housing estates. A whole new generation grew up associating the sixties with an environment like an open-plan prison.'

Vincent rose unsteadily to his feet. 'Well, pardon me for not keeping still in my grave. But I was around then and I'm still here, and I don't like being blamed for fucking up your dream. As I see it, most of us stayed alive and carried on trying to change things. But we couldn't. Because things – by which I mean *people* – didn't want to fucking change.' When he was upset, a few Scottish hills broke up the flatlands of his Brummie accent. 'Another round, eh? Before I get angry and start talking about the eighties, and then you'll be fucking sorry.' He negotiated the wooden tables to the back entrance and the crowd at the bar.

Matt lit a cigarette and sighed. It was a cloudless night, and the moon was tinged with red. Someone was burning leaves in a garden nearby; there were ashes in the smoke, and red sparks that winked and died in mid-air. A couple of people were burning leaves on a smaller scale at one of the tables, and the scent mingled with beer to give the air a faint, elusive sweetness. Neil didn't think he'd ever felt so calm. In a few seconds, his depression had blown away like dust. Even the shadows around him seemed full of the promise of light. He smiled at Matt, who smiled back. Their hands clasped across the table.

'Yer fuckin' queerboys.' The voice came from just behind him. It was choked with alcohol and contempt. A middle-aged drunk, hands shaking around an empty pint glass, was standing so close that Neil could smell his breath. His grey hair stuck out at various angles from under a cloth hat. 'Yer fuckin' students. Think yer so fuckin' cool. Nancy boys.'

Matt tensed, withdrawing his hand. Neil stared at the stranger's reddened face. Slowly, he stood up. 'What do you want?'

The drunk gestured vaguely around his head. 'Here – this garden – without you in it. Fuckin' ponce – think you know fuckin' everything. Think you're better than anyone else. Someone's taught you a lesson already, but you weren't listening. Were you?'

'That's enough,' Sean said. Neil waved him down. He stared into the stranger's eyes. Cracks in the wall.

'Shut your fucking mouth,' Neil said quietly. 'Leave us alone. Fuck off. Come near me again, I'll fucking kill you. I'll cut your fucking head off. Do you understand? Because my friends will be happy to explain it to you.' He raised an index finger. 'I'm giving you one chance. *Get out of my fucking face.*'

The man blinked at Neil as if he were a burning house. He backed off, turned and made his way to the exit from the back yard into Woodbridge Road. In the doorway he glanced back over his shoulder, as if Neil might be following him. It was suddenly very quiet. Neil sat down. Vincent was approaching their table with four pints balanced on a little tray.

Matt touched his arm. 'I never knew you could be so assertive.'

'Well, I did grow up in Macclesfield.' But Neil couldn't make sense of the way he'd reacted. That wasn't him. The peace he'd felt a few seconds earlier was destroyed. Like a car windscreen: one moment pure clarity, the next a maze of cracks you couldn't see through. Vincent put a straight pint of Dogbolter in front of him. Neil lifted it gratefully to his mouth. But before he could taste it, his hand twitched and the glass slipped away. It bounced off the table and smashed on the grey cobbles. Wordlessly, Vincent handed him another pint.

Neil's consultant at the QE suggested he should go on anti-depressants. 'They don't cure depression,' she said. 'They just hold it back, give you a breathing space. And for someone in your position, that might be all you need. Since these feelings have been brought on by a traumatic experience, you need some time to get over it. As long as you don't see medication as a cure, it can help you.' But Neil wasn't convinced. His friend Marc had gone on Prozac after splitting up with his boyfriend, and the drug had made him so violent he'd called on his ex and beaten the shit out of him. The ex was a rugby-playing muscleboy, and Marc was a skinny peroxide babe. Called in by the ex, the police had refused to take his request for protection seriously. But then, all muscle-boys were fucking cowards. According to Marc.

There was a deeper reason, too. Neil felt there was already enough he couldn't see clearly. If anything blurred the picture, he might be even more at risk. The idea of not being able to feel disturbed him too much. And what if the medication interfered with his ability to work? He needed to be able to find meaning in the negative.

The consultant had also given him the details of a self-help group for disfigured people. They met regularly in Birmingham. But Neil was afraid of going to see them. He didn't want to make friends with people just because they had damaged faces. He didn't want to be helped to accept himself. What was the point? The scarred face wasn't him. It was what had been done to him. When he looked in the mirror, he didn't see himself. He saw the blue mask. It was impossible for him to look closely at the image. He didn't want to think of it as a living face.

Out in the streets, in the shops or the Central Library, he was aware of people's questioning glances. Maybe they thought he was dangerous. They watched him from a distance – but face to face, they avoided eye contact. It was different at the University. People who knew him there kept smiling at him, trying to pretend nothing had changed. Looking through him as if they could pretend his damaged face was something they hadn't yet noticed. He had to look straight at people, because both sides of his face were scarred. The back of his head was his best side.

One night, he went to see a band at the Jug of Ale. He always enjoyed the passivity of live music: it was like going to the cinema. Standing in the dark, unseen, made him feel safe. The band were a low-key psychedelic outfit called Mocca. Two songs into their brooding set, he felt a moment of pure euphoria. The world seemed full of light. He'd only drunk a pint of cider, so it wasn't that. Walking home, he felt no better than usual. 'What do you want?' he said out loud, and felt stupid.

Another night, he said to Matt: 'I want to cry, but I can't afford to.' Matt said it was good to cry. It might help him get something out of his system. 'That's not what I mean,' Neil said. 'I don't mean the way you cry at a film, or after too much cider. I mean the way you cry when you know it won't help. When everything inside you is cold. I mean the kind of crying that never really stops.'

Being this low had its compensations. Everything felt sharper somehow, more in focus. Neil borrowed some of Matt's *noir* thrillers and read them at night when he couldn't sleep; their chords of terror and suspense rang loud in his head. One night, after watching *Question Time*, he wrote a furious tirade about intolerance: starting with quotes from Dick Gregory and Lenny Bruce, then quoting a Tory MP who, when recently asked whether British society was still intolerant of homosexuality, had remarked 'We have always been bizarrely tolerant of it.'

How much tolerance qualifies as bizarre? Neil typed. *Would only an iron policy of zero tolerance lack any taint of bizarreness? Or is there an ideal level of prejudice, a kind of homophobic bliss point, beyond which the bizarreness level would start to creep up along with the faggot suicide rate?* James at *Redbrick* printed a somewhat abridged version of the article. Neil got an unexpected e-mail from Gary, saying *I enjoyed your column.* He e-mailed back: *You wish.*

It was only the nights that were good. Or not. The days passed in a kind of apathetic haze. He often stayed in bed all morning, dreaming of a place without people where mountain-peaks shone through veils of mist. Out in the streets, there was only a thin layer of daylight that he couldn't take seriously. The sun never showed itself. It was like human nature, he realised: you took it for granted, but it was only a mask over empty space.

After a delay, the second operation came in mid-October. This time, they removed some tissue to even out the contours. When the doctor showed him his face in a mirror, it looked thinner and angrier than before. It was the face of a man he could become.

The phone rang just after midnight. Stefan answered it. 'Hello? Yeah, he's here. I'll get him.' He went into the living-room, where Neil was watching TV with the light off.' Neil? It's for you.'

'Hello, it's Anne.' Her voice sounded quiet and flat, like a poor recording. 'Sorry I haven't called. How are things?' He told her about the operation. 'How does it feel?'

'I don't know. A bit strange. You know something the doctor told me? Subjectively, the face has no regions. If it hurts, you can't tell where. You expect parts to be bruised that aren't. So even though it's sore, it feels numb. Looks OK, though.'

'You think it's an improvement.'

'Definitely. I just need to get away for a bit. I've been in the house too long. Can't see anything but my own shadow. I might go up to Macclesfield this weekend, have a look at the Edge. How are things at work?'

'Don't know. I haven't been there. Malcolm got me suspended.' She told him about the missing page. 'He wants me to know that he did it, because he knows I can't prove it. It's all some kind of fucking spy story to him. I bet he really loves himself for this.'

'Have you talked to the union yet?'

'They don't know what to do. They've offered to liaise with the *View* to get me a different job. They're also willing to back me if it comes to a tribunal. I don't know . . . I don't want those things. I went out and bought something for Malcolm.'

'What, a present? Why?' Something in Anne's tone was beginning to disturb him. He'd heard her angry, miserable, blind drunk; but he'd never heard her sound defeated.

'Not a present. It's *for* him. Until I can work out how to give it to him, I'll leave it in the kitchen drawer. With the other knives.'

Neil laughed. He knew she wasn't joking. 'When did this happen?'

'About three weeks ago now. The company haven't been in touch. I'm still getting paid.'

'Why didn't you tell me before?'

'I don't know. Didn't want to bother you. But I haven't told anyone. I've just been so tired. All I want to do is sleep.'

'Would you like me to come and see you?'

'Not just yet, Neil. I appreciate it. But I can't face anyone at the moment. When you come back from Macclesfield, I'll come to Moseley and . . .' She paused. Neil could hear her breathing.

'Anne. Are you OK?'

'Sorry. I was going to say, *we'll go for a drink*. But that reminded me of last weekend. I went out in Bearwood and got totally rat-arsed . . . I remember throwing up in some guy's bathroom. When I woke up, I didn't know what was going on. Didn't know who I was. All I could remember was lying there, not caring, while . . . It wasn't even good. How could I do that? You know me. I don't let myself get used. I'm not even sure he was careful . . . I couldn't look at him in the morning. Just got the fuck out, Neil. Came home and slept all day.'

'I'm sorry,' Neil said. 'You shouldn't feel bad about it. Mistakes happen, you were very down. Some people do that every weekend.' There was silence at the end of the line. 'Anne, take care of yourself. And phone me any time you want to talk. OK?'

'OK.' The line went dead. He realised she'd taken his words as meaning *Goodnight*. He should have been more careful. After all, he knew how that felt. When every sound was a door slamming in your face. He'd call her tomorrow and try to help. Not that sharing each other's despair was likely to help either of them. Maybe they should form a band.

4

From Birmingham New Street to Macclesfield was quite a short journey; but to Neil, it always felt much longer. The only seats that morning were in the smoking carriage, which was full of schoolkids with cigarettes. They smoked clumsily, puffing grey clouds into the air. Opposite Neil, a boy who looked about twelve whined: 'Shit, I need a fag.' Neil tried to focus on his battered copy of *Miracle of the Rose*. One sentence tugged repeatedly at his eyes: *I shall not let my child-hood escape*. He wondered if that was a deliberate inversion of the truth.

It always surprised him, when he went back, how little the place seemed to change. Compared to Birmingham, which was in a permanent state of reconstruction, the centre of Macc was frozen in time. But it wasn't preservation that achieved this, he knew: it was inertia. From the station he could see the Peugeot car showroom and the big hardware store, S & M Supplies, that he'd walked past as a child. Around the dark tower of the church with its four stone crosses, there were the same tilted alleys you'd never get a car along. And the same office buildings with red fire escapes. The Pig and Whistle had shut down, but the Nag's Head was still there. Of course, the market had been gone for years. According to Deborah Curtis, Ian had nicked records from it as a teenager, hiding them under his trenchcoat.

The Jackson house was out towards Prestbury, on a road lined with birches and other trees. There wasn't much pave-ment, so you had to look out for oncoming traffic. Strange: you couldn't drive in the town centre, and you couldn't walk outside it. Neil's father answered the door. He paused, glanced at Neil's weekend bag, then said 'Come in.' Neil was sure his father hadn't recognised him for a moment.

'You look wonderful,' his mother said. 'Doesn't he?' His father smiled assent. 'You look a bit like you did at fourteen. When the scars fade, you'll be as good as new.' *Scars don't fade*, Neil thought. But they seemed glad to see him. Maybe he was more welcome as a visitor than as someone who was trying to belong.

The spare room didn't look like his bedroom any more. There was a futon, and his old books were packed in boxes along the wall. Maybe he should ask his parents to get rid of them. He opened one box and blew the dust off the contents. Marvel comics, true crime, old copies of the *New Statesman*. In between the stacks were *The Thoughts of Chairman Mao* in its red plastic cover and a tiny address-book. Neil flicked through it. Victor – he'd surely moved away. Kerry – so that was her name. Des.

The phone rang nine times before someone answered. 'Hello?'

'Is Des there, please?'

'Speaking.'

'I don't know if you remember me. It's Neil. Neil Jackson.'

'Shit. Yeah. Neil, yeah. How are you?' His voice was heavier and slower than Neil remembered.

'OK. I'm a student still. But not for much longer. How are you?'

'All right. I'm a fast-food chef. Want a chicken burger, I'm the man. Pays the rent, don't it? And I'm married now.'

'Oh . . . Look, I'm here for the weekend. Wondered if you'd like to meet for a drink. Catch up a bit.'

'Yeah, why not? My shift finishes at nine. See you in the George and Dragon at half past?'

'Sure.' Neil hesitated. 'I might look a bit different. I had an argument with a broken bottle a few months ago.'

'So you'll look like most people round here. Have you heard the joke? A stranger in black goes into a Macc pub and says to the barman, *I'm looking for the man they call Scarface.* Barman says, *Can you narrow that down at all?*' Neil laughed, though he didn't find the joke comforting.

That afternoon, he walked out to Alderley Edge. There

was more traffic than he remembered, and not much time to get out of its way on the twisted, uneven road. Trees made a jigsaw of the light, and dead leaves covered everything. Birch, sycamore, oak, beech. The only buildings were churches, so old they were like dreams. He was tired already, not used to walking. The new skin felt tight and dry. He imagined the patches falling off, one by one, like dead leaves. *The bodies obtained.*

Someone was keeping pace with him, behind the trees. He could see a car parked by the walkway to the Edge. Then another car, next to a dry-stone toilet building with a lichen-covered roof. It was too isolated here. And too overgrown. Tension jarred his spine. An image from childhood came back to him: the Edge as a cliff you could fall down and never be found. He was safer on the road. Among the trees, you could be followed and not know it. The afternoon sunlight, coming through the tatters of yellow leaves, gave him the sudden image of a shadow with a mouthful of blood.

Further on, the view opened out like a map: electricity pylons marked out the fields like grid lines. Sheep grazed behind the sheet music of barbed wire. There was no threat of wilderness. Neil wondered if he'd ever trust nature again. The things you were told were instinct were really just imagination. When you fell back on your instinct, there was nothing there.

By the time he reached Alderley Edge, he was so tired his legs felt nerveless. The skin over his left cheekbone was bleeding. He paused and looked back down the steep hill he'd climbed: a river of dead leaves, burning in the sunset. There was no human figure in sight. Yet he still felt pursued, watched. For the second time, he asked out loud: 'What do you want?' He needed to know what he had to do to make this end. But for now, a quick pint and the bus back to Macclesfield would have to be enough.

After dinner, his father produced a small envelope. 'This is for you,' he said to Neil. 'It's really for your birthday, but you need to see it now. Matt helped us to plan it.'

'You talked to Matt?' Neil was amazed. He tore open the envelope. It contained two return tickets from Birmingham to Paris, by airline, at the start of November. 'My God. This is fantastic. Thank you.'

'We just thought it would be a nice break for you,' his mother said. 'It's where we went on our honeymoon.'

'It's just what we need,' Neil said. 'Thank you.' He knew there was more acceptance in this gift than in anything they would ever say. The silence wasn't one-sided. The rows he'd had to listen to as a child still echoed in his head. He couldn't erase the tapes, make the family real. He couldn't explain that even to himself. The cut on his cheek stung.

When he reached the George and Dragon, an old-fashioned pub with a largely middle-aged crowd, Des was nowhere in sight. As he glanced at a succession of tall men, he had to fight to avoid eye contact. He'd lost the knack of straight pubs. Worse, he could sense people looking at him: a kind of hostile curiosity, as if he was an alien. The cracked skin on his cheek wasn't helping. The barman eyed him warily before pouring him a pint of John Smith's.

When he turned round, Des was there. A redder face, less hair and a paunch; but the same nervous blue eyes and pale streak of moustache. He stared at Neil for a few seconds, then stuck out a hand. 'Neil! Good to see you.'

'What are you drinking?'

'Same as you. That guy really did some damage, didn't he? Did you do something mortal, like spill his pint?'

'I don't remember,' Neil said. He turned back to the bar. The Stranglers' 'Golden Brown' was playing on the juke-box. In the corner of his eye, he saw a hand gesturing towards him. Light flickered on the optics like a torch with a dying battery.

'Come back here often, do you?' Des asked when they'd found a table. The pub was filling up rapidly. Neil shook his head. 'Don't blame you. Not a lot to come back to. All Macc is now, a service industry for rich fuckers from the countryside. Fucking Thai restaurants and licensed tapas bars and Internet bars. What's here for us? The nearest cinema's in fucking Stockport.'

When Neil got up to go to the Gents, he saw two men staring at him from the bar. He made his way cautiously between the tables. Just as he reached the corridor with the sign TOILETS, a foot reached out between his ankles and he tripped, falling hard. The bare wooden flooring jarred his wrists. Suddenly everyone close by was looking the other way. He got up and stared at the silhouette figure on the toilet door. Too many mirrors, only one exit. He brushed the dust off his knees and limped back to the table. 'Why don't we drink up and move on?' he said.

'I saw what happened,' Des said when they were outside. 'I was ready to pitch in for you, like, but maybe it's better not. You really need to watch yourself around here.'

Neil shrugged. 'Do they think because of the scars, I must be hard?'

'Nah. If they thought you were hard, someone'd take you on properly. Face you down. It's 'cause you look like a student. Show me a student, and I'll show you a face as wants breaking. No offence, like.'

'Sure.' Neil thought of the Marion song 'Violent Men', inspired by growing up in Macc. *Because family men are violent men.* They paused outside the Jolly Sailor, a haunt of theirs in the old days. 'You know, I used to think education could change the world.'

'You used to believe all kinds of shite.' Inside, it was noisier than the last pub, but felt less threatening. Des bought a round of Carling. Mixing beer and lager was part of their old routine, Neil remembered. As they stood at the bar, he noticed the barmaid looking at him, then checking some photos in an envelope. Next, she checked a list of names pinned up on the wall, with the heading BANNED. He turned away.

They moved on quickly, compressing their pub-crawl into a sprint. Diamond Whites at the White Lion. Double vodkas at the Blueberry Inn. They got to the White Swan just in time for last orders. 'Classic,' Des remarked with satisfaction. This was a quieter place: a working men's pub, with small tables and a haze of tangy smoke from roll-ups. Neil didn't feel watched here. Maybe he was just too drunk to notice.

Throughout their trek, Des's anger at the state of things had been building. 'Fucking election might as well not have happened,' he muttered. 'We've still got a fucking Tory MP who's . . .' Raised voices behind Neil's back, a chair being pushed over, drowned his words. Neil forced himself to keep looking at Des's face. He willed the soundtrack to return to it. '. . . that's why nothing ever gets done. Our Labour councillor's a voice in the fucking wilderness. I tell you, Neil Hamilton was right at home here. Happy as a pig in shite. Him and that fucking horse he should have rode instead of married.

'I've got friends who've been evicted when they couldn't find work. Miss a week's rent, you're in front of the magistrate. *Who doesn't fucking live here.* The fucking town's collapsing round us fucking feet. Don't talk to me about the third way. It's not even a joke.'

Neil was used to this bitterness here. It was what had fuelled his enthusiasm for political theory, believing that the global truths would answer the local questions. But things weren't getting better. In fact, they seemed to be getting worse. He didn't know what to say.

In the hushed twilight of the White Swan, drinking Scotch on top of Brew XI, Des calmed down a little. 'Tell you something. I'd have been out of this dump years ago if it wasn't for Julie. We met just after I left school. We were working at the dye factory, before some crooked bastard had it burnt down. Been married three years, got two daughters. You know, it's not where you're born that matters. It's where you make your home.' He looked at Neil thoughtfully. 'So, you got a bloke?'

Neil choked on his whisky. 'How did you know?'

'Because I'm fucking Sherlock Holmes. We always thought you were. I don't give a shit.'

'Well, yes, I do have someone. Another student.'

'Goes without saying.' He drained the last of his Scotch, wincing as it bit his throat. 'Is that why you got your face rearranged?'

'I suppose so, yes. It's a long story.'

'Can I ask you something, man to man?' Neil nodded. 'I can't imagine what it's like, giving a blow job. Are you good at it?'

Neil shrugged uneasily. 'Suppose. Never had any complaints.'

'Well . . . would you mind explaining it to Julie?' Neil stared at him. 'Hey, I was only joking. Take it easy.'

When they left the pub, both of them were a little unsteady. Neil glanced up and saw a bridge with figures swaying on it. The streets were full of people. Some were arguing or squaring off for a fight. Some were looking for a quiet spot to piss or throw up. But most of them were just standing there, because they didn't know what to do next. A boy came running up the street and swerved to shoulder-charge Neil. He crashed into the wall and felt the back of his head smack the cold brickwork. Des turned in confusion, grabbed his arm. 'Are you OK?'

'Fine.' It didn't seem to hurt. They walked on towards the town centre. More to himself than to his stumbling companion, Neil muttered: 'I'm finally beginning to feel like I belong here.'

5

The problem with drama, Matt realised, was that every part of it had to be worked at. You couldn't just go with the flow. And given what Neil was like at the moment, that kind of pressure was the last thing he needed. He'd been worrying all day about *Nights of Insult*, making phonecalls and sending e-mails. He wouldn't leave the house in case someone got in touch with a problem. Tonight was the first night. Matt was doing his best to help by making coffee, cooking dinner, and otherwise keeping out of the way.

According to Neil, the dress rehearsal hadn't gone very well. Michael was still fazed after his attack of chickenpox; he seemed to have no energy. Sean and Theresa weren't communicating, except on stage. And Gary was dealing with his nerves by sniping at everyone. Matt had pointed out that creative tensions between artists often produced great performances. 'Look at the Smiths. Or the Velvet Underground.'

'Yes,' Neil said. 'But the operative word there is *artists*. Meaning, *people with talent*.'

At least there was a reasonable-sized audience in the Studio Theatre. October winds were shaking the Muirhead Tower to its jerry-built foundations, but fifty or so people had made it alive through the canvas-draped tunnel. On the stage was a white bed with iron rails, a wooden chair and a small dressing-table carrying an assortment of plastic dolls and cosmetics. Behind these were three linked walls covered with pale wood-chip wallpaper. Next to the right-hand wall was a tiny, empty cot.

Matt and Neil sat near the front, to the left-hand side. Neil had been with the actors for a while, and only took his seat with a couple of minutes to go. He looked pale and tired. As the lights went out, Matt squeezed his hand.

A blue spotlight fell on the stage, with Gary at its edge. He stepped into it, holding up a small clock. *This was always the worst time. Waiting for her to come home. At night, there was nothing between me and the ghosts. I stared at the clock to keep myself in real time. I'm not an instrument, only a metronome.* Matt could hear the clock ticking. *At last, she came home.*

Gary turned to face the bed, but didn't move forwards. Theresa came in, wearing a hat and raincoat. She took them off. Underneath, she was wearing a tarty black top, a red miniskirt and black stockings. She changed into a more conventional blouse and skirt that were hanging behind the wall. Gary watched in silence. She didn't appear to see him. As the light dimmed, she picked up a doll from the dresser and began to comb its long hair. *She never goes to bed until dawn.* Gary's face was expressionless, his voice cold with bitterness. *It takes her that long to feel at home. The night's not for sleeping.*

The scene changed. Matt recognised the track played in between: 'Sleep' by Marion, a Macclesfield band that Neil was inexplicably into. Then Gary again, talking about the other tenant. *Dave was a collector of light. He went out in the dark and stole the morning light. He stole the fire of the gods and used it to light his stolen cigarettes.* A light came up over the bed: Michael staring at a shelf of framed photographs, TV and film stars. Then he paced around the room, shifting from one role to another: a doctor in a hospital drama, a soft-spoken villain, an incoherent drunk. Gary mimicked his gestures.

A mobile phone rang, and Dave answered it. *Hello? Who? Oh, him. No. Dunno where he is. Look, I haven't seen him since I left Winson Green. Last I heard, he was in Stuttgart. Some kind of gun-running operation. Apparently linked to Colonel Ga— There's no need . . . OK. OK. Yes, I'll let you know. The second he gets in touch. Of course.* He put the phone down and stood there, shaking, his face in his hands. There was a knock at the door. Sean stood in the doorway, half in shadow. He raised his hands. There was blood on them.

The light faded, and a few seconds of Marion's 'My Children' led into the next scene. Matt felt uncomfortable watching this. It was too slow and contrived. Gary's character kept getting between the audience and the play. His lines were blackly poetic and bitter, like a drugged Robert Smith, calling up stronger images than Matt could see on the stage. The props looked cheap: dolls, framed photos, sweat-marked cotton sheets, a crap phone.

The scenes picked up pace as they became more violent. But the acting didn't improve. Gary's delivery was mannered and cold; it often sounded like he was afraid of losing the thread if he changed his pace. He took a couple of prompts. When the others got involved, it flowed more naturally, though Sean was clumsy and Michael sleepwalked through a nearly inaudible performance. Only Theresa, locked in her silent world, seemed to belong on the stage.

There was no interval. The play was two hours long. After a while, two people behind Matt started whispering to each other. He turned and signalled at them to shut up, but they didn't. A few times, when a sound effect was mistimed or a prop fell on the stage, a few of the audience laughed. Whenever that happened, Neil stiffened and gripped his chair. Near the end, a particular scene-change took several minutes; a few people took the opportunity to leave. Matt wasn't sure he'd have stayed if it hadn't been Neil's play. His knowledge of the dramatic art began and ended with Roger Corman; but even he could tell this was a mess.

The big love scene – or at least, fuck scene – between Corin and Dave had both actors bare-arsed, which surprised him. At the climax both men were silent, clamped together on the bed, staring at the audience – who'd be invisible from there, Matt knew. He could hear the couple breathing. Gary's languid commentary was as distant as a radio in the next room. The light faded and another Marion track came on, 'Time'. The next scene was in the same bedroom, but the broken glass had been replaced with the scattered petals of white roses.

The last few minutes of the play were strange and confusing. Rachel struck a match above the little cot in the corner of her room, then pulled back the blanket: a heap of red and orange tinsel spilled out. Smoke began to rise from between the walls. Rachel beat at the flames with her hands. Dave and Corin ran in. Then they put out the fire somehow; the smoke obscured them for a while.

The three tenants of the house began to talk about Gary's character – who, for once, kept quiet. They called him the landlord. *He never goes out*, Rachel said. *If we weren't here, I think he'd fade away.* Gary stood in the half-light as if in rain, shivering. When Corin opened an invisible pair of curtains, flooding the stage with light, Gary stepped behind a wall. Dave and Corin embraced and kissed slowly. Rachel rose from the bed, as if waking up. They all froze as another Marion track began to play.

Matt thought he saw the point. All the characters were living inside one person's head. When they stayed apart, the person was unable to change. Or maybe it had to do with capitalism and the need for people to unite. Whatever. Neil's loneliness was written all over the play. The way he moved, the way he made love. Maybe he'd always been fucked up, and he'd used politics to cover the uncertainties. But he couldn't any more.

The applause was muted. When the lights came up, Neil was still staring at the empty stage. His face looked waxy, nauseous. Matt touched his hand. 'You OK?' He didn't respond. 'That was good,' Matt said, not really sure if it was a white lie or a truth he'd believe in later. People were drifting towards the bar. Neil looked around as if lost. He gripped Matt's arm, then made for the stage door.

Matt bought two pints of Grolsch, then sat in the bar on his own. About half the audience were still here. Some Drama Soc people at the next table were talking about *Les Misérables*. A skinny first-year lad at the bar was saying: 'I'm not homophobic, but I don't see why I should pay money to watch men kissing on stage.' His friend nodded as if something important had been said, then commented: 'It was a load of pretentious twaddle. Where was the story arc?' Depressed, Matt looked away.

Sean and Neil appeared in the doorway. Neil still didn't seem to know where he was. Eyes on the floor, he walked slowly between the tables to join Matt. He'd been a bit like this when he'd first come out of hospital; Matt supposed the stress of the last few weeks had brought it back. 'Are you OK?' he said.

Neil looked at him, then nodded slowly. 'Sure. I'm just tired.' The rest of the cast joined Sean at the bar. Neil lifted his pint. 'Cheers.' Then he looked over his shoulder, as if somebody had touched him. There was no-one close by. He dropped his face to his shoulder and held the pint in front of it: a posture that might have looked natural if he'd held it for less time. Matt wondered what to say.

He noticed Gary pointing towards them. A young, fashionably dressed woman he recognised as a Creative Writing lecturer came over to their table. 'Excuse me,' she said to Neil. 'You're Neil Jackson, right?'

Neil looked blankly at her. 'Sorry, not me.'

'Oh.' She glanced at Matt, then back at Neil. 'Do you know where he is?'

'Think he's gone home.' The lecturer backed off, still looking confused. Matt stared at Neil, dumbstruck. Neil gulped the last of his pint. 'Can we go?' he said.

They were halfway to the door when Alan, a graduate friend of Neil's, stepped in front of them. 'Hey, Neil. Enjoyed the play. How you doing?'

Neil blinked at him. 'Who's Neil? My name's Jason.' Matt bit his lip.

Alan went red. 'Shit. Sorry.' He turned away. Neil made a quick exit. Matt fetched their coats from the cloakroom, then followed him outside. The wind was gasping for air in the makeshift tunnel. Neil was gone.

He was standing at the edge of the courtyard, looking up at the lamps in front of the University Library. When Matt reached him, he was shivering. A pale curtain of rain fell across the view. Matt slipped Neil's coat over his shoulders and held him from behind. The rain smeared light into Matt's eyes and across Neil's expressionless face.

6

Three days later, a review of the play appeared in *Redbrick*. It was written by Lisa Wohl, a drama student whom Neil had met once or twice the year before. Under the heading 'From a Broken Life,' it ran:

Neil Jackson's play *Nights of Insult* draws on his own experience of disfigurement to portray a household of damaged lives. Those beloved symbols of middle-class order and normality, the family and the home, are shown to be little factories of trauma and fragmentation. The improvised, non-linear scenes enact helpless rituals that could only have meaning in a different world. The stage is littered with detached signifiers. This is not so much a play as a disfigured text, a script of scars, whose raging incoherence reminds us that that there can be no true drama in a world where only power and profit hold sway. Don't miss it.

For the remainder of its six-night run, only a few dozen people followed Lisa's advice. After the last night, everyone concerned with the production got blitzed and trashed the set.

chapter 6

....

the bodies obtained

1

The sun burned a hole in the clouds, transforming the layer below them into a glittering ice-rink that was painful to look at. Neil shut his eyes. The low vibration of the plane's engine reminded him of standing on a bridge over a busy road. It soothed him, blanked out his thoughts. They'd been up since six, and he wasn't sleeping much these days. Beside him, Matt was reading to keep his mind off the flight. But Neil felt strangely detached. This wasn't part of the world. It was like being asleep.

The plane lurched. Through the eyeholes, Neil saw the frozen sea of cloud tilt upwards and back again. He tried to turn his head and couldn't. A crust had grown on his face, light but hard; it smelt like bleach. He touched it. The mask was as thin as paper. It didn't fit his face, but it was clamped hard on to it. There was no way to lift it off. Neil punched his left cheek, just below the eye. The shell fractured. Some pieces fell in his lap, over the seat-belt; others had to be picked off his face. Within minutes, the whitish crust had disintegrated and blown away like cigarette smoke. Underneath, his skin felt raw.

Matt was still lost in a battered copy of *The Haunter of the Dark*. He glanced at Neil as the plane began to descend. 'Y'all right, bab?' Their hands clasped between the seats. Things had been awkward between them since the play. Matt seemed to have decided that Neil needed looking after. He was always happiest in the role of carer. But that was part of the problem. Last week, they'd gone to see *Betty Blue* at the Electric Cinema. It was meant to get them into the mood for the trip to Paris, but it had left both of them feeling shaken and miserable. They hadn't talked until the next morning.

After a long wait on the runway, they were released from the tiny plane into the vastness of Charles de Gaulle Airport. Neil had been to Paris once before, with his parents, at the age of nine. This airport had seemed bigger than Macclesfield. Now, he realised that the eye of a child was not easily deceived. It was at least that big.

A coach took them into Paris, along wide roads seething with traffic. By now, both of them were having trouble staying awake. Their hotel was near the Gare Saint-Lazare. The wind blew streaks of rain at an angle between the tall buildings. They checked in and were shown to their twin room on the second floor. It faced inwards: a hexagonal courtyard, paved with concrete and enclosed on all sides. Neil could see into a dozen or more similar rooms, all empty. It was like looking at the window of a TV shop.

They kicked off their shoes, lay down and slept for an hour or so. It was cold in the room. Neil could hear the rain hitting the glass in slow waves. He thought of the narrow side-street the hotel was in. They'd passed a funeral parlour called POMPES FUNEBRES. And an alley where a man had stood in the shadows, watching them. He was smoking. But as he stepped into the daylight, Neil saw that it was his mouth that was on fire. Neil froze as the man approached him. Their faces merged.

He woke up and felt too depressed to move. The pale room seemed about to twist or distort. A few minutes later, Matt woke up and went for a piss. Neil started unpacking a few bits and pieces. When Matt came back, they stood together and kissed slowly. 'It's great to be here with you,' Matt whispered. 'This is going to be wonderful.' They made plans for the afternoon. Montmartre was close by, and seemed like a good place to start.

When they handed in their keys at the hotel desk, the manager – a middle-aged woman whose English had a strong American accent – said: 'How is your room?'

'Er, fine. Thank you.'

'Just one thing,' she said. 'Could you please keep the noise down? Only we've had a complaint from another guest. About the noise.'

'Umm, sure,' Neil said, utterly confused. 'Sorry.'

Outside, he asked Matt: 'What was that about? How were we making noise? Snoring?'

'No. They probably say that to every male couple. In case we were fucking. Or thinking about it.'

The rain had stopped, and the dark streets were glowing in the afternoon sun. They walked up the steep hill towards Montmartre, and stopped at a small café-bar for lunch: white beer and omelettes. 'This is fantastic,' Matt said between mouthfuls. Neil wondered how anyone could get so excited about food. He was struck by the total absence of fast-food outlets, chip shops and kebab houses. The French obviously preferred a better class of cholesterol.

In the rue d'Amsterdam, they stopped at a small bookshop. Neil bought two volumes of poetry: Genet and Baudelaire. They were surprisingly cheap. Genet's face on the cover of *Le condamné à mort* seemed both frightened and knowing, as if he was trying to warn the reader about something. The cover of *Les fleurs du mal* superimposed a naked woman on

Baudelaire's face. 'That looks like a Marc Almond album,' Matt said. 'You remember *Absinthe*, that brilliant Paris album he did?'

Matt was a committed Almond fan. Neil was a sceptic. 'Never really liked that one. He was trying to be too clever. It's a hollow record.'

'Why? It's an album about getting old. It's bitter, but that doesn't mean it's hollow. You have to see all his records as a complete statement, made over a lifetime.' They walked past a butcher's shop with a red queue of skinned rabbits hanging in the window.

'That's the problem,' Neil said. '*Absinthe* is just a retread of *Mother Fist*. He doesn't mean it any more. Actually his album of Jacques Brel songs was good. But not as good as Scott Walker.'

'That's like saying the Cure aren't as good as Joy Division. It's an unfair comparison. You're always ranking things, when you should just listen to how something is. Marc Almond is erotic and sensual. He's singing in the dark.' They seemed to be arguing about music more and more these days.

The roads around the Cimetière de Montmartre were set in the hillside, with tiers of stone steps and old-fashioned lamps. They reminded Neil of Macclesfield. The cemetery was a few yards below street level, sheltered from the wind. It was a labyrinth of vaults and headstones at different levels, connected by tiny staircases. All the tombs were overgrown with moss and ivy. Trees burned slowly in the fragile sunlight. Neil and Matt walked quietly through the stillness, drawn into its strange territory of paths and steps. Some of the vaults were topped by open shrines, with iron crosses and blacked-out windows. Others were almost featureless, rooms sealed in grey stone.

They walked for an hour or so, sometimes holding hands. There was hardly anyone else in the cemetery. The sun clouded over, but it still felt warmer here than on the street. This was really a place where the dead could live. The sense of peace was unbelievable.

As they left, Neil felt the downswing click into place. He shivered and walked faster. There were only a couple of hours of daylight left. The wind blew dead leaves along the roadway, scratching like a trapped stylus. Matt tried to unfold the map, but it flapped and tore. They stopped at a wine bar and drank tiny espressos, listening to 'Dazed and Confused'. Neil wasn't sure if it was Led Zeppelin or Willie Dixon's original. It seemed to matter.

They took a detour through Pigalle in order to reach the Musée Gustave Moreau. Even by daylight, Pigalle was manic: a neon centrefold with its caption spelt out in plain English. A Greek or Turkish man in a red jacket grabbed Neil's arm. 'In here, sir! Only fifty francs! Peepshow, live show! See everything!'

Neil shook his head and walked on; but the man stepped in his path, forcing him to stop. 'This way! Only fifty francs!'

Neil allowed his face to twist into a snarl. 'Va te faire baiser.'

The huckster snorted contemptuously. 'Ha, I see. Gay. Pair of queers.' He wheeled around, smashing his elbow into Neil's shoulder, and marched off. Neil felt his jaw tensing. He reached inside his jacket for the knife.

Then Matt's hands gripped his elbows, propelling him down the street. 'What the fuck are you doing? You'll get us in prison. Or killed. You said that thing was for self-defence. Not fucking stupid fuck . . . Do that again and I'm fucking leaving you. I'm going home on my own.' He broke away from Neil and walked off furiously, weaving between the sightseers.

Neil caught up with him in the rue Fontaine, opposite the windmill of the Moulin Rouge. He was crying. 'Matt, listen to me. Please. He hurt my arm. I was just checking the knife was there.' Matt stopped. They embraced briefly.

'Why did you have to say that?' Matt said as they walked on. 'Why couldn't you just say, no thanks? Or tell him we were gay instead of waiting for him to say it? Why do you have to be so fucked up?'

'Because I've *been* fucked up,' Neil said.

Matt turned to face him, angrily. 'That's becoming an excuse for too many things.'

At least the Musée Gustave Moreau calmed them down a little. It was impossible to concentrate on feeling hurt and angry while looking at a picture of two people with dragonfly wings fucking in mid-air. Or a harpy pushing her breasts – her only human feature – into the face of a bewildered goatherd. Or a pale-skinned nymph dancing naked, while a luminous goat approached her through trees that appeared to be rotting. Neil laughed quietly. These pictures were genuinely, not accidentally, funny. In a really twisted way.

One huge canvas showed a community of mythical creatures from various times and cultures in a subterranean grotto, taking part in some kind of orgy. Quasi-human figures were riding, caressing or otherwise playing around with completely inhuman partners. But the revellers looked peaceful, even fatigued. Shagged out. Their skin was pearly and translucent, like scar tissue. Behind them, a gap in the cavern wall revealed a modern city. 'It's just like Machen's "The White People,"' Matt said happily.

They didn't try to make up; they just pretended nothing had happened. It was easier. Neil let Matt choose a restaurant for dinner; they ate paella and drank white wine in a bistro near the Rome Métro station. Matt read out descriptions of gay bars from Gary's *Spartacus* guide, and Neil marked the more promising ones on the map. There was a kind of unspoken agreement between them that they would visit the more cruisy places tomorrow. For tonight, music and alcohol would do.

The Métro tunnels were dark and warm, breathing heat into the train through its open windows. Whenever they were out of sight of a station, Neil began to panic. Just before Hôtel de Ville, the train paused and the lights flickered and dimmed. Neil could see graffiti in the tunnel, white on black. He touched the folded knife in his jacket. A figure lurched from the back of his mind, running on thin legs, slamming through door after door. His breath was a trail of grey smoke.

The train pulled into the brightly lit station. There were letters on tiles all over the walls and ceiling. Neil couldn't make out any words. He went to press the green button, but froze when he saw a shadowy figure in the doorway. The doors opened, and it disappeared.

Even at night, the traffic was fast and furious. Crossing the road could take a long time. But indoors, the vibe was very different. Most of the bars were dark, quiet and calm. Central Café had high black walls and a mature crowd. Les Philosophes was full of students. Amnesia had a basement bar decorated with the fragments of a broken mirror, which made Neil feel watched. Le Cox was louder, more of a leather and denim bar, but still quite easygoing. Matt was gaining some covetous glances, though he didn't respond to them. Neil drew no attention at all.

They finished the night in a basement bar reached by a narrow spiral staircase. It had walls of raw stone, like a cave. Shirtless boys were dancing to 'Hava Negila'. Already very drunk, they bought vodka. You automatically got a double measure, in a glass so narrow the ice chilled it at once. As the music changed to 'Dancing Queen', Matt took Neil's hand and drew him into the crowd. It was the first time they'd danced together since the New Year party. Neil felt incredibly high, almost euphoric; but light was the only thing he could see clearly. The sense of shared energy and love was overwhelming. He pulled Matt close to him and they kissed frantically, their mouths dry with vodka.

As they stumbled out on to the pavement, Neil realised they'd missed the last Métro train. They'd have to get a taxi, or walk. He checked the map, but couldn't make sense of it. Piss artists of various nationalities were staggering back and forth. One of them blundered into Neil. 'Fuck me! It's the Phantom of the Opera! No offence, mate.' *Of course not,* Neil thought. *Why should I be offended at a crass insult from a fucking moron?* He was too drunk to say it.

More by luck than navigation, they found a taxi rank with a dozen youngsters waiting. But it was the wrong kind of luck. Neil and Matt got involved in an argument about the merits of Nico's solo career while a series of taxis went past, all with their roof lights on. After half an hour, Matt said: 'Have you noticed, all the people in this queue are English? I don't think this taxi rank works at night.'

By studying the map together, they decided on the route back to the hotel. It was very late now, and very cold. Neil couldn't stop glancing behind him. All the shadows had mouths of broken glass. The moonlight overlaid the street-lights, creating a kind of double exposure. After a while, he took out his penknife and held it, still folded, in one hand. Matt didn't say anything.

They were scarcely awake when they reached the hotel. The night receptionist was a florid-faced man with a mous-tache. 'We couldn't get a taxi,' Matt said in an oddly childish voice. 'We were at a taxi rank in the Marais. Nothing was stopping at all.'

The receptionist nodded. 'Taxis don't stop in the Marais at night. It's too dangerous.'

As they climbed the stairs, Neil said: 'See, I told you we were being followed. It's dangerous. I was right.' Their room was cold; they undressed and got into their twin beds, which shared a double duvet. Matt asked if there was any chance of a cuddle. Neil was too depressed to answer.

2

Early the next morning, Neil sat at the desk in their room and read Baudelaire's 'Spleen' poems. Their bleak rage knocked him out. Especially the last one: *un jour noir plus triste que les nuits . . . Quand la pluie étalant ses immenses traînées / D'une vaste prison imite les barreaux . . .* He wondered how you could translate that. *When the rain cuts out its endless lines / And reveals the world as a prison cell . . .* He picked up the Genet volume, remembering something he'd heard years earlier: a recording by Etienne Daho of part of 'Le condamné à mort', the words chanted over a feverish pulse of strings. He could still hear the voice: *Un assassin si beau qu'il fait pâlir le jour.*

Matt was still asleep, half of his face framed by the white pillow. With the help of a tiny pocket dictionary, Neil started reading through that section of the poem. It was a fierce cry in the night, a plea for love in the hours before execution. He thought *ma corbeille blonde* meant 'my white crow', a disturbing image. But according to the dictionary, it meant 'my white basket' – nonsense, unless Genet meant 'basket' in the Jeff Stryker sense. Still, he kept reading. It made him feel more in control of things.

Later, he woke Matt just in time for them to get up and go downstairs for breakfast. Which was horrible: lukewarm coffee, a croissant so hard you could break it, plastic sachets of pale jam. They were too late for orange juice. Matt looked rough: pale under the stubble, his eyes bloodshot and heavily shadowed. Neil suddenly wanted to fuck him. It would have to wait. They drank a jug of water between them and made plans for the day.

The Métro might be dingy and unnerving, but it was quick. Within half an hour, they were at the Pompidou Centre on the edge of the Marais. Pulled along by Matt's enthusiasm, Neil felt both physically and mentally lost in the collection of modern art. If they ever found their way out, it would be into a world of shattered wheels and metallic stars, a world turned blue. The disfigured Cubist faces both repelled and fascinated him. He felt sure some of the frames were windows through which malformed people watched the visitors go by. *What's a confrontational profile? A face as wants breaking.*

'I wonder if they have that lobster telephone here?' Matt said in one of the sculpture rooms.

'They couldn't keep it in France. People kept trying to eat it.'

The café was packed out, so they went outside and bought strange rarebit things. Neil realised that hardly anyone had stared at him since their arrival. Obviously, Parisians were used to ignoring tourists. He felt protected by his foreign status. Something glinted in the back of his mind, an answer he needed a question to reach.

Matt was keen to visit the Catacombes. They took the train to Montparnasse and hung around for a while, window-shopping and chatting. Even on a cold, overcast day, Paris was impressive. Its narrow tenement buildings had an air of quiet seriousness that offset all the tack and over-consumption. The duality was as confusing as French culture itself, with its mixture of radical geniuses and racist pigs.

They walked through the Cimetière de Montparnasse, laid out like a vast chessboard. The shared tomb of Sartre and de Beauvoir was decorated with stones, leaves and flowers. Baudelaire's tomb had messages, sketches and a folded map of Paris. Many of the tombs included small chapels: icons, photographs and candles were visible through the barred windows. Two stone angels were lifting a vault above the ground. A new headstone contained the perfect spiral of an ammonite fossil.

The entrance to the Catacombes was close by. A long spiral staircase led down into a series of tunnels below the streets. It was warmer here than at the surface. The lights cast huge, distorted shadows on the rough stone walls. Water dripped from tiny pits and cracks in the ceiling. Neil hadn't realised it was going to be so shut off. The only way out was the far end.

They'd been walking for about a mile when they reached a black stone archway. Beyond this, the burial vaults started. Along both walls, grey femurs were stacked like firewood. Skulls had been used to form the outline of an archway around a tomb with a cross above it. More skulls made a yellowish sleeve around a pillar. Their eyes were dark with rage. There was a sound of trickling water.

Behind some railings was a mad hill of bones, rock and mud. In one closed-off tunnel, a stack had collapsed and covered the floor. Neil could just make out a flickering red light beyond it. He looked away. A wall of skulls looked back at him, through him. One of them had a round hole in its forehead. *Can you see now? What the rules are. Can you see?* He kept walking, eyes fixed straight ahead, ready to jump to either side if the wall collapsed.

'This is fabulous,' Matt said quietly. 'It's like a city designed by Ed Gein.'

Neil glanced at him. 'But Gein's house was just a family home. This is the public domain.' A crack sounded in the distance: bones falling or burning. He stopped. The furnace was all around them. He couldn't breathe. His face was coated with a film of sweat. It was about to come down.

Crouching, he closed his eyes and rocked slowly back and forth.

'Neil.' A hand touched his arm and he flinched involuntarily. 'Neil, what's wrong?' It was Matt. A group of people were gathered around them, talking in a language he didn't recognise. Matt knelt beside him and touched his forehead. 'Your temperature's OK,' he said. 'Do you feel sick?'

He couldn't hear the furnace any more. The only sound was the slow drip of water from the ceiling. Carefully, he stood up and brushed the dust from his knees. 'Sorry,' he said. 'I just blacked out for a moment. I'm all right.'

Matt gripped his arm. 'Come on. Let's get you out into the fresh air. Get you something to eat.'

It was a long, slow climb back to the daylight. Matt walked behind him in case he blacked out again. But every step left the danger further behind. For a moment, the past had trapped him. But now, he was coming back to the surface. And the assassin wouldn't find him. He was the assassin.

3

That evening, they spruced themselves up: black silk shirts (bought cheap in Paradise Place), lots of hairspray and a late shave. Neil had to shave twice a day in any case, because his beard grew in odd patches and drew attention to the scars. Matt was getting used to Neil's face; but the changes in his personality were more worrying. Sometimes he seemed like a different person, or no-one at all. There was an odd tension between them as they showered and dressed: desire with an undercurrent of suspicion. When they'd discussed it in the past, a threesome had seemed like an exciting thing to share. Now, Matt wasn't sure what it might mean.

They ate at a bistro next to the Gare Saint-Lazare: snails, chicken, white wine. Neil was less edgy on the Métro than he'd been earlier. Alcohol seemed to calm him down. Towards nine o'clock, they reached their first destination: a narrow alley in the Marais called the rue des Mauvais-Garçons. The bar at the end had tinted windows. Its interior was a labyrinth of dim corridors and alcoves. Clutching bottles of strong beer, they slipped between the shadowy male figures that lined the walls.

Upstairs, the music was louder – a techno remix of Madonna's 'Rain' – and the shadows were denser. They glanced at each other and carried on into a long room that smelt of poppers and flesh. It was crowded: standing room only. Invisible hands brushed Matt's shoulders, nipples, arse. Eventually, they stood together in a corner that was almost completely dark. They kissed, then turned to face the room. Nothing too heavy was going on. It was more like a gradual dance than an orgy.

A young man wearing glasses approached them. He and Neil moved into a gentle snog: mouths locked together, hands exploring. In the twilight, Neil's scars were invisible. His eyes were shut. Then he reached out for Matt, drawing the three of them into a clinch that seemed to dissolve their identities. Matt didn't know who was kissing his neck, or who was stroking his crotch. Then things clarified: he and the stranger were kissing, while Neil was on his knees between them. He reached down and ran his fingers through Neil's hair. The lad was still wearing his boxer shorts, his cock sticking out the front and into Neil's mouth.

Matt kissed the stranger's still face, then bit his neck and sucked at the smooth flesh. He knew it would leave a mark. The boy tensed, then shuddered. Then relaxed. There was a moment of stillness. Neil stood up, wiping his mouth. 'Merci bien,' the boy said.

'Et toi,' Neil replied. He looked into the stranger's eyes. 'Comment tu t'appelles?'

'Alain.' The boy pulled up his jeans. 'Et toi?'

'Jason.' He stroked Matt's hair, which was sprayed hard. 'Et mon copain est Matthew.'

'Enchanté.' The boy kissed them both, then turned and was lost in the shadows.

Neil seemed in a daze. Suddenly worried that he might have another blackout, Matt tugged at his sleeve. 'Shall we go?'

Outside, it was raining again. A bunch of partygoers wearing ghost and vampire masks staggered past, making half-hearted 'wooo' noises. Neil walked away rapidly, ignoring them. Matt caught up with him and said: 'The return of Jason is *Friday the 13th*, not *Halloween*. You've got the wrong film.' Neil didn't respond. 'OK, what now?' What he really wanted to do was take Neil back to the hotel, where they could fuck their way to oblivion.

Instead, they went to QG. Even the *Spartacus* guide had sounded uneasy about this place. But it was free and close at hand. They had to knock for admission to what seemed a normal, if poorly lit, bar. Matt bought two beers and received a condom and sachet of lubricant with each. 'Are we up for this?' he said as they watched two stiff-backed clones walk down the black staircase to the basement.

Neil's face mimicked fear for a moment, then went blank. 'No harm in having a look.' There didn't seem anything real about Neil's reactions. A place this full of shadows would have spooked him completely a few days before.

They both drank quickly. *OK*, Matt thought. *Let's get this over with.* 'Are we together?' he asked.

'I'm on my own.' His eyes and mouth were full of darkness, holes in a paper mask. *Then so am I.*

The basement was crowded, lit by weak red bulbs. It was a long room with alcoves and sweaty brick walls. Some of the men were naked. Matt couldn't believe any of this was real.

It was like Neil was some kind of insane guide, leading him into the underworld. *Waiting for a guide to come and take me by the hand.* All around them, people were fucking, sucking, wanking . . . and watching. Always watching. It didn't feel sexy. It felt like a dream. The forest you had to pass through to come out the other side.

The music was overwhelming: hardcore techno that seemed to pour from the walls, echo upon echo, remixing itself. A shirtless muscleboy grabbed hold of Neil and shouted into his ear. Neil shouted something back. Matt imagined the words: *Je suis Hansel. Et mon copain est Gretel.* The rough wall of the alcove looked like gingerbread. The air smelt of aftershave and rotting stone.

Depressed, he backed off and stood against the wall. A blond queen eyed him sympathetically. 'Don't worry, love. They'll *all* respect you in the morning.' He kissed Matt on the cheek, then skipped off to watch a man being spanked over a barrel. Matt closed his eyes.

A hand touched his neck, then his face. A mouth clamped on his, a thick tongue probing. He opened his eyes, but could only see a silhouette against the vague red light. He felt a hairy chest, a taut belly. They unzipped each other. The stranger put a condom and tube of KY into Matt's hand. Matt put them on the stranger. Practised hands turned him round and pressed him to the wall. He knew it wasn't Neil, but he pretended.

The man took his time, holding Matt in a secure embrace and jerking him off slowly. Only at the end did he lose control, breathing hard and crying 'Marc! Marc!' They came almost at the same time. Matt wiped himself with a tissue and pulled up his jeans. His shirt was torn; there was brick-dust on his hands. The stranger had gone. Someone else was standing just inside the alcove, watching him. It was Neil.

They walked back to the Métro station in a daze. It wasn't

much after eleven. Neil rubbed his neck, wincing. 'Someone get rough with you?' Matt said. He meant it sympathetically.

Neil stared at him, then laughed. 'You can talk. Jesus, Matt, I didn't know you were going to go that far.'

'Why do you think they gave us condoms?' Matt said. He was getting pissed off. 'It's not a place for cuddling. A crafty snog before the lights go up.' Neil flinched. On their first date, they'd gone to see *Maurice* at the Electric Cinema and kissed all through the end credits. He was about to say 'I'm sorry' when Neil lurched towards him, eyes glinting like ice in the sodium light.

The first blow caught him in the chest and knocked him back at an angle. The second missed his face and smashed into the wall behind him. Then three more blows landed hard, in rapid succession, on the wall. It looked as though Neil was trying to beat up his own shadow. Not unaware of the risk to himself, Matt grabbed Neil's wrist. 'Stop! You fucking lunatic!'

Neil punched the wall again with his free hand. Then he stopped. As if blind, he reached up and touched Matt's face. There was blood on his fingers. As they embraced, he began to shake and then to cry. Out loud, like a child.

'Neil,' Matt kept saying. 'Neil. Neil.' As if to prove that his name hadn't changed. 'What's happening to you?'

'I don't know,' Neil said. His voice was calm again. 'But I know what I have to do.'

4

The plane took off, wavering a little as it rose against the wind. The runway was gleaming with rain, like a black mirror. Flying at night was different: more real, more uncertain. Matt was biting his lip; his eyes were shut. Neil gripped his hand gently, wincing at the contact. Matt had cleaned his wounds and covered them with Elastoplast, back at the hotel. He'd also quizzed Neil about the bruises on his neck, where the muscleboy had half-strangled him while tossing him off. Neil had said it was an accident.

The madness of that night had calmed things down between them. In the morning, they'd gone shopping for food and souvenirs in Montmartre before walking on to Sacré-Coeur and down the long flight of stone steps. Another reminder of Macclesfield, whose 108 Steps Neil had counted as a child. Looking down over Paris, they'd held hands and said they loved each other. It was true, but it didn't exactly help. In the afternoon, they'd gone to Notre Dâme. Matt had gone crazy over the Gothic spines and crests of its exterior. The inside was glowing like a weird kaleidoscope, with candles floating in stone bowls of water. The air stank of burning wax. Neil had tried to pray, but it was like tuning into a blank frequency.

The plane rose unsteadily into the dark. Its wing lights reflected from grey streaks of cloud and pale, oblique lines of rain. Beside him, Matt began to relax. Darkness sheathed the plane as it left the clouds behind. Nothing could be waiting here to cut it from the sky. For the first time since the attack, Neil had no sense of a hidden figure pursuing him. But someone was waiting for him. A blue mask. A life in pieces. The lights in the plane went out, and he was free.

5

The next weekend, they had tickets to see Echo and the Bunnymen on the Wolverhampton date of their reunion tour. Neither of them had seen the band live in the old days. Matt cried off with a severe cold, so Neil went on his own. The audience were mostly in their thirties or older. It was a loud, furious gig. The Bunnymen played as if desperate to make

up for lost time. In the aching choruses of 'The Cutter',
McCulloch's hunger for experience seemed more raw than
ever. The new song 'Nothing Lasts Forever' was a bleak
encore, denying faith in the future even as it kissed off the
past.

On the train back to Birmingham, Neil couldn't escape
the knowledge that something had ended. Since coming back
from Paris, he'd told his supervisor he was putting his Ph.D
aside for a while. 'I need an epistemological break.' He'd
been to an employment agency in town; they were trying to
get him some temporary work subbing at the Post and Mail.
Failing that, the University Library had a vacancy for an
assistant. The hardest change was going to be walking away
from Matt. Part of him was sickened at the thought. He
stared into the window, looking through his own reflection at
the Black Country landscape. Roofs of terraced houses. Brick
factory walls. Windows without glass. Lights from below
ground.

*Matt, you know I love you. But we're changing. You need
someone who can make you happy. And I need to sort myself out.
On my own.* Bullshit. *Matt, I'm sorry. You're the best friend I've
ever had. But I'm not happy. I don't want to find someone new.
I just don't want things between us to turn sour. It's better if I
leave.* Wank. *Matt, I can't face a future of your recipe books and
childish tantrums. And your record collection gets on my tits. Fields
of the Nephilim. Jesus wept.*

When he got home, the house was dark. The music from
behind Matt's door was so subdued he couldn't name it. He
knocked. 'Come in.'

Matt was sitting in the dark. He switched on the bedside
lamp. 'Neil, Sue phoned. You know, Anne's flatmate. She got
your message. But Anne's not there. She's in hospital. Sue
says she took an overdose, but she's OK. There's nothing you
can do until the morning.'

Neil sat down on the bed. 'Thanks. What happened?'

'I don't know. Sue didn't say much. She gave me her number at work, if you want to call her tomorrow. But she said not to worry. They used a stomach pump. It was all right.'

It didn't sound all right. Neil realised he'd forgotten about Anne. This episode was like some dramatic statement of her self-disgust. But surely that couldn't be what she'd done it for? If he was sane, he wouldn't even be thinking that. 'I'll go and see her tomorrow,' he said.

'Well, give her my love.' She and Matt had never got on. 'Did you enjoy the gig?'

'Oh . . . it was brilliant,' Neil said. 'Exciting and sad at the same time, you know? Mac still has a voice to die for. How's your cold?'

'Getting better. Neil . . .' Matt hesitated. 'I wasn't really too ill to go. I just . . . I didn't want it to be something else I'd remember later and feel sad. Because of you and me.'

Neil hugged him fiercely. Matt's embrace was weak, neutral. His eyes were full of pain. 'I'm sorry,' Neil said. 'I love you. It's not fair for you to have to deal with me when I'm like this. Nothing I can do is right. I don't know when it will change. There are things I have to do to be . . . alive again. If you'll want me back then, I don't know.'

Matt drew away, then looked hard at him. Neil looked back. A minute passed before Matt said: 'What do you have to do?'

'Find the man who did this to me.'

'And then what?'

'I don't know. Make him understand, somehow. What he's done. Make him see.'

They sat together for a while, in silence. Then Matt said, 'It's getting late.'

'I'll go back to my room. If you want me to.'

'I want you to stay.' They kissed. 'Just one thing,' Matt said as he unbuttoned Neil's shirt. 'If you ever say *We'll always have Paris*, I'll fucking kill you.'

6

Anne hadn't wanted anyone to visit her in hospital. She met Neil two days later, in the sandwich café at the top of the City Plaza. It was a strangely anachronistic place: bone china coffee-cups, silver platters, a waiter in an elegant DJ with tails. If the Crane brothers came to Birmingham, they would eat here. She saw Neil's face in profile on the escalator. From a distance, you couldn't see the scars. What struck her was how much more confident he looked. Just from the way he stood there. Either things had really improved for him over the last few weeks, or he was over-compensating desperately.

'Anne! How are you?'

'Not so bad. I'm OK. Really. Just tired.'

'So what happened?' He touched her hand.

'It's a bit confused. The *View* were still playing the waiting game. I got drunk. It doesn't matter.' She didn't feel like talking about it. The waiter approached with menu cards. The café was beginning to fill up.

They drank coffee and ordered sandwiches. Neil told her about Paris. It sounded lovely, though she sensed he was keeping things back. Then he said, 'I'm moving out of the house. Matt and I need a break from each other. Things have been a bit strange.'

'I'm sorry,' Anne said. 'Hope it's not permanent.'

'I don't know. Just doesn't feel . . .' He looked confused, more like the Neil she was used to. 'Too much has happened. I can't explain. Matt's OK about it. I think he's relieved that it's come to a head. It'll get worse later, I know that.'

Anne smiled. 'People change. It's sad. As long as you care

about each other, you'll be OK.' Their own break-up hadn't been easy, though the relationship had been quite brief. They still didn't spend much time together, probably never would.

The excellent sandwiches distracted them for a few minutes. Neil told her about the Moreau paintings. And the Catacombes, which he described as 'an incredible symbol of the class system. Above, there's the cemetery: the family vaults, the names, the little shrines. Down below, there's a pit of bones. And some platitudes about how death is the great leveller.' Again, he didn't seem to be telling the whole story.

'Are you going to be all right?' he asked as they waited for the bill.

'I think so. I've got to see this counsellor for a while. But I didn't really want to die. I just . . . wanted to feel better. Sleeping pills. Went too far.'

Neil looked at her. 'Was it Sue who found you?'

'No. I phoned 999. Something in me just wasn't having it. I know you don't believe in instinct. But there was something. When I had nothing left, there was still this voice saying *fight back.*'

As the escalator took them down through the City Plaza, past the mock-Italian paintwork and the plaster doves on wires, Anne wondered exactly what had changed in Neil. He didn't seem to *say* things any more, just use words to cover them up. Maybe he'd always been a bit like that. Recovery or over-compensation? After an hour in his company, she still had no idea.

7

The final break with the past was, in many ways, the easiest. In late November, the government announced that from now on, students in higher and further education would have to pay their own tuition fees. This meant the end of universal access to education beyond school. On the day the Teaching and Higher Education Bill was passed, Neil and Matt tore their Labour Party membership cards into tiny pieces. They mixed the scraps of cards together, put them in an envelope and sent them to Millbank Tower.

chapter 7

this far apart

1

He couldn't take his eyes off the young man at the juke-box. It was like watching someone in a 1940s film: the black clothes contrasting with the pale features. The left side of his face was quite badly scarred around the eye and jawline. Still, damaged goods had a certain weird appeal. Like a puzzle it might be exciting to solve. He edged closer to the juke-box, trying to see what records the lad was selecting.

The CD collection was a mixture of new chart stuff and classic pop. The scarred boy flicked past Abba, the Supremes and Kylie Minogue without pausing. Evidently straight. He stepped back from the glossy juke-box and glanced sideways at Kevin. His eyes were very dark. Under the poorly-repaired skin, he had good bone structure.

Kevin smiled at him. 'Not much on the juke-box, then?'

'Fucking crap. Don't know why I come here.' He looked around as if astonished to see men chatting each other up. Kevin couldn't quite place his accent – Mancunian, possibly. And very drunk. His glass was empty.

Kevin gestured towards the bar. It was crowded with the

usual assembly of leathermen, accountants in suits, *faux* rent boys and theatre queens. 'D'you want a drink?'

'Cheers. Vodka and orange, please.' The bell was ringing for last orders. Kevin bought him a double, a move that always worked with drunk lads and never with sober ones. He bought himself a Coke. He'd once had a hot date completely ruined by being stopped, breathalysed and arrested. No phone number, not even a goodbye.

They chatted for a few minutes. The boy's name was Jason. He kept glancing up as people passed by – not in an appraising way, but as if he was expecting someone in particular. But when Kevin asked who he was waiting for, he said 'No-one.' His accent, and the level of background noise, made it hard for Kevin to catch most of what he said. But then, he wasn't really listening.

As the bar staff began the lengthy task of persuading the lonely to move on, he offered Jason a lift home. He was looking forward to a preliminary snog in the carpark, but Jason seemed so ill at ease that he drove off straightaway. Outside the city centre, the streets were quiet. Frost coated the pavements like mismatched skin grafts. Glass from a shattered bus shelter crunched softly under his wheels.

Jason lived near the Swan Centre in Yardley. That might explain the state of his face, though Kevin didn't like to jump to conclusions. Maybe his fondue set had blown up during a dinner-party. He parked in the road outside the square block of flats where Jason lived. There was a small courtyard, but it was poorly lit and scattered with rubbish from two overturned metal bins. He sat back and stroked Jason's thigh. The boy took Kevin's hand and moved it to his crotch. 'Shall we go inside?' Kevin said.

Jason's flat looked like he'd just moved in. It was sparsely furnished, with no pictures on the walls and no ornaments to speak of. But hundreds of books lined the narrow bed-sitting room: in cheap bookcases, in boxes, or just stacked up against the wall. 'You sell books?' Kevin asked.

'No, I read them.' A lot of the books looked serious, even academic. Politics and stuff. Hadn't Jason said something about working at the University? Kevin wished he'd paid more attention.

'So you're an educated girl,' he said.

'Yes, and I can write my own name and everything. Now why don't you just shut up?' The thin arms that gripped him felt capable of violence. They sat on the fold-down bed and kissed slowly. Jason's mouth was soft and yielding. He let Kevin press him down on to the lilac duvet. Behind him, their joint shadow on the wall writhed and began to shed its skin.

He found the contrast between Jason's prematurely aged face and his almost hairless, adolescent body painfully exciting. Jason sucked him fiercely, bringing him off before he'd had a chance to suggest going further. He tried to make Jason come, but failed; either the boy was too drunk or he wasn't really turned on. You didn't need to be aroused to have a hard-on: you just needed to be male and breathing. He gave up and kissed Jason tenderly, imagining the perfect face under the scars.

While they were getting dressed, Jason said: 'Tell me something. Do you know a boy called Ian Moore? Cropped hair, skinny, walks with a stoop?' Kevin shook his head. Jason fumbled in his wallet, pulled out a small photo. Like a bus pass snap or a police mugshot. 'Ever seen him?'

'Shit.' Kevin felt himself going red. 'Yeah . . . rings a bell or two. I never knew his name. He used to hang around the Sandwell Valley a couple of years ago. That's him all right. Why do you want to know?'

'I met him last year. We made a date. But I was ill, couldn't make it. He never gave me his phone number. I thought he might really be the one. Know what I mean?' Jason sounded like a child. 'What's he like?'

'To be honest, I don't think he's worth chasing. He was a druggie. Probably still is. When he was on speed he'd talk non-stop, jabbering away like a lunatic. When he was on downers he'd just stare at you, or drawl some nonsense in a spaced-out kind of way. I think he might have been a rent boy. Selling it to feed his habit. You're better off without him.'

'Did he do pills or inject?' Jason asked.

'Both, I should think. He had needle tracks.'

'Really?' Jason looked bewildered. 'Where?'

'All over.' The dismay on the boy's face made him feel both guilty and aroused. 'Yeah, I suppose we had . . . a bit of fun.'

'You mean, you paid him for sex.' His voice was expressionless.

Kevin hesitated. 'You could put it that way, yes. I was really lonely. It was a bad time.'

'And you think he might have been a rent boy. Have you ever thought about becoming a detective?'

'Have you ever thought about starting up an Internet company, *www.smartremarks.com*? You'd make a fortune.' Kevin looked at his watch. 'I'd better go. Early start tomorrow.'

They kissed again, swaying together. 'Look after yourself,' Kevin muttered. 'Don't waste your time chasing people who don't care.'

'What, and leave show business?' Jason opened the door. A cold draught came through. 'Will you phone? That's FON. Fuck Off Now.'

'Funny. So funny. See you around.' The door closed behind him, leaving him in darkness. He felt his way to the front door. His car was still there with its tyres intact. Kevin drove carefully, fighting exhaustion. He'd have liked to bring the boy home with him, tuck him up, cook him breakfast in the morning. But that called for a level of tenderness he was no longer capable of. Besides, his boyfriend would have killed them both.

2

Sundays in Yardley were always miserable. There were two good options: going to the launderette and walking around the cemetery. Otherwise, it was best to stay in and avoid the angular drunks who tracked the district from pub to pub. This morning, he'd waited in the grocery shop behind a sandy-haired man in red braces, who was clutching an open lager can in one hand and haranguing the Asian shopkeeper about his prices. After a few minutes, the drunk had turned around and remarked to Jason: 'Holding you up, am I? *Tough shit.*'

Just beyond the cemetery, on the edge of Acocks Green, the road crossed over a canal. On the left side, the trees framed a derelict house. On the right side, there was a gap in the trees and a staircase going down to the towpath. Jason bit his lip: one more fear to be overcome. It looked harmless by daylight. On the near side of the canal, a narrow walkway ran between a chain-link fence and the black water. Across the water, the backs of factories presented rusty pipes and bricked-up window-frames. Bits of a torn plastic sheet were scattered along the far bank.

No-one was fishing here. The only person Jason passed was an old man walking his dog. The water was so still that it reflected the graffiti painted on the underside of a bridge. He thought he remembered walking with his parents along a canal in Stockport. There was a field with a horse in it. And the skeleton of a horse in the canal. And a derelict house where he'd found a black brooch shaped like a butterfly, which he'd given to his mother. *Bullshit*. He was just remembering dreams.

There'd probably never been a canal, or a derelict house. Or a time when his parents had liked each other. When he wasn't calling her stupid, and she wasn't calling him ugly. Why had they stayed together? Because neither of them had the strength to start again. And because their mutual spite was a bitter, addictive kind of love.

Another bridge. Its alcoves reminded him of that club in Paris. And the Nirvana song about living under a bridge. He couldn't listen to music any more. It brought too much back. Everything was the past. The smell of dirty water filled his head. He stood in the shadow of the bridge, trembling. Sunlight flashed from the black mirror. *An assassin so fair he can fade the day*. It wasn't just the real Ian he needed to find, Jason realised. It was the Ian inside himself. Their faces merged.

Half a mile further on, the towpath went past an abandoned warehouse. Its interior was a mosaic of graffiti, from multicoloured tags to carefully printed messages. *It's a dog eat dog world out there & I've got bigger teeth than you*. Steel girders were torn and twisted under a roof of corrugated iron. The ground was a crazy paving of clinker and broken glass. At one end, a brick wall had been botched together any old how, the bricks jammed in at all angles. On the far side from the canal, some weeds and a branch of a shrub had forced their way in under the wall. Pigeons were clinging to the ledges outside the empty brick window-frames. Beyond was the garden he'd wanted all his life to escape to.

It couldn't be much further to the city. The tall buildings on the skyline were hazed by the pale sunlight. On his right, a brick wall topped with coils of razor-wire shut out the view. Across the canal, dead and living factories were indistinguishable seen from the back. Birmingham was a city of frontages and façades. Down here was the backstage, where they kept the props. It was only by losing faith that you got to see. What the rules are.

When he reached the small brick bunker with its arched entrance, a ruined or unfinished bridge extension, he stopped. Somehow he'd known all along it would be on this route. Maybe that policeman had shown him a map in hospital. He could smell ashes, burnt paper or cloth. The sunlight crept along the edge of a cloud as he stood there. It was such a tiny building, smaller than some of the Montmartre vaults. He wanted to go inside, look for some trace of Ian or himself. But he couldn't. He couldn't even look through the black opening.

A few minutes later, he reached a flight of stone steps going up to street level. The canal widened here, zig-zagging between factory buildings. Jason climbed the steps. The first thing he saw was a church with a glass mandala design. He was at the edge of a busy road with a blue metal bridge overhead. There were no signs anywhere in sight.

3

Christ, the Nightingale was boring these days. With its magazine shop and its restaurant and its big seated area, it was more like a shopping mall than a nightclub. Maybe that was why it was so full of Marys: they were expecting to find Next on the top floor. Like the zombies in *Dawn of the Dead*. The old place had been a bit more stylish. There'd been a nice central dance floor, and each room had had its own distinctive vibe and mode of lighting. There weren't any *rooms* here, just floors. You spent half the night going up and down the stairs from one boring vista to another. They should install fucking escalators.

Subway City, under the bridge where the Jug used to be, wasn't much better. Nothing but light shows and hardcore techno, a lot of skinny kids dancing their non-existent butts off all night. It only made sense if you were off your face, and Gary didn't like E. It stripped away all his anger. And without his anger, he was nothing. As for Boots . . . he gave a delicate shudder. Dungeon chic, steel bars across the bar, the reek of amyl nitrite and leather and testosterone. What girl ever flourished in such company?

But the Jug, late and generally unlamented – now *there* was a nightclub. It had still been there when he'd first come to Birmingham, but had closed down a few months later. You had to knock on an unmarked door in a brick wall to be let in. The manager sat outside the cloakroom in an old-fashioned suit and half a ton of slap. The lounge had a water feature with green and blue lights, like the crystal garden he'd made in a fishbowl when he was eight years old. The main bar had drag queens singing old show numbers and telling filthy jokes. The first time he'd gone there, a boy with a quiff and red fingernails had taken him round, introduced him to everyone, got him drunk – then taken him home and fucked him hard until daybreak. Losing the Jug had been like losing a part of himself. A part you could live without, but couldn't be *yourself* without. Your hair, for example.

He might as well give up and catch the night bus home. Any more gin and he'd be a basket case tomorrow. Spend the afternoon watching old films on BBC2 and crying. And he had a seminar to prepare for Monday, 'Wilfred Owen and the Death of Humanism'. He lit a cigarette and gazed over the pool tables. What was wrong with him? It was like he'd been feigning boredom one day and the wind had changed, and now everything felt like a waste of bastard time.

As he stubbed out the cigarette in a little foil ashtray, he saw a familiar ex-face approaching him from the bar. Neil.

He was drunk, but otherwise didn't look too bad – at least in the subdued lighting of the club. Gary thought of the 'pale rain-flawed phantom' in Owen's poem about the newspaper boy. He felt a momentary stirring of tenderness.

'Hello Neil,' he said. 'How are you?'

'Not bad. Actually, I'm not Neil any more. I'm Jason now.'

Gary raised his eyebrows. 'How very trendy of you. Why Jason?'

'I don't know. Neil just wasn't . . . me, somehow.' There was more Macclesfield in his voice than before. It was funny how people changed their nature. A makeover of the soul.

'Jason sounds like the kind of name a rent boy would have. Have you sold all your books and bought a big pile of old boxing magazines and a teddy bear?'

'You're evil,' Jason said. 'Do you want a drink?'

'Why, thank you. A gin and tonic, please.' Gary lit another cigarette as Jason stepped past the human refuse cluttering up the pool tables. He was feeling significantly less bored.

The G&T was strong, presumably a double. Was Jason trying to get him drunk for sexual reasons, or just to share his own alcohol buzz? Either way, Gary didn't mind. They sat by a window overlooking the old-fashioned neon signs of the Chinese quarter. 'How many divas does it take to change a lightbulb?' Jason asked. Gary said he didn't know. 'Only one, but she needs two assistants. One to refill her glass and one to make sure the light only shines on her good side.'

Gary winced. 'So have you come here to take beginner lessons in bitchy humour, or do you have other things in mind?'

'I just go with the flow. Whatever.'

'I heard you broke up with Matthew. I'm sorry.'

Jason looked at him. 'Are you really? I thought you didn't like him.'

'That's not the point.' Gary looked away. Across the dark

skyline, he could see ghosts sitting and walking. Anger played its quiet tune in his head. 'I just felt you were overdoing the domestic bliss thing. It bothered me. I wanted them to build an expressway through your living-room.'

'Bitch.' There was an awkward silence. Then Jason touched Gary's hand and said: 'Last year, you told me every issue came down to gay versus straight. Do you still believe that?'

'Not really. I don't know.' Gary drained the last of his G&T. Its cold spread through his chest. 'Something about gay politics just fucks me off. It's the whole "identity" thing. D'you know what I mean? If you write about a man fucking a woman, it's "the erotic". If you write about a man fucking a man, it's "homosexuality". As if we only had sex to show how *gay* we are. I don't feel like a *homosexual* when I'm fucking, I just feel good. All the *rest* of the time, I feel like a homosexual. Why is this expected of us? This feeling like you're not real.'

He stared bitterly across the twilit room. 'And then to make a religion of that . . . it's adding insult to injury. So no, I don't think it all comes down to gay versus straight. I just say things like that to wind up cunts like Sean. If you don't belong, you're fucked. It's as simple as that. Want another drink?'

Gary bought a double vodka for Jason and a double gin for himself. He was starting to lose sensation in his fingers. They sat close together, looking out of the window. Car lights melted across the darkness like fireworks. Jason began to stroke Gary's thigh. Gary turned and kissed him lightly, then muttered in his ear: 'I like you. But I don't do relationships.'

'Neither do I,' Jason said. His fingers brushed Gary's crotch. Gary arched his back and let Jason kiss his neck. He realised he'd wanted this for a long time. They kissed fiercely.

Close up, Jason's scars were dead white, like enamel. Like freshly bleached hair.

'What do you want to do to me?' Gary whispered. 'Tell me.' Jason told him, in more detail than he'd expected. 'Sounds good.' At the other tables around them, couples were snogging or arguing about where to go next. Those standing were still playing the waiting game. For most of them, he suspected, it would be a long wait. It was funny how ugly people never fancied other ugly people. Nirvana to the contrary.

As they walked down the twisted staircase, Gary began to feel a little unsteady. Outside, the damp March air gripped his throat. He swallowed a thread of bile. Jason touched his arm. 'Are you OK?'

'Think so.' They walked slowly up towards the Bristol Road. At this time of night, he knew, the entire population of Halesowen would be camped outside the minicab office. When his head had cleared a little, he waved down a black cab outside the ruins of the Lee Bank estate. Fortunately, they didn't have far to go. He concentrated on breathing.

The cab stopped outside the terraced house Gary shared with two other queens. No lights were on downstairs. He led Jason straight up to his bedroom. 'Look, I'm not being funny,' he said, 'but I don't really want you to stay the night. It's just . . . I get very down in the mornings. Can't stand to have anyone around. Do you understand?'

'That's OK.' They sat on the kingsize bed and kissed, exploring with their hands. Then Gary lay back and let himself be stripped. Jason's mouth crawled over his body like a hot insect, licking and biting. Then it gripped his cock, and he ran his hands through Jason's close-cropped hair. He'd let the red grow out.

After a few minutes, he lifted Jason's head and they kissed again. Then he reached into the bedside cabinet and took out a condom and a tube of KY. Jason applied them, then pushed Gary's knees up to his chest. 'So gefällst du mir,' he said. Gary recognised the line: it was from *Querelle*. He arched his back as the scarred man penetrated him. They rocked together for a while.

Then Gary pulled Jason towards him, kissed him, folded his legs around his thin back. They gazed into each other's eyes. 'Tell me how it feels,' he said. Jason gripped his ribs with both hands. There was real aggression in his grip, as well as a desperate need. He thrust hard, pushing Gary back against the headboard. It hurt. Gary shut his eyes, holding on. Jason was talking, gasping words he was surprised to hear from such a well-brought-up young man. Then a hand grabbed his cock and he came suddenly, muscles tightening against Jason's violent thrusts. They struggled together as if fighting to the death.

Then Jason became still. His face was a gleaming mask of sweat. The silence made Gary aware of how much noise they'd been making. Alan and Steve would be taking the piss for days. If they were here. Jason pulled out. The condom was torn, flapping at half-mast. 'Fucking shit,' Gary said.

Jason slumped. 'God. I'm sorry.' He pulled off the useless scrap of rubber and sat holding it. Gary stepped past him to the door, walked into the bathroom and locked the door behind him. He showered, rinsing as thoroughly as possible. Alcohol, disgust and fear reduced him almost to a state of collapse. But he wouldn't cry. Not until later, when the visitor had gone. He would have felt safe having unprotected sex with Neil. But Jason was someone else again.

When he got back to the bedroom, Jason was dressed. Gary put on a dressing-gown and took him down to the front door. 'It's better if you leave,' he said.

'I'm really sorry. It was an accident.'

'I know. Don't worry about it. But you'd better go, it's late.'

They embraced in the hallway. It was a friendly embrace, not a sexual one, and it meant something. 'See you around.'

'Take care,' Jason said. Gary closed the door without waving goodbye. Then he turned out the hall light and climbed the stairs in the dark. God only knew what time it was. He felt sick, but it was too late to vomit now.

4

Somehow, he knew Ian hadn't left Birmingham. That was what kept him going out, night after night. Expecting to find him around the next dark corner, in the next manky pub or half-imagined backstreet. Or find someone else who had the key to Ian's life. Who'd shared a bed or a drug with him and kept in touch. Some people thought they recognised the photo. A few had seen more than the thin face. But the trail was cold. *As cold as fuck.*

He was looking for a boy who talked too much. Or didn't talk at all. Who did smack. Or speed. A teen queen on the make. Or a dog-rough straight who robbed his pick-ups. Rumour was another world. Like newspapers: everything was true for a day, and then not. He couldn't think any more. He just showed people the photograph, and asked questions. Usually after a drink, or even sex. If you just asked straight away, they wouldn't tell you anything. When he found the right person, he'd need to have the right approach worked out.

The drugs connection had taken him to housing estate pubs in Newtown and Highgate, where you certainly wouldn't start asking questions. They'd think you were police. Not that anything much was going on, apart from middle-aged black couples dancing to reggae and a few white loners hoping for a shag. The atmosphere was easygoing, even warm. People left in groups, clearly afraid of the streets outside. It was completely different in the city centre. He'd gone to a wine bar in the Chinese quarter where people just stood, posing so the angled lights would catch their jewellery. The toilet was packed with clubbers buying and selling pills and tiny wraps. After some hesitation, he'd shown the doorman his frayed photo of Ian. The response was immediate: 'Fuck off. If I see you here again, you're dead.'

When he woke up in the morning, he felt convinced there was some kind of underworld he hadn't discovered yet. A labyrinth with Ian at its heart. But in the evening, after a couple of drinks, he soon realised the mean streets were more in his head than on the map. Tonight was no exception. He'd gone to the Fountain, an old-fashioned pub on the edge of the gay cluster. It was the kind of place a listings mag would describe as 'mostly men'. At once, the sight of leather and chains had prepared him for a bleak atmosphere. Then he'd looked at the bar. Among the optics, there nestled a collection of Sesame Street puppets.

Clutching a happy hour double vodka (around here, the happy hour lasted all night), he'd slipped through the narrow and crowded bar area to the tiny, even more crowded lounge. At the back, a doorway led through into a recently built extension: a poorly-lit room decorated with wire netting and an overhang of green cloth torn to look like ivy. A few tough-looking men stood against the walls, sipping pints of real ale. This was probably because they only seemed tough as long as they didn't actually move or speak. Right at the end, another doorway led to a brick-lined room that had obviously once been a garage. Inside, two men were playing pool.

Jason would never really understand the Brummie sense of style. It seemed to be a kind of knowing under-achievement. A pretension so half-hearted that its mocking nature became obvious. Birmingham had been postmodern before it was even modern. To someone from the North, it all seemed a bit sad. He passed back through the camouflage room, where he noticed a tall man watching him. He'd seen the guy before. Maybe one of his drunken nights that seemed more like dreams than memories. There was no point in saying hello just to be embarrassed at not remembering his name.

An attractive skinhead in blue denim walked past him, slowed and glanced at his face, then walked on. Jason wondered if the guy had been following him, but had found his arse more appealing than his face. He'd done the same thing himself with older men, quite a few times.

Depressed, he pushed through into the main bar and gave himself up to thoughts of Ian Moore. He'd run through their encounter in his head so many times, it hardly disturbed him now. A face clouded with smoke. *I want to show you . . . something.* The sunset burning through a wire fence. *Do you like playing rough?*

'That's kind of a big question.' Jason opened his eyes. A lad with red hair, about his own age, was looking at him.

'Sorry,' Jason said. 'I was just thinking aloud.'

'Yeah, but were you looking at me and thinking? Because I'd hate to catch you on the rebound from an important fantasy.' His voice was a mixture of Black Country and Irish.

'I might have been. What are you drinking?'

'Bacardi and Coke, thanks.' He looked like he'd had a few already.

'You shouldn't drink Bacardi,' Jason said. 'They're a right-wing company who support the blockade of Cuba. Starving the people to free them back into the arms of the Mafia.'

The boy smiled. 'True. But it's the only white rum they serve here. Get me a dark rum and Coke if it's easier on your conscience.' He followed Jason to the bar, as the crowd was almost impenetrable.

'Aren't you a bit young for this place?' Jason asked as he

waited for one of the frantic clones behind the bar to spot him. Having a weird face could be useful in a place like this – though in other places, it could result in your not getting served at all.

'Well, I've always been the kind of boy who wanted to play on the field with the bigger boys. Even if I got a few bruises.' He looked sad. 'I was never a kid at all, really.'

They found a relatively quiet corner where they could talk, standing by the wall. The boy's name was Aidan; he worked as an electrical engineer. 'So *do* you like playing rough?' Jason asked.

'Sometimes. I just like to have fun. I'm not walking around with a chain on my neck like some fucker's slave. I'm a disappointment to my parents, though. Once they accepted I was queer, they expected me to have a nice boyfriend and a cat and a collection of Streisand albums. But I'm not that kind of person.' He smiled. 'So what are you looking for? Love?'

'Peace, I suppose,' Jason said. 'But I've no idea how to find it.'

'Most people know where that is. It's just everyone else that stops them getting there.'

Aidan lived in one of the two huge tower blocks at the top of Bristol Street. It was only a few minutes' walk from the pub. As they passed a Chinese restaurant, a drunken boy emerged with his girlfriend on his arm. He waved at Jason and Aidan. They stopped. He lurched forward, then ran full tilt into Aidan, slamming him against the wall. Then he turned and swung an arm across Jason's chest. 'Fucking queers!' His face was twisted into a snarl of rage. Then he doubled over, retching. Jason clenched his fists and stepped forward.

The girl jumped in front of him, screaming 'Fuck off! Fuck off out of here! Go on, get the fuck out!' Aidan grabbed

Jason's sleeve and pulled him to the side. They walked on in silence. It had happened too quickly for Jason to feel anything but confused.

By the time they reached Cleveland Tower, they'd both calmed down enough to establish that neither of them was hurt. Aidan found it quite funny. 'They should go into business,' he said. 'Bang and Blame. We add insult to injury. No opportunity too small. Doesn't Tony Blair say he believes in enterprise? People making something of themselves. They're making cunts of themselves, but it's a start.'

'Has this happened to you before?' Jason asked.

'All the fucking time. Where have you been?'

The entry and hallway in the tower were so impersonal, it was hard to believe anyone lived here. The lifts were behind a row of steel doors. The interior of the lift was metallic and smelt of bleach. Jason shivered as it rose towards the nineteenth floor. He was thinking of the hospital ward: the cracks in the wall, the hidden furnace.

Aidan's flat was small but tidy, decorated in black. They drank coffee in his living-room, which had a view over the city centre. He had a large collection of videos, mostly taped off TV. Jason's knowledge of science fiction was mostly derived from Matt, but he tried to nod intelligently while Aidan raved about *Blade Runner* and *Alien*. And some new American series on Sky, about a girl who killed vampires. Fighting monsters was clearly a big theme with Aidan.

Around midnight, they went through into his bedroom. A double mattress on the floor, some weights, a punchball. Aidan dimmed the light to an after-image. 'How about a wrestling match?' he said. They stripped to their underpants and grappled fiercely on the mattress. Aidan was stronger, but Jason had quicker reflexes. They pinned each other down, threw each other, twisted arms and legs. Then Aidan started jabbing him with quick, light blows. He fought back. Soon they were kneeling face to face, exchanging hard punches. By some kind of unspoken agreement, head blows were not allowed. Jason sensed a kind of rage gripping him, a frenzy that made the pain fade.

Then Aidan threw up his arms. 'Enough!' He reached out and stroked Jason's cropped hair. Then he pulled Jason's head gently down towards his crotch. They were both shaking, coated with sweat. It look him less than a minute to come in Jason's mouth. Then Jason pushed him back on to the mattress, rubbed against him and shot over his belly. They lay cradled in each other's arms, kissing tenderly and recovering their breath.

In the near-dark, you had to get very close to Aidan to see that his torso was patterned with tiny scars and discoloured bruises. Jason thought he might be imagining the marks, though he touched some of them with his lips. 'Have you done that before?' Aidan said.

'Never.' He vaguely remembered getting a hard-on in a playground fight at eleven, rolling and tearing at clothes. But that hardly counted. 'You have.'

'Every now and then.' Aidan looked at him thoughtfully. 'You know, there are really two kinds of S&M. There's pain before sex, and then there's pain instead of sex. There's probably a deeper way of putting it, but that's what it amounts to.' Jason felt the bruises starting to ache on his arms, then all over. Cold sweat ran off him on to the sheet. 'You wanna stay the night?'

'Thanks.' Then he thought of the photo. 'By the way . . . there's someone I used to know. You might have met him.' He fumbled with his jeans, found the wallet. 'Ever seen this guy?'

'Hold on.' Aidan stood up and turned the light switch. Now the marks on his body were obvious: purple and yellow welts, like the sky before a storm. He studied the picture carefully. 'Is his name Ian?'

'Yes.' Jason suddenly found it hard to breathe. 'You know him, then.'

'Used to.' He looked into Jason's eyes. 'No, I haven't slept with him. He's from a part of my life I don't often talk about.' They sat together, looking at the photograph. 'Two, three years ago, I was into barbiturates. And then heroin. I loved that sense of not feeling, not caring. There were four of us met up when we were all scoring off the same dealer. We agreed to look after each other, use clean needles, help any member who was in trouble. It was drug bullshit. We were hardly even friends.

'We used to meet in this one guy's flat, in Balsall Heath. Listen to his old records and get wasted. I used to do pills and smoke heroin, injected it a few times. Ian was one of us. The youngest. I didn't know if he was gay or not. Never really fancied him anyway. He was up his own arse most of the time, either totally withdrawn or talking rubbish. Fucked up before he touched the shit.

'Anyway, our supplier got busted and obligingly gave the pigs our names. Like a good law-abiding Englishman. We all got charged and agreed to go on a rehab programme. Ian split – I heard he went on the rob and got jailed. Me and Vince stuck with the programme, got clean. I was glad to get free of the stuff anyway. Not as fun as I'd thought it was. I don't know what happened to Mike, the fourth guy. He went to Germany. Way he was going, I'd be surprised if he's still alive.'

'The guy with the records,' Jason said. 'That was Vince?'

'Yeah. Older than the rest of us, hippie type. I think he was trying to relive his youth.' There was a pause. Then Aidan said: 'I had the test, you know. We were always careful with needles. But even so. I'm negative.' Jason held him close. Finally, he asked: 'Why Ian? Why the photo?'

'We were almost lovers. I missed a date. Never saw him again. Always thought he was . . . you know, special.'

Aidan twisted to face him. 'I know Ian,' he said. 'And you're lying.' Jason looked away. Suddenly he wished the room was dark again. Then he felt Aidan's fingers touching his face, tracing the scars. 'He did this, didn't he?'

They went through to the living-room and sat in the dark, looking down over the constellation of distant lights. The central heating kept them warm. Jason thought of the hotels, the tower blocks, the rushing cars. The people inside them, and the links that held it all together. Aidan stroked his hair, as lightly as rain. Then they went to bed and made love. There was no numbness any more: just touching the bruises brought the pain back. They fell asleep marked with each other's semen. This high above the streets, the sound of the traffic was no louder than the scratch of a retreating tide.

5

He was just plucking a few interesting chord sequences out of the air when the doorbell rang. He sighed and put the guitar down on its cushion. It was almost certainly some generic Moseleyan hoping to blag a tenner or a smoke. But it could be a haunted, deeply spiritual female singer beating a path to his door. You never knew.

The face in the doorway was unfamiliar. Then he realised it was Sean's friend Neil. The one who'd been in a fire or something. His face looked different now: thinner, more symmetrical. He must have had more plastic surgery. 'Hi Neil. Come in.'

Neil looked around the living-room as if expecting

someone else to be there. 'I live alone,' Vincent said. 'What can I do for you?'

The boy stared at him. 'I need to ask you about someone,' he said. 'A guy called Ian Moore.'

Vincent shivered, as if Neil had brought in the chill of the March night. 'Sit down,' he said, hastily shifting a pile of old magazines from a chair. 'There's a name I've not heard in a while.'

'So he's not around? You're sure?'

'No, I'm not sure. But I haven't seen him since he went to prison in '95. He might still be there for all I know.' Vincent sat down on the couch, whose pattern had almost entirely faded. He knew how it felt. 'What's the problem?'

'It's kind of private. Between me and him. I just want to know where he is.' Neil gazed at him helplessly. *I'm the end of the line*, Vincent thought. The idea amused him, but he managed not to smile.

'If I knew, I'd tell you. We haven't kept in touch. Who told you I knew him?'

'Aidan.' For a moment, Vincent could see trails of smoke in the air. Still figures huddled around the gas fire. He shut his eyes. 'You remember him?'

'Of course. He was all right. I liked him.'

Neil smiled. 'Yeah. Last night we . . . you know. He told me about the four of you, what happened.' So Neil wasn't with Matt any more. But then, Matt was a bit of a pain. A Brummie trying to be a Californian. Or was that just the pot having kettle issues?

'How is Aidan?' Vincent asked.

'I'm not sure. He looks well.'

There was an awkward silence. Vincent tried to think of something to say. 'I never got on with Ian,' he said at last. 'Put up with him, because . . . when you're in that state, who you're with doesn't matter. And I suppose it helps to have someone around who's more fucked up than you.' He paused again. 'He never seemed to know who he was or what he thought. Said he took drugs to see things clearly, but all he ever did was gaze into himself. And all he ever saw there was rage. I think he hated everybody. Too young to know any better.'

'So with maturity comes universal love?'

'Fuck you.' Vincent hated being patronised by the young. What did they know? 'No, you just get to understand that everyone has something to contribute. Even Margaret Thatcher was a good chemist. Hitler could paint pictures. No, fuck it. They're all cunts.' He realised he badly needed a smoke. 'Sorry I can't be more help.'

Neil looked up. 'You can.' He hesitated. 'Could you get me something? Some gear?' Inwardly, Vincent laughed at the kid's attempt to sound streetwise.

'I didn't know you were into that.'

'I'm not. I just . . . want to know what it was like. For Ian. The four of you.' He glanced around the room. 'Sorry, I've no right to ask. But it's important.' He drew his hands to his chest and shivered. It was cold in here.

Vincent hadn't scored anything stronger than weed in two years, unless you counted his birthdays. But he knew someone who knew someone else. It wasn't that difficult. 'All right,' he said reluctantly. 'I'll get you some. A tenner's worth. You can smoke it here if you want. You can even pass out on my sofa, as long as you don't throw up over June here.' He stroked the neck of his acoustic guitar. 'But listen, I'm not Mr fucking Tambourine Man. You want a regular supply, you go to someone else. And I won't come to your funeral. I won't even send flowers. All right?'

'Got it. Thanks.'

They arranged to meet the next Friday. Just before he left, Neil said he'd changed his name. It was Jason now. Vincent said he thought Jason was supposed to wear the golden fleece, not smoke it. After the boy had gone, he looked around the cluttered living-room in some confusion. It was hard trying to deal with someone else's obsessions, when he had enough trouble dealing with his own.

And there was something scary about Neil. Or Jason. Maybe the boy needed some smack just to calm himself down. Vincent thought he'd settle for a pint at the Moseley Arms.

Outside, it was starting to rain. Two teenage boys were fighting outside the off-licence. Vincent remembered when prostitutes had used to stand there all night, smoking to keep their faces warm. Some things changed for the better. But not many. He passed the school on the corner of Tindal Street. In front of him, two rats jumped out of a rotting mattress and crossed the road in no particular hurry. He walked down past the children's playground to the pub, then stood looking beyond it to where the city's lights hung like a blurred watercolour. Standing here, he always felt he was on the threshold of another world. He drew up his collar, turned round and walked back to his flat.

6

'Would you like some coffee? I thought we'd wait till it gets dark. Daylight just doesn't feel right.' While Vince busied himself in the kitchen, Jason scanned the record collection that filled three shelves above the stereo. Fairport Convention. Joan Baez. Patti Smith. Richard Thompson. The Rolling Stones. June Tabor. Ewan MacColl. Nico. Janis Joplin. Nick Drake. Kirsty MacColl. Dick Gaughan. Marianne Faithfull. No discernible order. And that was just the bottom shelf. Most record shops didn't have this much vinyl.

'You like female singers, don't you?' he said as Vince reappeared with two mugs of coffee.

'Good ones, yeah. The truthful ones. I can't stand *divas*. That showbiz crap is strictly for brain-dead queens. No offence . . . All the music business wants a woman to be is a pretty face and a sweet voice. They can cope with male anger, because it's part of the rebel mythology. But female anger's not marketable. So it can't exist.'

When the last traces of daylight had faded behind the red curtains, Vince disappeared into his bedroom. He came back with a folded piece of silver foil and a twist of paper. 'Have you seen this done?' Jason shook his head. 'OK, it's very simple. They call it "chasing the dragon". You burn the powder and inhale the smoke through a straw.' He rolled up a five-pound note and passed it to Jason.

The golden powder darkened, melted. A thin plume of white smoke rose from the foil. Jason sucked it into the tube. He imagined Ian doing this. Breathing the fire. The crucible. The furnace. Vince moved the lighter about under the foil, until nothing was left but a black crust.

'Now just sit back and relax,' Vince said. 'If you feel sick, there's a waste bin just there.' Jason felt a bit light-headed, as if he'd breathed in too many traffic fumes while waiting for the bus at the Swan Centre. He sat very still and let his eyes gather light from the dusty surfaces. He felt certain this would help to bring him nearer to Ian. And maybe to Aidan as well, though he wasn't sure what to hope for there. The red-haired boy hadn't called him.

Vince had picked up his acoustic guitar and started tuning it, strumming gently. Jason realised he hadn't moved in a while. He was aware of every sensation in his body: his breathing, the settling of food in his gut, the dull ache of bruises from his night with Aidan. He could feel the bruises, but they didn't *hurt*: it was like seeing them. He remembered

Aidan coming in his mouth, and the memory was intensely sexual; but nothing stirred in his crotch. Then he thought of Ian, the desire he'd felt for the thin-faced boy. He remembered the bottle cutting his face in the dark. But there was no pain, no fear in the memory. He was a screen.

It was like being awake while your body was asleep. Was this the peace he'd been searching for? He felt happy, but he wasn't happy *about* anything, and the irrationality of that worried him. But not much. Vince put a record on the turntable. It was Led Zeppelin: 'Dazed and Confused'. Images of Paris flickered through his head, like someone else's holiday slides. He couldn't imagine why he'd gone there, or why he'd come back again.

The room seemed to get brighter and duller in waves. The music too ebbed and flowed: one minute the chords were tearing at the air, the next they were barely audible. He could hear the echo from every surface in the room. The music was in his head. Fire in stone. The furnace. For a moment he was back in hospital, wearing a mask of bandages. They should have given him more stuff, so he'd feel as little as this. He became aware that the music had changed. Why should that be? Then he realised Vince had put a different record on.

Fragments of melody drifted. Strings, a clarinet; then harsher, electronic sounds. Nico's voice, wailing in a strong German accent. About loneliness, waves, her mother *facing the wind*. There was a terrible realm of loss and disorientation in her voice. Jason heard that as clearly as he heard the vowel sounds and the slow, careful phrasing. He understood what these bleak songs were about. But it meant nothing to him. It was just music, around him and in him. The last thing he heard was a child's voice behind hers, like a bright shadow.

When he opened his eyes, it was silent in the room. Vince was reading a copy of the *Socialist Review*. He glanced at his watch: it was just after midnight. A rush of nausea hit him and he reached for the waste bin. He retched twice, his mouth filling with bile. Then his gut settled and he sat back, breathing cautiously. Vince looked up. 'How you feeling?'

'All right. A bit spaced.' The room still wasn't real. Ghosts hid in the shadows, covering their faces.

'The effects won't completely wear off until tomorrow morning,' Vince said. 'Did you get where you wanted to be?'

'I don't know.' His feelings hadn't seemed to matter. It had been like his first couple of days in hospital: the same detachment, but without the terror waiting at the edge of his vision. 'It was strange. Like nothing was real any more. It wasn't bad or good. There was just nothing.'

Vince nodded. 'It's a new method of birth control. You take it, and it's like you were never born.'

Jason contemplated that for a few seconds, then laughed. The laugh tore the net of apathy that had held him since breathing the smoke. 'I'd better be going,' he said.

'Look after yourself. You'll feel pretty rough tomorrow. All a drug can give you is an overdraft on your own life. The payback happens a lot faster than you expect. That's why people keep going back for another loan. You've had a few hours of feeling nothing. Tomorrow you'll feel everything . . . most of it bad.'

'Maybe I will go back,' Jason said.

'Up to you. I don't recommend it.' Vince looked uneasy. He was seeing ghosts as well.

They shook hands in the doorway. 'Thanks,' Jason said.

'No problem. See you around.' The street was empty. Jason started walking towards the crossroads. When he glanced back to see whether a taxi was coming, there was still a light in Vince's doorway. A shadow was standing there, watching him.

....

7

Aidan rang him the next day and suggested meeting in the Village. That meant he wanted to talk. The Village was not a tacky venue. It was the kind of place where you'd meet to plan a march. Jason was still feeling drained from the after-effects of the previous night. He didn't tell Aidan about that. They were into their second pint when the Irish boy said: 'You know, what happened last weekend was really special. But I'm not ready to get serious about someone yet. And it would be. I've been scared all week, thinking about you. We've both got too many issues. You know? And there are things I do I'm not ready to give up.'

'So what do you want to do?' Jason said.

'I want to take you home and love you. But I can't. There's this guy I'm half-seeing.'

Jason blinked. 'What, like a ghost?'

'More like a fucking vampire. You know . . . sometimes you go for the wrong people.' He gazed around the pub, his face blank with despair. 'He's someone I was at school with. I don't even like him any more. But I can't stop needing him. We hardly ever have sex. It's a bad joke. But I can't stop thinking about how it could have been. He's the only thing that brings it back. The time when everything seemed pos-sible. One day I'll end it, or he will.'

He looked at Jason, examining his face in the way people had used to before the attack. 'I think you're tied to someone, too.' Jason couldn't answer. Did he mean Ian? Or was he guessing about Matt? How could he know what Jason felt when Jason wasn't sure himself? He shrugged, feeling tired and a bit pissed off.

They finished their drinks. Aidan reached out and clasped Jason's hand. 'I'm sorry this hasn't gone very well,' he said.

'It's OK.' Jason felt himself tuning into the blankness he'd felt under heroin. 'Maybe we'll talk about things, later.'

'I'd like that. You will keep in touch?' Jason nodded. He didn't know. In the past, he'd have condemned such evasive tactics. But then, he'd thought he knew who he was. Aidan leaned over the table to kiss him. Their tongues met briefly.

Over the next fortnight, he stayed in and drank. The Yardley off-licences were reassuringly cheap, and allowed for some browsing in the same way as bookshops. He bought strong cider, British sherry, Special Brew. After weeks of trying to forget the past, he painted the walls of his skull with memories. And he went back to playing music: *In Utero, Closer, Pornography.* He thought about getting hold of some more smack, but couldn't see how that would help. At least when he was crying, he felt like something mattered. In the library, where he worked as an assistant, he catalogued and repaired books with a kind of detached tenderness. His own life had become strange to him.

He had the same dream three or four times, but couldn't make sense of it. A dark corridor that seemed to have no end. Through arched doorways, he saw pale figures stretched out on the naked frames of beds. People were crying, but the sound didn't carry. All he heard was the drip of water from the stone ceiling. Eventually he came to a huge vault like a railway station. People were huddled on seats and behind pillars, wrapped in blankets to keep out the cold.

At the far end of the room was a full-length mirror. He could see a chalk design on his face, like a white tattoo. Before he could touch it, his reflection broke free of the glass and floated away. He saw it break the surface and pass easily into a white marble tomb with carvings of angels. He looked back at the mirror, but saw only a doorway into a tunnel full of bones. He felt himself come apart as he stepped through it. The clean bones of the dead caught between his own.

Then he went to the Nightingale, got drunk and danced himself into exhaustion. Faces shuddered in the silent film of the strobe light. Colours bled from the shadows, signs whose meaning he'd forgotten. He let the stark music drive not only his movements, but his breathing and heartbeat. It kept getting faster. He stumbled, missed a beat, carried on. The figures around him were puppets on strings of sound. If the music stopped, they would all cease to exist.

Cold water struck his face. Someone was holding him: an arm under his ribs, lifting him from the floor. 'Y'all right?' A young man with close-cropped hair, almost a skinhead, and blue eyes. 'Come on, let's get you some coffee.'

His shirt was damp. He didn't know if that was the water or sweat. 'You have to be careful here,' the stranger said as he guided Jason up the crowded stairway. 'They see you lying on the floor, they'll throw you out. What have you had?'

'Enough.' Jason realised that wasn't a good answer. 'Vodka.'

'No pills? Are you sure?'

'Yes.' They sat down in the restaurant area, where a group of leathermen were devouring burgers. Jason shook his head, but his vision wouldn't clear. The walls were streaming with light. The stranger reminded him vaguely of Ian. A similar thin face and wariness of manner. His eyes were an unusually deep blue.

Two coffees arrived. Jason watched the steam drifting from the black surface. He forced himself to drink it, feeling as if grains of ash were falling through his bloodstream. 'Are you feeling better?' the stranger said. 'I'm Anthony, by the way.'

'Jason. Yes. Thanks. Thanks a lot.'

'Don't mention it. We have to look after our own. There's a lot of scum out there.' He shot an angry glance at the window, where the lights inside and outside were blurred together. 'So what happened to your face? Were you mugged?'

People almost never asked about that. 'Not really. A pick-up who turned nasty.'

'You're really not good at looking after yourself. Are you? I'm serious. You've got "crime statistic" written all over you.' That was the difference between him and Ian, Jason realised. Ian wanted a victim to hurt. Anthony wanted a victim to comfort.

The restaurant area was filling up with tired, hungry queens. Listening to them was like having a steamroller drive over your vowels. Jason finished his coffee. The bitterness of the last mouthful made him shudder. 'What now?' he said.

'It's up to you. We can carry on dancing, or get something to eat. Or you can come back with me if you like. You don't have to.'

'Where do you live?'

'Five Ways.' Anthony stood up and shrugged his leather jacket on to his thin shoulders. 'You coming, then?'

The block of flats was quite similar to the one where Jason lived. Anthony glanced uneasily up and down the street before unlocking the steel door. The inside was half-lit by the yellow streetlight, shining through a window of reinforced glass. 'The timeswitch is fucked.'

Anthony's flat was chaotic: clothes strewn across the bed, fantasy novels and action-movie videos heaped on the dusty floor. 'Would you like some coffee?' he said.

'No thanks.' Jason was feeling strangely wired. He'd have trouble sleeping as it was. Anthony cleared the bed and started unlacing his DMs. 'Umm . . . can I hang up my shirt?'

'Sure. But sit down first.' They embraced on the worn black duvet. Anthony looked into his eyes. 'Have you ever subbed?'

'Well, I had a temporary job at the *Birmingham Post*. Worked over Christmas.' It had bored him half to death.

'That's not actually what I meant. Have you ever been a slave?'

'No.' He thought of Camus' story, the renegade slave talking with a tongueless mouth. 'Never been into that.'

'No problem.' Anthony started undressing him. They were both aroused. Their bodies were similar: thin and nearly hairless. Anthony didn't seem to like kissing, but he bit Jason's nipples and licked his cock before turning him over. He paused to sheathe himself, then mounted Jason and screwed him with short hard thrusts. He kissed the back of Jason's neck.

Their breathing fell into a shared rhythm. Anthony's body went completely rigid, then relaxed. Still inside him, he gripped Jason's cock and tossed him off slowly. They lay together on the bed, legs still tangled, as their breathing slowed and their sweat cooled. 'I needed that,' Anthony said. 'I think you did too.'

He turned away to drop the condom over the edge of the bed. Jason watched his muscled back twist as he reached to the bedside cabinet to pull himself up. There was a row of hardbacked books in the cabinet. He looked closer, tilting his head. *None Dare Call It Conspiracy. The Turner Diaries. Race Mixing: the Master Plan. Mein Kampf. The New Lords.* He felt cold. 'Fuck me.'

'I just have. Didn't you notice? You've hurt my feelings now.' Anthony lay back, staring at the ceiling. 'What's up?'

Jason couldn't speak. He'd often wondered what he would do if he met a fascist. *Receive his hard six inches* was not a possibility that had crossed his mind. How could someone be gay and a fascist? Then, suddenly, it hit him. With a trembling hand, he reached down to the floor and took the photo out of his jeans pocket. It was badly creased and worn, hardly recognisable.

'Anthony . . . there's someone I'm trying to find. Do you

know who he is?' He passed the photo to Anthony, who held it up to the light and studied it for a few seconds.

'I'm not sure,' he said. 'It looks like Ian. Ian Moore. Do you know him?' Jason nodded, his chest painfully tight. 'So you're one of us? The Aryan brotherhood?'

Jason looked away. 'I just want to see him. Do you know where he is?'

'No idea, but I think he's still around. I saw him a couple of times when he'd just left prison, but then he dropped out. I heard he'd joined Combat 18. They're a bit much, if you ask me. Because I believe in racial purity, doesn't mean I believe in smashing up Paki shops and torching mosques. They're playing into the hands of the people who portray us as cowardly thugs.'

Jason started pulling on his clothes. 'I'd better go.'

Anthony sighed. 'Don't tell me you're another politically correct moron. You shouldn't believe everything you read in the papers.'

'It's just late. I can't stay. Thanks for your input.' He aimed a kiss at Anthony, who turned his face so Jason could kiss his cheek. 'Maybe we'll talk another time.'

There were still a few people in Broad Street, dazed clubbers waiting for taxis. Jason walked slowly back towards the city centre. He was so tired that nothing seemed real. The '18' in Combat 18 stood for the 1st of August. The Führer's birthday. Or the numbers corresponding to the letters AH. Whatever. At last, he had it. The link that would take him to Ian. He had to join the BNP, pretend to support them, find a way into Combat 18. Except . . .

Except not. This was where it ended. He'd come to the limit, and beyond was not a world in which any version of himself could walk. No more.

When he reached the top of New Street, instead of going to the taxi rank at the station, he walked down under the bridge to the markets. In the moonlight, the huge grey buildings seemed no more than film sets. He walked on to Digbeth High Street, where the kebab shops had closed for the night. And turned left, through the black viaduct at a slight angle to the roads. Under another bridge, past an antique metal urinal. A guard dog barked at him from behind a factory gate.

The only people he passed were homeless, wrapped in blankets in doorways or the alcoves of bridges. Some of the factories were lit up; he could hear the whirring of extractor fans. He tried not to think about where he was going, since he had no conscious memory of the route. It was like finding your way home when you were too drunk even to remember the address. There was the boarded-up pub with the message WELCOME. The yard full of rusting car bodies. The steel fence with a gap across darkness. The moonlight glinted on ripples below.

Going down in the dark was like falling. Mud caked his hands and arse. The towpath was barely visible even when he reached it. The city's ambient light was lost here. But as he began to walk along the path, his eyes adjusted to catch the shreds of moonlight reflected from the canal and the paler types of stone. He drew the penknife from his jacket pocket and flicked out the blade. It was grey, like a wisp of smoke.

Where the canal widened between small buildings with corrugated-iron windows, he saw a group of four or five vagrants sitting round a dying fire. The smell of burning wood stung his nostrils. Further on, a man was fucking a young woman against a brick wall; a second man stood close by, watching. As he passed under a bridge, a rat scuttled away and leapt into the water. It was cold down here. Threads of music passed through his head, not much more than single chords and vowels. His thoughts made no sense.

Under the next bridge, the wind made a strange echoing

sound. Then he saw the figure crouched in an alcove, motionless. It was an old woman wrapped in an overcoat, hair falling
around her face. She was weeping. He stopped in case she
wanted to talk. But she either didn't see him or felt safer
ignoring him. The moonlight cast his shadow on the towpath,
as vague and momentary as he felt.

Another bridge. The alcoves on the near side were bricked
up. He walked on to the bunker and stared into its black
entrance. The dead heart of a dead landscape. He shivered,
looking from the stone block to the cloudy water and back
again. *How cold is fuck?* This cold. He wrapped his arms
around himself and stood there for a while, waiting for some
thought to come to him. There was no light inside, and no
sound. He reached out and touched the damp stone as if it
was a face.

As he walked on along the ghost of a towpath, he remembered a game they'd used to play in junior school. It was part
of a drama lesson where they all had roles that were being
fleshed out. One of their teacher's favourite tricks was called
'conscience alley'. A child in role had to walk between two
lines of children, who called out the character's thoughts.
Voices echoed from the grey walls. *What have you got to lose?*
What the rules are. Can you see? Do you think we should be
celebrating? The fucking town's collapsing round us fucking feet.
What's happening to you? One day I'll end it, or he will. If I see
you again, you're dead. He tried to focus on the path ahead,
the lights floating somewhere in the distance. *Like a fucked-*
up face.

By the time he climbed the steps to the road outside the
cemetery at Yardley, dawn was just starting to displace
the night. There was no traffic on the road. It was less than
a mile to his flat, and the prospect of food and sleep. The
world seemed real again. But was he? On the corner of Stock-

field Road he picked up a dried-out newspaper and held it up to the streetlamp, scanning it for news. Any kind of news.

8

The morning was bright, but cold. She'd got up at seven to finish packing, then gone out for some milk and the morning paper. The government were celebrating the end of their first year in power. But from the report on the press conference, it sounded like it was their victory over the Labour Party, not the Tories, that they were celebrating. Anne gazed up the terraced street to the familiar silhouette of the engineering works, where the dayshift was just beginning. Smethwick was one of the oldest parts of Birmingham, at least in its lack of redevelopment. The part of Sheffield she was moving to had seemed oddly similar. She preferred old housing to tower blocks or conversions. It felt more like a part of something.

Sue was still in her room. They'd had a lot to drink the night before, recalling the past and talking about the future. She was the only friend Anne was really going to miss. It had happened quickly. After the union had written to the *View* on her behalf, she'd had a letter from the management offering her a job in another department. On a reduced salary. She was sick of being manipulated. The Sheffield *Echo* had agreed to take a reference from her previous manager. Being able to start at once had helped her get the job.

Her clothes, her tape player and a few books and tapes were packed in two large suitcases. Everything else was in boxes, to be stored in the loft until she was able to collect it. She looked out the window at the tiny overgrown garden. A pigeon was calling in that strange, cold way they had. Like a distant train. It was time to go. She glanced around the room nervously, aware that she always left things behind. The alarm clock was already packed, and her stuff from the bathroom.

Then she remembered to check the bedside cabinet. A broken chain she might as well leave. A packet of aspirins and a half-full bottle of sleeping pills that she slipped into her handbag. An old photo of Neil that she looked at for a moment, then placed between the pages of a book in one of the boxes. She couldn't remember what he'd changed his name to. Just before taking her suitcases down the narrow staircase, she fished in her handbag for the bottle of pills and dropped it in the waste-paper basket.

The last thing she did before leaving the house was to knock on Sue's door, go in and say goodbye. Outside, the streets were full of traffic. Sunlight flashed from car windscreens, like a message she couldn't put into words but still knew.

chapter 8

the room without a light

1

He hadn't intended to go out tonight. The off-licence had everything he needed. But a phonecall from Anne in Sheffield had left him feeling restless and lonely. He hadn't been able to say anything to her about his new life. Because he didn't have one. Standing outside the Jester on Bristol Street, the two tower blocks massive silhouettes against the fading light, he remembered coming here almost a year before. He'd been desperate for something that would make the previous night the past. Well, he had a past now.

The basement bar was half empty. That lull between the early evening and late evening crowds. He spotted the blond boy over in the lounge area, looking bored; Jason waved, but the boy didn't recognise him. Over by the cigarette machine was a balding guy Jason thought he'd slept with, but he wasn't sure. He bought a Diamond White and waited for it to lift his mood. According to Marcuse, the key to revolution was memory. Oppression worked by making people forget. After four or five drinks, Jason usually felt he could remember everything. Half an hour later, there was nothing but the present moment.

He'd been drinking every night since that insane walk through the silent underworld. Nothing had ended. He'd had a huge argument with Anthony about racism, but only in his head. The last non-socialist he'd tried to argue politics with was his father. Maybe society needed to sink right into the shadow of capitalism, into violence and despair, before a true revolutionary spirit could grow. But he didn't really believe that. He wasn't sure that he really believed anything.

From the Jester, he went on to Partners, the Old Fox, the Village, then Route 2, drinking in gay and straight bars indiscriminately. They all sold happy hour doubles. The Friday night crowd were younger and more drunken than the Saturday people. He didn't care about meeting someone. In the Fountain, that tall guy was watching him again. Jason still couldn't remember where they'd met. There was a kind of stillness about him: not a rigid pose, but a calm detachment that was oddly soothing. He was maybe thirty-five, with a long face, clean-shaven. Jason was about to go up and say hello when he glimpsed Aidan's red hair by the wall. He was kissing someone. Jason pushed his way to the exit with a roughness that drew appreciative glances, pausing only to drain his glass of Smirnoff Red.

The night was stained with unstable blotches of light. Van Gogh stars. Jason couldn't be bothered to head back towards the Nightingale, but he was too drunk to stop drinking. He walked on down the road to Boots, a small building nestled at the edge of a housing estate. Its interior held a semi-darkness he might once have found exciting. And before that, threatening. Its steel bars, fabric netting and red-lit corridors suggested a cross between a dungeon and a forest. Like the set of a Roger Corman film. All you needed was Vincent Price screaming *She's alive, I tell you!* Jason bought some more vodka and slouched against the cold wall.

Nobody much was talking. Incongruous happy handbag

echoed through the gloom. Jason remembered there was a smaller, brighter bar on the first floor. At least he'd be able to see people's faces. Just like heroin took away everything but sound, alcohol took away everything but light. He could feel eyes on his back as he climbed the narrow staircase. At the end of a murky corridor, a few more steps led to the doorway. A dozen or so queens, mostly in leather, were crowded into the tiny room, drinking bottled beer. Jason bought another vodka, then realised he couldn't drink it. He sat on a low metal stool and waited for the room to settle. The man sitting next to him turned round, and Jason saw his face.

In the same moment, he realised they hadn't spoken before. 'I knew you'd say hello sooner or later,' the stranger said. 'When you left the Fountain, I guessed you were coming here.' His voice had a slight accent, Midlands but not local. 'Are you feeling OK? You look a bit shaky.'

'It's nothing. Too much to drink. So why did you follow me?'

'I've seen you a few times. You're always on edge, but usually you look like you know what you're after. But tonight, you just seemed lost. When you looked at me, I could see you were desperate. Not desperate for sex, just desperate.'

Jason sipped his drink. It helped him to focus. 'So what? Are you from the Jesus Army or something?'

'Wash your mouth out,' the stranger said. 'I was in the Territorial Army once. But I dropped out. It was a great game. Then I realised the other men thought it was real.'

Jason swallowed another mouthful of vodka. He couldn't taste anything except cold. 'I see,' he said, not seeing at all. Was this guy another fascist? 'So what . . . what did you join then?'

'Nothing. I don't believe in organisations. I'm an anarchist. Still, the army past comes in handy when I'm chatting people up.' He eyed Jason thoughtfully. 'Just how much have you drunk?'

'I don't know.' He tried to add them up and felt dizzy, as if he were still out on the street. 'A few.' The glass was empty. He put it on the floor, then felt his head tipping forwards. The stranger caught him. Jason reached up and they clung together in a strange embrace, rising slowly to their feet. The stranger drew Jason's head on to his chest and stroked his hair. It felt reassuring and strangely humiliating at the same time. Bodies moved past them, converging like moths on the light behind the bar.

The next thing he knew, they were in a cab. From the elaborately lit-up balti houses, he recognised the Stratford Road. He didn't remember being asked if he wanted to go home with the tall man. He thought he'd rather just sleep it off. But it was too late now. The cab turned off on to the Warwick Road: terraced houses, glass-fronted shops, black silhouettes of factories. He reached for the stranger's hand. 'What's your name?' he asked.

'Mark. What's yours?'

'I'm Neil.' He realised his mistake, didn't bother to correct himself.

The Asian cab driver laughed quietly. 'Romance is a wonderful thing.' He was young, Neil saw: probably younger than himself.

'I told you we should have caught a black cab,' Mark said.

The cab stopped in a spiral cul-de-sac just off the Warwick Road, in Tyseley. To one side, the lights of a factory night shift glowed through tinted glass. Mark unlocked the black door of a narrow terraced house. 'Come in.'

As the door closed behind him, Neil saw a dark shape leaping from the stairs. Teeth flashed in the sudden light. Mark stooped to stroke the creature's sleek fur. 'Easy, easy there. Solo, this is Neil. Neil, this is Solo.' The three of them went through into the living-room, which had two bookcases, a stereo and a TV. A large print of an old painting hung on the wall: a blast furnace burning in the night. 'Have a seat. I'll make some coffee.' Neil sat at the rectangular table. He was too drunk to focus.

Mark came back with two small mugs. It was filter coffee, bitter and so strong Neil felt his heart accelerate. 'How long have you lived here?' he asked.

'Nearly ten years. I keep meaning to move, but I don't earn much and I always blow my money on drugs or holidays.' He said this with no hint of irony.

'So what do you do for a living?'

'Varies. I work in a recording studio. And I write pornography. For Prowler Books, Idol, that kind of thing.' He yawned. 'I'm tired. And you look fucking shattered. You can have the spare bed. I'll show you.'

Neil stared at him. 'Are you serious? You don't want to sleep with me?'

'I like to get to know someone first. Establish roles.' He stood up and moved behind Neil, ruffled his hair. 'Are you back at work on Monday?'

'I've got the next week off, actually.' He had no idea what he was going to do with the time. Except drink and stay in bed.

'Maybe you'd like to stay here for a while,' the voice behind his head said quietly. 'Not as a boyfriend. As a prisoner. It's up to you, obviously. Think about it tonight.'

'You're completely mad.' Neil wondered if his dismembered body was going to be found by teenage lovers in Edgbaston Reservoir a week from now. But like the cat that was now stretched out in front of the barely visible blue glow of the gas fire, he didn't really care. He let Mark lift him from his chair and guide him up the naked stairs, into a tiny room with a single bed and a blind over the window. Then he was alone.

The first time he woke, the blind had gone and the window was open. There was someone beside him in the narrow bed, turned away. Neil lifted the blanket. He remembered holding a man, touching his barely-healed wounds, kissing his eyes shut. But now the wounds had opened like dark flowers, bleeding shadows on to the cotton sheet. He could feel the warmth of the sleeping body. In the morning they'd have to make a run for it. He closed his eyes.

The room was still dark. So dark, all he could make out was the blurring threads of light he saw when his eyes were shut. He needed to piss. He felt for his watch by the pillow, lifted it, pressed the glow button. Nearly ten o'clock. Surely it couldn't be night again? He stood up, crossed to the window and pushed the blind to one side. His fingers touched cold glass, sticky with dust. There must be a shutter or boards over it. He was still wearing his underpants.

The next door along was open: the bathroom. Daylight shimmered behind frosted glass. He remembered the bathroom in Moseley, the sick figure he'd glimpsed leaning over the washbasin. Neil pissed, splashed some cold water over himself, drank a mouthful from the tap. Then he went back to the dark room for his clothes. His head felt like a cinema screen with the fire curtain over it.

Mark was sitting in the living-room, reading a crime novel. 'Hi. Did you sleep well?' There was a glass of whisky by his hand.

'Fine. Why's the window boarded up? I overslept.'

'You obviously needed the rest. The window was like that when I came here.' Mark smiled. 'Sit down, I'll get you some breakfast.'

While Mark was busy in the kitchen, Neil examined his bookcases. The first one contained a variety of paperbacks: thrillers, science fiction, true crime, horror. He noticed titles by Genet, Burroughs and Purdy mixed in with the collection. The second bookcase was all gay porn, mostly American. Lots of S&M titles with black spines. The top two shelves were all devoted to one author: Mark Question. There were several copies of each book. One title sounded familiar; he pulled it out.

The Violent Skin. On the front cover, a sketch of a young man standing in an alley. His face was half in shadow. Something in his hand glinted from the darkness: a knife? Neil flicked through the pages, surprised at how much he remembered. At seventeen, he'd found a porn shop in Manchester that had a shelf of gay titles. This was the one he'd bought, read in his bedroom, then thrown away in case his mother found it. Every chapter had at least one fully detailed sex scene; but there was a story. Teenage dock workers who were also gangsters, dealing in stolen and smuggled goods. The psychopath who was killing them one by one, after making love to them. At the end, the hero discovered that the killer was his own boyfriend. They fought on the dock, then in the harbour, one of them drowning. You didn't find out which one.

Memory guided Neil to his favourite scene. The part where a minor character was being interrogated. He was tied naked to a chair and forced to watch as the boy he desired passionately was fucked senseless in front of him. It went on for hours. Only when he told them where he'd buried a stash of heroin did they untie his left hand and let him bring himself off. Then they left him, alive, for his boss to discover. Neil closed the book and put it back on the shelf.

When he turned round, Mark was watching him. There was a tray of toast and coffee on the table. 'I've read that,'

Neil said. He felt himself blushing. 'Enjoyed it. You make being humiliated seem . . . I don't know, special. Like a ritual.'

'There's no point in humiliation without dignity. You have to learn to walk before you can crawl.' Mark had a weird tendency to make outrageous statements as if he were talking about the weather. 'Honey or marmalade? Or Bovril?'

Neil ate slowly and sipped the jet-black filter coffee. He could still taste vodka in the back of his throat. 'How did you get into writing porn?'

Mark hesitated. 'It's a long story. Let's save the difficult questions for this evening, when we can talk about the rules. Ask me something easier.'

Have you always been mad? Neil thought. But he didn't want an argument. The stillness he'd sensed in Mark at the beginning was still drawing him in, soothing him. Ordinarily, with a hangover like this, he'd still be crying into the pillow at this time. 'What else do you write?'

'The occasional shopping list.' Mark shrugged. 'I wrote an avant-garde novel once. About a day in the life of an alcoholic coprophile. But my agent didn't like it. She said it fell between two stools.'

'Arf arf,' Neil said wearily. 'Did you ever see Mat Coward's "Backchat" column in the *New Statesman*?' Mark shook his head. 'Just before the Scott Report came out, he wrote a special column apologising for calling William Waldegrave a dog turd. He said the *New Statesman* building had been picketed by thousands of dog turds. The editor had called him into his office and said "Mat, this is all down to you. And to be honest, my sympathies are with the turd brothers and sisters."'

Mark laughed. He was slightly drunk, Neil realised. Then his face became serious. 'OK, here's the plan. This morning, I'll do some work while you wash up in the kitchen. Then I'll go out and do some shopping while you get the vacuum cleaner and do all the floors. That's just a bit of training for you. Things don't get heavy until this evening.'

'What happens then? I dig up the garden?'

'No, we get into role. That's when you become a prisoner.'

'What if I don't want to play?'

'Then you can go home. And do whatever you were going to do. But you can't come back.'

Neil thought about it. Then he nodded. 'OK. But I can stop whenever I want to?'

'Only by coming out of role. To do that, say my name. Mark. That's the safe word.' He winked, then embraced Neil and kissed him gently on the cheek. 'Get to work now.'

Through the day, Neil got to know the narrow house. The kitchen with its ancient gas cooker and cheap pots and pans. The back room with its long bare table and locked store-cupboard. The main bedroom, with its black double bed and shelf of porn mags. All the lights seemed to be about 40 watts. Finally, the study where Mark worked was the sparsest room of all: just a small table with a computer and a pile of notebooks. The collection of tapes and CDs in the living-room was a mixture of classical music and rather moody pop – Abba, Gerry Rafferty, k.d. lang, Yazoo, Boy George. Mark evidently had a maudlin side.

After a break for lunch he went round again, dusting and tidying. He felt an odd sense of freedom. Whatever he did here was controlled by Mark's will. It wasn't a part of his life. While here he had no past, no choices to make, no name. By mid-afternoon the house was cleaner and he was exhausted. Mark gave him a large glass of whisky and left him in the living-room, watching TV. His mind was almost completely blank.

Over dinner, which Mark had cooked, they shared a bottle of red wine and talked about books. Mark was a huge fan of Genet. 'I often think his scenarios are built up, not just from solitary fantasies, but from real sex. The books are a fundamental part of his love life. What he does on the page, he does in himself. That's how he survives.' His own favourite Genet novel was *Miracle of the Rose*, 'because it's the most liberating. It's about the freedom of the imagination. It makes you feel that anything is possible. *Funeral Rites* is beautiful, but it's a book without hope.'

Neil told him about *Nights of Insult*. 'You know, when people didn't like it, I felt like my whole view of things was being fucked upon. Even sitting and watching it, knowing that it wasn't very good, I still wanted to kill anyone who laughed at it. Because they were laughing at me. It was scary.'

'There's more than one way of losing face,' Mark said.

Afterwards, they went for a walk. The pale streetlights blended with the reddish glow of the sunset. Signboards outside the industrial estate in Wharf Road advertised INDUSTRIAL COATINGS and SIGNS & SIGNWRITING. Two black funnels stood like inverted rockets just behind a construction site, where scaffolding was heaped on a concrete surface. Neil thought of a children's playground. Next to a muddy crater, waste filled a metal tank to the brim.

Nearer the Warwick Road, they crossed a bridge over the same canal he'd walked along recently. He shivered, suddenly convinced that he was still down there and the streets were a dream. They walked on to the Greet Inn, an isolated building where they drank Jack Daniels and listened to some truly dreadful karaoke. Hearing REM's 'Everybody Hurts' being murdered by a pale youth in a tank-top, he suddenly realised what it was about. It wasn't meant to comfort. Stipe was arguing that those who'd been through bad times had a responsibility to help others in the same position. The song was about the need for solidarity. But whether that went as far as condoning karaoke, Neil wasn't sure.

When they got back to the house, Solo clamoured silently

to be fed. Mark emptied a tin of prawn-coloured jelly on to a saucer, then poured two more large whiskies. They settled on to the black sofa by the stereo, with piano music playing softly. 'All right,' Mark said. 'Question time.'

Neil hardly knew where to start. He fixed on the question he'd already asked. 'How did you get into writing porn?'

'It was thirteen years ago. I was very into drugs at the time. Got caught in possession of some heroin, and the police convinced the court I was a potential dealer. Anyway, I landed a six-month sentence. There I was in prison, bored out of my mind, started writing porn stories to turn myself on. Showed them to a friend. Word got round, and soon I was in demand. Writing fuck stories for cigarettes, wraps of coke, whatever. The whole of *The Violent Skin* was written like that. Under commission, you might say.'

'What did you mean earlier about roles?'

'Hold on. My turn to ask a question.' Mark looked at him thoughtfully. 'What happened to your face?'

Neil swallowed a mouthful of whisky. 'It was a year ago. There was this party to celebrate the election result. I went with my boyfriend . . .' He explained about the party, meeting the boy in the Jester, what had happened by the canal, the two operations. Then he explained about the search for Ian, the things he'd found out, the final hopeless walk along the canal. None of it seemed to make much sense.

Mark listened attentively. Then he refilled their glasses and said: 'I'm sure you can do better than that.'

'What do you mean? I told you, it's over.'

'It's a reasonable first draft. But there's no character motivation. No real plot.'

Neil stood up, swaying a little on his feet. 'I think I'd better leave.'

'Calm down,' Mark said. There was a hint of anger in his voice. 'You think I'm accusing you of lying. I'm not. I'm just

accusing you of not being creative. *Sit down.*' Neil obeyed.
'Let me explain about the rules. The first rule is: every time
you tell the story, it has to be different. The second rule
is: you work backwards from the end. Like telling a joke. Or
fucking.'

Neil shook his head. He was beginning to feel tired. 'I'm
getting lost here. Give me an example.'

Mark refilled their glasses. There was more light in the
room now: the reflections were stronger. Solo wandered in
and lay down somewhere, out of sight. 'Let's go forward
about five years,' he said. 'To the end. Ian's gone down to
the south coast. Cornwall, maybe. But he's not free. His
victims stalk him in his dreams. The thought of their damaged
faces paralyses him. That's why he lives by the sea: he's
terrified of silence.

'Across the country, things are getting out of hand. The
Hague government is losing its grip. Violent battles between
protesters and private security firms rage in every city. Ian's
joined a local militia dedicated to maintaining a patriotic
order. Then a gang of rebels come into town. Their leader is
a tough lad of Romany origin. Nobody knows his name.
They're about to move on. Ian volunteers to infiltrate them
and kill their leader. But deep inside, his desire for the boy
is growing like a slow fire.'

'Lost in a Roman wilderness of porn,' Neil slurred. 'Travelling to the heart of Cliché City.'

'All right, Boy Wonder. Why don't you contribute? Give
me something else.'

Neil tried to focus. His mind was blank. Then he described
his dream about the wounded man in the bed. 'I knew we
were on the run together. But I didn't know what from.' His
voice sounded childlike in his head.

'Ian doesn't know what he's running from,' Mark said.
'The militia he supposedly belongs to? Or the damaged

victims in his head? He's on the loose, but he's not free. The whole world's an underground. That dream is when the rebel boy comes to him, wounded from an ambush.' He stared into the darkness behind Neil's head. 'And he realises, as they're lying in bed together, that Ian belongs to the militia. That's why his wounds have opened.'

He sipped his whisky, lost in thought. A question was stirring in the back of Neil's mind. 'You still haven't told me what you meant about roles.'

'Oh that? It's very simple.' Mark slipped his hand under Neil's shirt. 'We create the story. From now on. I'm the rebel leader. And you're Ian. Unless you break out of the role, you can't leave the house.'

'Why not? I thought they were on the run.'

'You're not listening, are you?' That hint of anger again. 'Ian's trapped. You're trapped within him. A prisoner of the past. A prisoner of your fears. And a prisoner of love.'

Neil moved closer to Mark. 'Do you always use your pick-ups to get material for your books?'

'It's the other way round,' Mark said. 'The stories are just a by-product. The real story is between us.'

'I'm not sure I believe you.'

'Your point being?'

Neil was confused now. Too many words; he needed contact. 'My point being, as long as I get a fuck out of this, I don't really care.'

Mark's fingers brushed Neil's thigh gently. 'All in good time. Whatever happens is in role now. Don't forget that.'

'I can't just stay here. I'll need clothes.'

'Wear some of mine. You'll stay for as long as it takes.'

'I've only got a week,' Neil said. He wanted to stand up, move away, assert some control; but he was too drunk.

'That's long enough.'

Another question rose slowly towards the light. 'Long

enough for what? What's the end? You said it started with
the end.'

'Isn't it obvious?' Mark said. He turned his face and looked
directly into Neil's eyes. 'When the rebel boy knows Ian
belongs to the militia, he stabs him. At that moment, all the
ghosts come back. To watch him die.'

The whisky bottle was empty. Neil said goodnight, then
went up to the tiny bedroom on his own. He undressed in
the dark, slipped into bed and lay there on his back. He felt
as though he had never existed.

2

The next day was chilly and overcast. Rain trickled gradually
down the windows. They stayed in all day, working on their
roles. It was pure improvisation: there was no script, nothing
written down. They spoke narrative as well as dialogue,
framing their own actions. The nameless boy did most of the
talking. Ian privately thought of him as Shadow. He kept
confusing the boy with the vengeful shadows in his head,
especially when the dim light blurred or marked his face. It
was all right to break off and pour a drink, make a sandwich,
go to the toilet. These basic things weren't part of the story,
so they didn't interfere.

Slowly, in a piecemeal sort of way, the story moved
forward. The strangers arrived on motorcycles, lighting a fire
in Ian's cold world. There was a closeness between them, a
trust, that he both envied and despised. The local people
were too cowardly to deal with them. He saw Shadow on the
street corner, a gun bulging the side of his leather jacket. It
was a face he wanted to carve up.

A fight was staged between Ian and two militia men in the
pub where the rebels were drinking. They went further than
he'd expected: pinned him to the brick wall and beat his

shoulders and arms with a stick. His face slammed into the wall and his nose bled over his shirt, but he didn't cry out.

After that, it was easy to approach Shadow and ask if he could leave town with them. The gypsy boy took him aside and cleaned his face with a damp cloth, his hand resting on the back of Ian's neck. That evening, they ate and drank together by firelight on a black-pebbled beach, the sea crackling like static under the music of a portable tape player: Thin Lizzy, the Clash. They stretched out on blankets, beyond the reach of the tide. Then Shadow took his hand and led him to a dark room with a narrow bed.

After all the build-up, the sex was something of a disappointment. Neil felt himself being manipulated efficiently and forcefully, but without tenderness. He came early, sitting on Mark's long cock. Then they went through a series of positions, with Mark increasingly dominant: Neil on his back, then on all fours, then flat on his stomach with his face pressed into the pillow. It was beginning to hurt. Eventually Mark pulled out, removed the condom and got Neil to suck him off. Even like that it took some time.

A few minutes later, the sleepers lay huddled on the beach. Ian sat on the toilet, shivering. The pain made him grimace with rage. The militia were the only family he had. Why was this queer threatening his chance to belong? Lights hung in the cloudy windows, like faces without normal features. The rebels were sleeping when he couldn't. Why didn't he cut all their throats and walk away? When he wiped his arse, there was blood on the paper. He limped back to the dark room and closed the door.

The next day, he scarcely left the room. They lit candles and rolled up the blind, so he could touch the dusty boards over the window. When he went to the toilet, the mirror in the bathroom had gone. The dark room had become a tent, an alley, a cellar. The rebels fled by night and hid by day, hijacking vehicles and keeping their faces covered. The militia used Ian as a source of information. They were looking for a way to break up the group, undermine its purpose. Killing them all would only create a myth.

One night, Shadow and two others went to meet the leaders of another anarchist faction. They didn't come back. Ian paced the floor, worrying. He knew it was a set-up. Even Shadow had seemed to know, making love to him with an intensity that had left him bruised and silent. He wondered if Mark found it hard to get off because he'd seen too much pornography. Even petting the nameless cat brought him no comfort. 'I've betrayed your master,' he said miserably. He'd betrayed his own too. The camp settled down for the night in their tents and beat-up vans. He let the candle burn down to a pool of clear wax, a twist of smoke, nothing.

Hands shook him awake. 'Ian! It's me.' The smell of blood and sweat. Shadow lit a candle to let Ian see his wounds. There was blood, still drying, all over his face and chest. Ian stared at him, unable to move. 'They jumped us,' he said. 'Simon was killed trying to fight them. Militia men. Fascist pawns of the army. Cowardly scum.'

He spat blood on to the floor. 'They told us, "You can't trust anyone. The enemy is always under the bed. Or in it. Your war is not only futile, it's based on delusions. This is the reality." Then they cut Jonathan's throat in front of me. I went crazy. Would have fought until they killed me. But they let me go and drove away.'

'Let me clean your face,' Ian said. He reached for a handkerchief. But Shadow stopped him.

'What's the point? The cuts will heal faster like this. I'll wash in the morning.' His breathing was still ragged. Ian held him close, kissed his bruised lips. They lay together on the bed, naked, innocent as children. Ian felt despair pulling him down into the refuge of sleep.

From the traces of light in the cracks between the boards, he knew it was morning. The gypsy boy lay curled away from him, one arm clutching the edge of the bed. Dark blood was trickling down his back on to the sheet. The candle he'd lit was still burning. Ian felt tears run down into his mouth. 'I'm sorry,' he murmured. 'I'm sorry.'

Slowly, wincing with pain, Shadow raised his head and turned round. 'Don't cry, little one,' he whispered. 'The war's not over.' He reached up and stroked the side of Ian's face. There was blood on his hand. 'And I'm still alive. Let's drink to the future.'

He stood up and went to the door, then returned with two glasses of wine. 'Drink.' Their glasses clinked together. It was red, slightly acrid. Ian looked into the rebel's eyes, but he couldn't see them. The candle was jittering, breaking into frames.

They were lying together in the dark when he said: 'You don't know what I've done.'

There was a pause. Then the answer came: 'Yes I do.' Shadow gripped him from behind. 'I know everything.'

Ian froze. In his mind, a line of dead or wounded men waited to accuse him. He had no will to escape. 'What are you going to do?'

'I don't know. I don't really care what happens any more.' Suddenly Ian realised how the militia had used him. They'd freed Shadow to kill him – and in doing that, to lose his belief. But he was too tired to explain. Soon it would be over.

He could hardly even speak. 'You put something in my drink,' he whispered.

'I don't want you to feel too much pain.' The gypsy boy fumbled among his clothes on the floor, then placed something against Ian's cheek. An edge of cold steel. 'Keep still.

I'll make it quick.' The accusing faces hovered closer. All he could see of them was the scars.

The boy slipped an arm under Ian's side and gripped his chest, drawing him up close. His knees slipped into the crook of Ian's knees. Ian arched his back. He felt a sudden cold shock under his left shoulder-blade: the knife going in, cutting down, the wetness of blood. His own breath pouring from his mouth like smoke. Lips touching his ear, whispering 'I'll never forgive you.' A heartbeat. Then nothing.

3

There was no light. Was he underground? He stirred, and the blanket moved. The sound of traffic came from far away: rising and falling, like slow waves. No trace of light anywhere. His face was stuck to the pillow. He pulled free and touched the stiff cloth. The smell of dried blood. The blanket was stuck to his back too. He reached there, almost expecting his fingers to disappear into the wound. But the skin wasn't even broken. It was because he was dead, he realised. After death, the body is perfect.

He pushed himself up on one arm. At once, nausea washed over him and he retched twice. Only a thread of saliva came up. He needed to piss. Did the dead piss? He stumbled to the door, nearly taking a sheet with him, stumbling over a plastic bowl at the foot of the bed. The door was locked. He couldn't even see the keyhole. He found the chamber-pot again and used it. Then he climbed back into the narrow bed and lay there. This was a dream, a dream of his corpse. If he kept still, he'd awake into rigor mortis and decay.

After a while, he got up and felt his way around the room. The only other object was a glass jug, filled with something cold. It didn't smell of anything. He dipped in a finger and tasted it. Water. He drank a few mouthfuls, feeling the return of nausea. Then he went back to the bed and slept. When he woke, a pigeon was calling from somewhere outside. His past life seemed like a film he'd seen a long time ago, then seen again recently. The second viewing was less powerful than the memory of the first. But neither seemed to mean anything now.

For hours he lay and stared into the darkness, feeling part of it. No dreams pulled him away. He felt no need for words, pictures or any kind of action. In death, he was complete. If he tried to live again, he'd be torn apart. Even the hunger slowly growing in his belly and throat was part of the darkness. Only this room was real. The sounds he could hear – traffic, someone moving below the floor, a cat's unanswerable voice – were part of the film.

Some time later, he needed the chamber-pot again. It was empty. There was fresh water in the jug, and a chunk of bread beside it. Did these things happen naturally in the land of the dead? As he ate, he felt the bruises aching in his back and shoulders. He thought about the hands that had held the stick, the bread, the jug. There was something he had to know. Before it could slip his mind, he went to the door. This time it opened.

Grey daylight filtered through a net curtain in the hallway. Flakes of dried blood drifted from him, like ashes from something burnt. The smell of floor-cleaner made him aware of his own bitter smell. He made for the bathroom. His clothes were inside, folded neatly on a chair; so was his watch. It was nine o'clock. He didn't know what day.

He stepped into the bath and turned on the shower. The hot water stung his shoulders. The blood became red again, flowing across his face and torso. There were greyish bruises on his legs, his sides, his shoulders; and a few recently healed scabs. But no wounds. He wasn't bleeding anywhere.

Putting on his shirt was so painful he cried out, astonished at the sound of his own voice. He walked slowly down the uncarpeted stairs. From behind a door, music was playing. He pushed it open. Mark was sitting on the black sofa with a glass of Scotch in his hand. The bottle was open on the table beside him. Someone with a high voice was singing over muted piano chords. As Neil stepped towards him, Mark looked up. There were lights in his eyes, tears. They embraced. 'Welcome back,' Mark said.

If this was morning, which it had to be, he must have got up early to start drinking. His eyes were blurred with red. The CD cover was red too: the Communards. 'What's the matter?' Neil said.

Mark looked away. 'Here's another story for you. I've been up a while, trying to work on it. But it doesn't want to change.' He picked up the glass, then put it down. 'There were three students in the mid-eighties, sharing a house. In Brighton. They were studying at the University of Sussex. And having a good time. As soon as they heard about HIV, they started taking precautions. But it was too late for two of them. They died not long after graduation, within a month of each other.'

He paused. 'When you read *The Violent Skin*, did you see the dedication?' Neil couldn't remember. Mark took a copy from the bookshelf and passed it to him. On the verso page facing the start of Chapter 1, it said: 'In memory of Jonathan and Simon. With all my love.' The CD had stopped playing.

'I started writing pornographic stories to turn them on,' Mark said. 'Took them to the hospital. That was the only commission. They both died before I'd finished the book. You can change the script, you can redraft your own memories. But you can't resurrect the dead.' He picked up the glass again; the light shone from the amber fluid. He drained it slowly.

They embraced again and kissed gently, sharing breath.

Then Neil remembered his question. 'When I told you what had happened to me, it seemed like you'd heard it before. Did you know already?'

Mark nodded. 'I have friends. You caught my eye a couple of times. Then I saw you with someone I know. So later, I asked him about you. He said you frightened him. He was sure you were going to kill yourself. Or get someone to do it for you.'

'Aidan?' Mark didn't react. 'And that story – Ian and the militia – you made that up beforehand?'

'*We* did.' Mark laughed. 'All that rebel stuff, anarchists fighting the government – that's pure Aidan. The romantic revolutionary.' He shook his head, then relapsed into silent thought. Neil suddenly realised how lonely he was. A man who could only make love in role. Badly. It was time to go.

'I owe you a lot,' he said. 'Both of you.'

Mark kissed him lightly on the mouth. 'Don't worry about it. I enjoyed it more than you did. Now it's time to go backstage. That's all the world is. Backstage.' He ruffled Neil's hair. 'You've got to get a flat-top or something. You look like a student.'

At the door, he reached into a pocket and gave Neil a card. 'Keep in touch.' The card was handwritten: 'MARK' and a phone number.

'I will.' They embraced again. 'Goodbye, Mark.' The door closed between them. Neil turned and walked up the narrow road towards the industrial estate. The bright April sunlight – or was it May already? – gave everything a faint glow. The negation of the negation. He could feel its warmth, as if through a sheet of glass.

chapter 9

never dream

1

The dreams were the worst thing. No matter what he took to cover it, the fear always surfaced. A shout echoing under the bridge. A face like a scar, skin pulled tight over the cheekbones, teeth exposed. Then the crash of glass, the sudden light glinting from a newly created blade. The blinding pain. And the helplessness, as if his nerves had been cut. Like it was the school playground and everyone was watching him. But he couldn't see them.

Every time, he'd wake up and touch his face to check it was still there. The wetness was only saliva, or tears. The yellow streetlight made the furniture in his room appear huge, bulked by its own impenetrable shadows. Through the window, he could see the grey façades of the houses opposite. He couldn't sleep with the curtains shut. Sometimes he kept the bedside lamp on.

Getting back to sleep was never easy. He'd pour himself a glass of water and try to drink it without gagging. Maybe some whisky after. A few Nurofen, maybe a Suprax if it was still early. Then he'd read for a while, have a wank, or draw patterns with a razorblade on the inside of his arm until some kind of calmness descended. He could still see the thin mask of a face, but now he felt secure in the knowledge of what he would do to it. He had faith now, like a chant that lulled him back into uneasy sleep. He believed in getting the bastard. The bastard would pay. They'd all pay.

Daybreak woke him from a churning half-dream of fire and bloodshed. An oil slick burning on the North Sea. A flame-thrower clearing an alley of slow zombies, wiping away their idiot need. He got up and showered, turning the water up as hot as it would go. As the steam cleared from his reflection, he knew what had to be done. He shaved his face slowly, removing the uneven stubble without drawing a single fleck of blood.

2

The Birmingham Pride Festival was a fairly new event. Neil had skipped it last year, because he'd kind of overdosed on the scene by then. And in '97, he'd not been long out of hospital. This year, it was quite a spectacle. The whole area defined by Hurst Street, Bristol Street and Wrentham Street had been marked off, a kind of giant pink triangle with a few thousand people crowded into it. Back in the late 1980s, during the controversy over Section 28, a Tory councillor in the West Midlands had asserted: 'It's not a matter of prejudice. We are trying to get back to the time when, if this sort of thing went on, it happened out of sight and out of mind.' Well, tough shit.

A soft-rock band were playing in the carpark; the wall of speakers made them audible all through Hurst Street. There was a Ferris wheel on the corner of Bromsgrove Street, which was lined with stalls: books, T-shirts, jewellery, health information, porn. The policing was low-key and relaxed. Aidan pointed to a fetish stall. 'Look at that.' Three policemen were examining a pair of handcuffs, unable to restrain their laughter. 'Do you think they're impressed or not?' Two teenagers walked past, arm in arm: a white boy and a black girl, disguised as Nathan and Gail from *Queer As Folk*. Neil had loved the series, particularly the idea of three characters representing different sides of the male psyche. What would life be like, he wondered, if all the parts of ourselves could talk to each other? Bones, skin, memory, need, hope?

Neil and Aidan wandered up and down in the crowd, enjoying the sunlight and the music. Every now and then, they stepped through the open door of a bar to consume some bottled cider. Neil tried to ignore the number of men who waved to Aidan, kissed him or ruffled his hair. They weren't officially a couple, though they'd been sleeping together regularly for six months now. Sometimes, but not always, their lovemaking included some violence. They were both wearing long-sleeved shirts this afternoon.

Having an open relationship wasn't easy for Neil. When he was out on his own, he avoided places Aidan might go to. Jealousy caught in his chest like a stitch that made him stop and breathe slowly. But for Aidan, being in any kind of relationship was a strain. The closer they became, the less able he was to express his feelings. His claustrophobia affected Neil, pushed them apart whenever things became too domestic. Whereas Matt had craved physical contact and signs of affection, Aidan needed to walk his own path. A joint mortgage was not a possibility. Yet they were in love.

The part of Neil that had sought out the darkness was quiet now. Had Jason faded away or just gone underground? Neil could hardly believe some of the things he'd done. How was it possible? The closest he'd got to backroom sex since Paris was seeing Ash play live in Wolverhampton. The memory of a shirtless Tim Wheeler still haunted his lonelier nights.

Weaving slightly from the effects of alcohol, they made for Wrentham Street via one of the short backstreets. Derelict factories blocked the sunlight; broken glass glinted from a high window. Unexpectedly, Aidan gripped Neil's hand. 'Relax,' he said. 'You're not alone. You're with me.' They stopped and kissed in a doorway. Neil closed his eyes.

After the bright sun, the near-dark of the Boots bar took some getting used to. No music was playing. 'Be the ideal venue for a blind date,' Aidan said. Around the main bar, a number of leather queens in fake police hats were hiding in alcoves and shooting each other with toy pistols. It was like a silent film, absurd and unsettling at the same time. Neil saw Mark among them, and waved. Mark raised a hand, then ducked back out of sight. The floor was littered with empty Diamond White bottles.

Aidan assessed the scene and observed: 'Tacky.' Neil suppressed the urge to giggle. This place was another kind of theatre. He and Mark had kept in touch, but they'd never talked about what had happened between them. There was a mystery about it that they both needed. The magician could never reveal his tricks.

Back in Hurst Street, the party was still warming up. Rumour had it that Dannii Minogue was going to appear on the carpark stage towards midnight. If he managed to hold on to Aidan that long, it would be a miracle. Just now, the red-haired lad was chatting to some boot boy with a Mohican. To his relief, the punk took off in the direction of a burger van. Then Aidan said: 'I told him we'd meet him in Route 2 at ten. Is that OK?'

'I suppose. Whatever.' Did that mean Aidan was planning a threesome? Neil thought he could handle that. Even though he knew it would push them further apart. Evidently Jason was still in there somewhere. But you had to adapt when you were going out with someone who regarded the world as a frontier. The rules were liable to change.

Most of the stalls were starting to pack up now, as the first hint of evening chill crept into the air. But the SWP stall was still going strong. Neil glanced at the array of books and pamphlets. The bearded man behind the stall handed him a copy of *Socialist Worker*. 'Hi, Neil. How's it going?'

Neil did a double-take. 'Oh, hi. Sorry, I didn't recognise you for a moment. Yeah, I'm fine. You?'

'Not bad.' Sean looked at him and Aidan thoughtfully. 'How many Maoists does it take to change a lightbulb?'

'I don't know.'

'Only one. But first, we have to sit down and discuss why it didn't work out with the old one.'

Neil thought about that. Aidan picked up a pamphlet on gay rights and trade unionism. 'You know what bugs me about the SWP?' he said. 'You think you've got a stake in every struggle that's going on. Do you really think it's that easy? That you can become part of something just by turning up with a bundle of poxy magazines?'

'Umm, yes. That's about it.' Sean grinned. 'Seriously, we're not trying to take over anyone else's cause. But someone has to join up the dots, and show how all these different kinds of protests have common ground.'

'Oh yes,' Aidan said, 'the part where you explain that capitalism's really to blame. That's really important.'

'If it's so obvious, why don't more people see it? Maybe people need to have the truth shoved in their face every now and then. Think of it as a kind of performance art.'

Neil laughed. 'Fabulous. You've gone from theatre as politics to . . . politics as theatre.' He could hear an echo of Gary's sarcasm in his own voice.

Oddly, Gary was the one person he'd expected to see today

who wasn't here. But then, he'd seemed a bit withdrawn
lately. Maybe that HIV scare from last year had affected his
confidence. They'd both tested negative, but Gary had been
very tense about it. Neil had never imagined he could provoke
that kind of fear.

It was getting dark now; the Ferris wheel, vans and pub
doorways stood out in the gloom. People streamed down the
half-lit roadway, coming from the station or the Arcadian
Centre to join the party. They didn't look quite as friendly
any more. You never knew what men wanted. Neil felt himself
tense involuntarily. The distant faces were blank in the
sodium light. He wished he'd brought the knife. But if necessary, he'd manage without it. It wasn't only Jason who was
hiding inside him.

3

He didn't know what he was doing here. This wasn't his
crowd at all. And some of them weren't just strangers, they
were truly *strange*. Or they were pretending to be. It was
Matt's fault. He was trying to kick-start Neil's social life at
the University, but he'd forgotten that his own friends were
neither social nor lifelike. Some of the figures in the dimly-
lit meeting room had the pale faces and brittle hair of extras
from a Lucio Fulci film. Others were dressed like characters
from *Dr. Who*. Neil drank white wine from a plastic cup and
wondered how soon he could leave. He was afraid some of
these people would morph once the sun went down.

Maybe trying to rejoin the student world was a mistake.
He had to supervise undergraduates to help finance the last
year of his research, but that didn't mean he belonged among
them. Most of them were so fucking materialistic: obsessed
with their laptops, mobile phones and futures in management

consultancy. At least this bunch were into something other than themselves. Even if they didn't really know what it was.

According to Matt, the speaker they'd just heard was a famous TV and film scriptwriter. A middle-aged shithead from Florida with a mustard-coloured suit and hat. He'd shown them endless slides of key moments from productions he'd worked on, while sullenly informing them: 'All that shit writers come out with about exploring human nature – what's there to explore? People are boring. Psychology is for second-rate minds.' Then he'd droned on for a while about the technological benefits of warfare. His remark that there should be a lunar colony for the members of CND failed to raise a laugh, which clearly disappointed him. 'You know, peace campaigners.'

Matt tapped Neil on the shoulder. 'Did that take you into an exciting new world?'

'Only a very depressing old one. Cheers.' They tapped their plastic glasses together, making no sound. Matt was looking well, he realised. Evidently getting out of medicine had been good for him. Or maybe it was the new boyfriend. 'So . . . how's Gordon?' They'd been living together since Easter. Matt had taken pains to make it clear that Gordon was a music graduate who played the violin superbly, and was thus definitely not a moron. He *was* a puff, however. There was hard evidence of that.

'Oh, he's fine. Couldn't make it this evening. Actually, we were wondering . . . if you'd like to come round for dinner some time. See the flat. If you'd rather not, obviously . . . we'd understand.'

Neil wondered if the use of *we* was deliberate. He missed Matt more than he missed living with him. 'I'd like that. Thanks.'

'If there's anyone you'd like to bring . . .'

Neil shook his head. 'Not really. At least, not yet.' He finished his beer. 'I'd better go. Take care.'

He got off the bus in the middle of Acocks Green. A crowd of teenagers were standing outside the pub on the corner. They weren't talking or waiting for anything, just standing. As Neil passed, a young girl ran after him. 'Excuse me, sorry. Have you got 10p? I need to phone my Mum, tell her I've missed the bus.'

Neil took a handful of change out of his pocket and examined it. The girl tried to snatch the coins; his fist closed involuntarily, blocking her. He turned away. 'You fucking bastard!' she screamed. He didn't look back, although she followed him across the Warwick Road, cursing. That was the second time he'd been almost caught that way. Eventually, her voice faded and there was only the sound of traffic.

Back in his flat, he switched the computer on and turned out the light. Feeling slightly drunk, he scrolled down the last article he'd written for *Redbrick*. The new editor had told him his views were 'outmoded'. Maybe that part about Princess Diana was a bit heavy-handed. *The survival of the aristocracy is essential to the strategy of the ruling class for maintaining its grip. Royal relics allow the business class to preserve the illusion of its own aspirational nature, disguising its own supreme power, wealth, inertia and corruption.* He closed the file. Boring.

Aidan believed in a kind of Fortean politics: a shifting of ground from one ideology to another, depending on the circumstances. If you kept shifting your ground, you stayed in touch with reality. Neil supposed he agreed, but he didn't want to. That made it too much like fiction. Or roleplay. He still felt the need for a compass to guide him through the dark. The shadow area between what the Labour Party had been and what the SWP thought it was. If you lived in that shadow, it was hard to know where you were. Or where you were going.

There was a need, he realised, for theory that didn't just restate a comforting ideological perspective. That got up close to experience and explained the mechanisms, the specific reasons why justice didn't come. A need for someone like Chomsky, who called himself an anarchist rather than a socialist – as Foucault had. His ideas were like pinpoint fractures in the screen of modern culture. Reading the *Socialist Review* was calming, it filled you with a sense of righteousness. But it didn't really illuminate things, because it didn't step into the dark. It could never admit that not having the answers was where the truth really started.

In *Powers and Prospects*, Chomsky argued that saying Eastern communism 'hadn't worked' in comparison to Western capitalism was like saying that a kindergarten 'didn't work' because the children there knew less about physics than the students at a university. But that metaphor was too detached and objective for the new revolutionaries. They needed a clearer narrative of betrayal to read an uplifting message in the scars of the twentieth century. Being in the SWP committed you to so many condemnations, so many unconditional verdicts. No-one could possibly disagree. The leader column in the *Socialist Worker* even had the strapline *What we think*. When had the righteous become the self-righteous?

Watching a broadcast by the BNP for the council elections last week, he'd been taken aback by their attempt to sentimentalise and Torify their message. How dare a neo-Nazi party refer to Dunkirk? The mendacity of it had left him barely able to breathe. You had to lose your beliefs to find out what your convictions were. It had taken him a year of pain to discover his own anger. It was the furnace of his dreams.

The screen was a grey square. He left it switched on as he

undressed and got into bed. The shadows around him weren't ghosts but possibilities. It might work out with him and Aidan. After Blair, the Labour Party might rediscover its conscience. Springsteen might record with the E Street Band again. No, that last one was just wishful thinking. As Neil's eyes closed, the screen saver kicked in and the grey square faded to black.

4

Even down here, it was bright. The sunlight reflected off the still water, briefly making him feel as though he were on some kind of bridge across the sky. They'd been walking for an hour without encountering a living soul. He needed the quiet, these days. Dean sensed his mood and kept pace with him calmly, not intruding on his thoughts. That allowed him to switch off, become part of the stillness. As if the canal were a stretch of tape running through his head. He couldn't distinguish it from memory.

They were nearing the end. The canal became wider here, its surface cloudy with weeds. It smelt worse than usual. No doubt the approach of summer speeded up the decay rate of the submerged leaves and stuff. Sunlight flashed from the corrugated iron windows of a roofless building. He paused, trying to breathe only through his mouth so the stink couldn't get in. The rotten-paper feeling in his chest was back again. And Dean chose this moment to pull away from him, heading for the murky water. 'Hold on,' he said irritably. Then he saw what Dean was dragging him towards.

He was on his knees, eyes shut. But now the stink had a shape. He couldn't keep it out. When he opened his eyes, the light reflected on the water dazzled him. The body was half-submerged, folded in on itself. What he could see of the face was dark with blood – not spilt, but somehow clotted under the skin, like a birthmark. Black flecks crawled across it. The shape of the face was wrong.

It was a young man, he realised: dressed in a white shirt and blue jeans, hair bleached and cut so short he could see the scalp. The lad's ribs stood out through the soaked cloth. The buzzing of flies made him want to tune the picture before it blanked out completely.

Dean was sniffing at the trough of water between the towpath and the corpse. He was preparing to jump. Andy didn't want to think about why. He fumbled for the lead, pulled Dean sharply away from the water's edge. 'Come on. Let's get out of here.' There was still no-one in sight.

The next stone staircase took them up into Bordesley Green, a district he didn't know. There was no phonebox in sight, just a street of identical terraced houses like the hall of mirrors in *Citizen Kane*. If he could only find a shop, he could use their phone. Dean padding softly at his side, he walked faster; then, heedless of his angina, he began to run.

5

DC Willetts had been spending a lot of time in Acocks Green lately. A spate of armed robberies had pushed up the insurance premiums so high that half the local shops were closing down. Gangs of teenagers and younger kids hung around the streets at all hours, waiting for entertainment. You couldn't pin much on them, but they made good informers.

However, he doubted they'd be any help in this case. Avoiding the constellations of broken glass in the dark roadway, he drove past the train station into Yardley. The long, tree-lined road was strangely restful: it broke up the harsh light into shifting patterns. Jackson lived in one of the small blocks of flats near the Swan Centre. Willetts parked as discreetly as was possible in a relatively new car.

The door opened on the first ring. Jackson was pale and red-eyed. There was only a faint tracing of scars on his face now, as if he were wearing a mask of himself. 'Hi, Neil. Can I come in?'

'Sure.' The flat was poorly furnished, but cluttered with all kinds of books, clothes and other bits and pieces. It would be a bugger to search.

'You're looking well,' Willetts said. 'Give or take a few hangovers.' Jackson didn't say anything. 'How's work?'

'OK. I'm back at the University. Tutoring and finishing my Ph.D.' He glanced around the room nervously. 'Why have you called? You didn't ring. I mean, I could have gone out.'

'We're just making some routine enquiries. Don't worry about it. Can you tell me where you were the night before last?'

'I was here. I mean, I went out in the evening. There was a group meeting, a science fiction group. I came home about half-eleven.'

'Did anyone see you here after that time?'

'I'm afraid not. I live on my own.' He was very tense now.

'What about the night before?'

'I stayed with . . . a friend.' He blushed slightly, which made the scars stand out more. 'My boyfriend, sort of. In Cleveland Tower. You know, near town.'

'You don't say. Could you give me his name and flat number?' Jackson hesitated. 'Yes, it *is* necessary.' He wrote down the information. 'Now, can you tell me where you've been over the last four days? Take your time.'

Apparently, Jackson had mostly been either in this tiny flat or at the University. It wasn't the kind of lifestyle the *Mirror* ran special reports on. 'If you talk to Aidan, can I ring him first? Just to let him know things are OK?'

Willetts shook his head. 'No, I'm afraid you can't.' There was a silence.

'What's happened?'

'You'll find out. It's all over tonight's *Evening Mail*. But first, I'm afraid we need to talk to you. Do you mind coming back with me to the station? We'll have to take a statement.'

'Will it take long? I've got a tutorial to give at five.'

Willetts looked steadily at him. 'You can phone from the station to cancel, if necessary. And I have to tell you that we're going to search your flat.' Jackson's eyes widened with shock; then his face went blank, as if he'd switched it off. He nodded.

Once they were settled in the interview room at the Acocks Green station, Willetts said: 'We never did find the guy who attacked you, you know. What was his name again?'

'Ian Moore.' Jackson took a deep breath. 'This is about him, isn't it?' There was a note of relief in his voice. Willetts wasn't sure what that meant.

'Did you ever try to find him?'

Jackson hesitated. 'Sort of. I mean, I asked around. People who'd seen him. I just wanted to know who he was. Then I heard a few . . . rumours. That he was into drugs. That he was involved with Combat 18. You probably know all that.'

'So you didn't literally try to find him?'

'Not really. He didn't seem to be around. I found out enough.' Willetts raised his eyebrows, waited. 'Enough to know it wasn't personal. He hates everyone.'

Willetts smiled. 'So you think he has enemies?'

'I don't think he's got anything else.'

'You could be right.' He eyed the young man's damaged face. It wasn't hard to see why villains in films were usually scarred. You had to guard against the tendency to interpret the scars as a second face, a dangerous *alter ego*. Some people were attracted to that. 'Would you like some coffee?' This was going to take a while.

6

It wasn't so much the heat that wore him out as the brightness. A red echo of it had been trapped in his head all day. Tonight, he just wanted to relax and forget everything. But it wasn't that easy. Only half of his mind registered the uniform black furniture and shelving, or the way Gordon's pictures and CDs blended neatly with Matt's videos and second-hand vinyl. The evidence of domestic bliss didn't make him either regretful or jealous. He felt as though the furnace in his head had burnt him out.

While Gordon and Matt argued in the kitchen over cooking ingredients, Neil browsed through Matt's record collection. He remembered the party at the house in Prospect Road. One of Matt's Goth friends smoking heroin off a piece of tinfoil. And Robert Smith groaning: *You know I believe you, but faith isn't everything.* Later, he'd tried to find that line on the lyric sheet. It wasn't there. He'd eventually found a line with roughly the same vowel sounds. He must have supplied those words in his head.

Finally, the meal was ready. They ate grilled prawns and home-made pizzas, and drank the white wine Neil had brought. Gordon, a friendly and broad-shouldered lad from Leeds, talked about his music. He was building a career as a concert violinist, working with three other graduates from the Conservatoire. 'It used to be the School of Music,' he said. 'But the University decided that sounded too ordinary. Now people get it mixed up with the Botanical Gardens.'

Neil tried to describe his thesis, but found himself struggling for the right words. The wine made him realise how tired he was. When Gordon went to fetch a second bottle, Matt said: 'Are you feeling OK?'

'It's been a bad week,' Neil said. 'Did you hear about what happened?' Matt shook his head. 'They found Ian Moore. Dead.'

'Oh, my God.' Matt closed his eyes briefly. 'Look, I can ask Gordon to go upstairs for a bit if you don't want to tell him about it. He'll understand.'

'No, it's OK,' Neil said as Gordon reappeared with an opened bottle. When a glass was passed to him, he took a deep swig. 'Something's happened. The guy who attacked me two years ago . . . they found him in the canal on Saturday morning. He was . . . someone had smashed his face in. Literally. With a brick or something. He choked on his own blood. It was all in the *Evening Mail*. The police don't know who did it.

'They took me in for questioning. The police. I was there for six hours. The night they thought it had happened, I was at home. But I couldn't prove it. They searched my flat.' He paused. 'They gave me a formal warning about . . . I had a gram of smack hidden away. I smoke it occasionally, when I'm stressed. So I got really told off about that.'

'I thought you didn't like drugs,' Matt said in a quiet voice.

Neil looked at him. 'People change.' Matt flinched from his gaze. 'Anyway, once they'd done the search and talked to the forensics people, they let me go. There's plenty of other people might have had a reason to attack him. Maybe it wasn't even personal, the killing. But I'm still kind of shaken up. That they could think . . .' He drained his glass. Without intending to say anything more, he heard himself add: 'And it feels strange. Like a kind of loss. A part of my life that has ended. I didn't even know he was still here.'

Silently, Gordon reached out and took his hand. Matt took his other hand. They sat like that for a short while. Then

Gordon refilled Neil's glass. 'To a better future for all of us,' he said. They clinked glasses.

The bottle was empty. Matt put on a Tindersticks CD at a low volume. By now, it was dark outside. 'Who'd like some filter coffee?' Gordon said. Neil and Matt both said yes. Gordon disappeared into the kitchen.

Neil sat on the black couch. His mind felt dry and empty. The music, a slow litany of piano and violins, seemed to come from somewhere behind the wall. He realised Matt was sitting beside him. They looked at each other. Then Matt reached out and hugged him, as if he were a child. He felt himself begin to shake, but he didn't cry. Eventually he was still.

Matt drew back, holding the contact only with his eyes. 'Neil,' he said. 'Was it you?' His voice was only just audible.

Neil hesitated. He looked into Matt's eyes, as if something had to be understood between them before he could speak. He didn't know what. Trust, perhaps. An acceptance that faith was enough.

'No,' he said. 'It wasn't me. But it could have been.'

Matt didn't say anything. Gordon came back in from the kitchen with three small cups of coffee. They listened to the rest of the CD, losing themselves in its bleak romance, and talked about nothing in particular.

When Neil left, the light was beginning to fade. He walked through the quiet Kings Heath streets to the number 11 bus stop. The trees along Vicarage Road were losing their colour, becoming autumnal with the twilight. He felt unable to trust anything. Matt had kissed his cheek in the doorway, but they'd avoided each other's eyes.

A flickering streetlamp made a thin tree appear to jitter. He thought of the girl he'd danced with that night at Edward's No. 8. Did people really see into each other, or just see their own fear reflected? Perhaps it didn't make much difference.

The loneliness was real. More real than anger or revenge. Did he wish he'd had the chance to kill Ian? Was that how it had sounded?

The death of the man he hated felt like the death of an ex-lover. Not of someone he still knew. Mark had helped him to kill the enemy in his head. But somehow, the hatred remained. Would it trail behind him until it found someone to destroy? Or was it finished now, a mask with no face behind it?

He didn't have any answers. As the bus came up the steep hill, empty and staring, he said out loud: 'I miss you.' Who he was thinking of, he had no idea. Somehow, he felt it was everyone. Even himself. And Aidan as well: the perpetual outsider with his violent love, his inability to feel at home. What sense would it make to rebuild the cosy domestic life with him?

As the bus waited by the shelter, its engine running, he thought about that. Then he thought about the dark streets. How complex and endless the world was. How the idea of revolution was just a dramatic way of saying, *Can we start again?* And as the bus finally jolted back into life, he realised that where he'd gone wrong with Matt was in trying to make a home. It didn't matter whether you could make a home. What mattered was whether you could leave it.

Acknowledgements

The author would like to thank West Midlands Arts for financial assistance, given through a Creative Ambition Award, that was of great value in the writing of this novel.

Thanks are due to the following for their help, advice, support and insight: Steve Bishop, Nicholas Royle, Gul Davis, Mum, Jonathan Oliver, Simon Bestwick, Kate Pearce, Mick Scully, Chris Morgan, John Howard, Jan Edwards, Dad, Mark Jones and Mair Evans of the No Future? Collective, everyone at Tindal Street Fiction Group, John Williams, Jerome Paillette, everyone at Serpent's Tail, Elly Tams, Paul Drohan, Helena Hempstead, Sarah Crowther, Simon Avery, Peter Coleborn, Helen Dann, Conrad Williams, Anna Oliwa, Jo Saxelby, Emma Hargrave, Jackie Gay, Alan Mahar, Penny Rendall, Sister Harper of the Queen Elizabeth Hospital, John Morrison, Zak Webber. Any medical, political or other errors in this book are entirely my own fault.